In the Shadow of Demeter

Vic Malachai

Published by Vic Malachai, 2021.

While every precaution has been taken in the preparation of this book, the publisher assumes no responsibility for errors or omissions, or for damages resulting from the use of the information contained herein. This is a work of fiction. Any resemblance to actual persons, living or dead, or actual events is purely coincidental.

IN THE SHADOW OF DEMETER

First edition. August 17, 2021.

Copyright © 2021 Vic Malachai.

Written by Vic Malachai.

All rights reserved.

To my Mother, Nana, and Sister.

And friends in the peanut gallery.

Thank you for your patience and contributions.

No one can do this alone.

0

The girl sat alone in the clearing. The air was warm, and she sat in the shade of a tree for hours trying to forget.

The sound was and wasn't like thunder. A cacophony streaking across the sky. The girl squinted against the sun to make out the black streak that glittered in places and was so very loud. She almost screamed when it dived down towards her, resolving into a black chariot pulled by four black horses. Everything about it gleamed and glittered, including the god in dark armor and cloak holding the reins. The chariot hit the ground heavily, throwing up clods of dirt in the crash.

But the ensemble seemed unharmed, and the god turned a great helmet straight towards her, reaching out a hand across the alarmingly small stretch of grass between them. The girl felt as if she were underwater, sound echoing at her from far away.

She bolted before she had any time to think, only to slam into the unyielding metal shoulder of the god's armor. His arm wrapped around her, cold metal against her shoulder blades. The chariot jerked beneath her and the horses screamed. Dazed, the girl tried to twist her head to see what was going on. But suddenly they were in the air the ground falling away distressingly quickly. The black manes and tails of the horses streamed in the wind. The air was cold as it tried to pluck at her curls. The god pulled her closer, wrapping his cloak around them both. She could hear his voice rumble through his chest, tone low and soothing as if she were a frightened animal. But the horses and the wind were too loud to make out the words.

The horses were driven faster and faster, but the ride began to take on a dreamlike quality for her. Exhausted after the days of the festival, the girl squirmed in his arms against the unyielding breastplate. A sliver of sunlight was visible through the gap in the cloak and she watched the green trees rush by so far below.

The ground grew bigger, the horses pulling them down faster than falling. The girl arched her neck, looking for the town or clearing or *something* they were heading for, but all she could see was a rocky cliff face dotted with dark spots. The biggest of the caves yawned in front of them, and she let out a soft scream before screwing her eyes shut for the crash. The light seeping in through the cloak was suddenly extinguished. The girl blinked against the darkness, but nothing revealed itself. The cave seemed to do something strange to distort the sound...sometimes echoing strongly, sometimes sucking away all sound. It was spooky. If before they were in what she was sure was a large, if normal cave, the sounds were her first hint that that was no longer the case. What before had been ordinary darkness began to push in on her, pressing at her skull. The temperature fluctuated wildly, the usual cold punctuated with brief blasts of heat. Her heart began to pound and she focused on his arms around her. They seemed to keep the worst of it away. The girl could sense that the cave...tunnel...whatever it was wasn't used to visitors and did not like the fact that they were here. It felt almost alive, and most definitely did not like guests. Maybe that's what was making the horses so unsettled and loud.

It belatedly occurred to her as the path wound down, down, down that she should probably be frightened. They were in the dark, far underground, with no idea when they would see light again...and in this place that seemed so angry and clearly wished they would disappear.

I

There was a time before even the memory of the Theoi. But still, there are impressions. We did not exist when this ball of rock cooled and the first rains fell. And whatever Zeus tries to tell you we did not exist when the lightning bolt—if that's what it was at all—first made life. We came much later when the first creatures looked up from the mud and realized they were alive, and in doing so knew death, for one cannot exist without the other. Those first sparks of knowledge beyond route survival grew with the creatures as they spread across the world, more complex every millennium, and as the first proto-humans discovered I, so did we. Theoi, by whatever names we go by, are the forces of powerful ideas. And the first ideas of the world became curious and went to meet the new inhabitants of the earth who contributed such strong thoughts.

Kore trailed her fingers through the soft tufts of wheat, giggling to herself. They tickled her fingers as they bobbled in the breeze. Looking up, Kore hurried on her short legs to catch up to her mother and the Melides who were sowing the other field. Kore grabbed a handful of seeds out of the basket and kicked off her sandals, racing across the dark earth. She dumped her handful of seeds onto the ground and stared at them expectantly. Nothing happened, and Kore began to cry. When her mother and the nymphs did it, the gold seeds turned to bright green leaves. Kore had wanted to see the magic. She flopped down onto the dirt, smearing it across her white chiton.

Demeter walked over to Kore, and knelt beside her, running her hands over the dirt stains, making the fabric white again. Kore stopped crying, fascinated by the way her mother could sit on the ground and not get dirty. Kore always got dirty, and one of the Melides would have to make the stains go away.

"You have to wait for us, Kore," Demeter said gently pulling her daughter to her feet and leading her over to one of the nymphs. Calligeneia shifted her basket of seeds to her hip and held out her hand for Kore to take. The party moved on, walking up and down the field trailed by Kore and Calli.

This is taking forever, Kore thought as she looked away from the field toward the road that led to the village. A little mortal boy sat next to a girl, watching them with wide eyes. *Maybe they will play with me,* Kore tried to tug Calli over to the mortals on the road. The nymph barely noticed the tiny pull, busy following her mistress through the tilled earth. Kore smiled and waved at the brother and the sister, who froze and ducked behind their mother. The smile fell from Kore's face. *Why are they always scared? I'm little, and I can't even do anything.*

The sun set, and Kore was finally, finally allowed to walk beside her mother along the path to the village. Kore had seen many villages, and this one was tiny. And poor. There was only one agora, surrounded by tiny houses and a bathhouse, but the fire was burning merrily, and Kore could smell roasting meat and bread. Even the worst villages always had delicious food. Demeter sat on a stone bench in pride of place right next to the fire, and Kore hopped up next to her. The Melides sat behind them, and an old man and woman sat on the other side of the fire. Villagers milled about the agora, and Kore looked around eagerly for the mortals she had waved at earlier.

There weren't many other children, so Kore found them easily, sitting right across the fire behind the oldest mortals. They were looking at the meat as hungrily as Kore felt. They couldn't reach into the fire to get any, it was too hot for mortals, but Kore could. She was hungry too, and they could share. She slid down off the too tall bench, and picked up a plate from the ring of stone surrounding the fire. The wall was very high, and Kore strained to reach over it, let alone get to the roast. She was just about to try to climb on top when she noticed the frightened gasps and her mother pulled her back.

"We must wait to be served," Demeter told Kore. "It is rude to take from the cook fire."

"But we're hungry," Kore said softly, looking down at her dusty sandals.

"Soon," her mother said, and she was right. Whatever the mortals were talking about was over, and plates were being filled.

Kore bounced up and down on her toes. *Wonderful! Sometimes the adult mortals never seem to stop talking.* Demeter was given the first plate, but Kore was given the next one. She ducked out of the way of the servers passing plates to the Melides and walked towards the bench where the young humans were. It was easy to get through the crowd—all of the mortals stepped quickly out of her way—but when she reached the bench, the young humans scooted quickly away too. Kore hopped up with a sigh then slid the plate halfway across the gap, and picked up a piece of meat. The others looked longingly at the food, but it would be a long time until they were served. Kore held the piece of cooling meat in her fingers and waited, watching the boy. He was closer. The boy's eyes rose from the plate to Kore. His dark curls bounced as he looked back down. Kore smiled and pushed the plate closer.

He slowly reached out and took a tiny piece of meat. Never taking his eyes off Kore, the boy passed the sliver to his sister and hesitantly took another for himself. Kore smiled and ate her piece. The other two did the same. She tore off a chunk of bread, smiling to herself this time. After a few rounds of everyone-has-a-bite, Kore began sliding closer to her new friends. They didn't notice, and soon only the plate rested between Kore and the mortal boy. When both the boy and the girl were distracted eating, Kore quickly picked up the plate, plopped it down in the boy's lap and closed the final handbreadth of distance between them. She felt the boy stiffen for a second, but he relaxed quickly. *Good, he didn't run. Sometimes they run.*

The plate had once been generously filled, but now it was empty. As the girl ate the last bite, Kore turned to the boy. "Would you like to play?" she pulled out a colorful top from her pocket.

The boy looked a little scared, but his sister reached eagerly for the toy, before bounding off to an open area between two of the houses. Kore skipped happily after her, and the boy trailed behind. The girl sat on the hard-packed ground, trying to get the toy to spin. Kore settled next to her and reached out after a few minutes. "Hold it here," she said, wrapping her fingers around the top and spinning it quickly.

The little girl laughed like bells and spun the top again after it had fallen down. Kore felt the boy kneel next to her but kept her eyes on the spinning top. When it had fallen down, she handed it to the boy. He was a bit older, and didn't need any help. It whirled even faster than Kore's try. Kore and the girl laughed and clapped their hands as it finally wobbled and fell, the red and green leaves ceasing to blur.

They played with the top as the adult mortals talked with Demeter and the fire burned low. Kore asked about their village and the stream that ran nearby.

"I like to play with the rocks," the boy replied. "Sometimes I splash my sister and she screams."

"That sounds like fun!" Kore replied. "We could go stack the rocks into towers."

The boy frowned. "It's too dark. They wouldn't let us."

It didn't seem very dark to Kore, but the top was fun too. "My name is Kore, what are you called?"

"Kore is a silly name," blurted out the girl, and her brother looked momentarily frightened again.

Kore just shrugged, "Lots of people have funny names." Many mortals thought her name was odd. The little ones sometimes laughed, and the big ones got funny looks on their faces. That was fair. A lot of their names were funny to Kore.

"I'm Bion and that's Doris," said the boy.

Kore nodded, and spun the top again. "I bet I can make it hit that rock."

Kore played with Bion and Doris until the moon was high in the sky. They slumped sleepily against the wall and Kore looked up at the moon and wondered if Artemis would come visit. Sometimes she did. Kore was almost asleep when her mother scooped her up into her arms. They walked towards the tent the villagers had pitched next to the field. *This one is nice,* Kore thought sleepily. It had a woven grass floor and white sides that fluttered. *Most of them don't have floors.*

Kore woke up when the sun shone in through the tent flap. The nymphs were already awake, and Calli held out a piece of toasted bread for her. Kore took it and tried to run out to find Bion and Doris, but Calli caught her.

"We need to leave soon, Kore. There are lots of other villages Lady Demeter needs to help during planting season." Calli kept tight hold of Kore's hand as the other nymphs gathered up their blankets and baskets.

Kore made sure that the top was in her pocket as they got ready to leave. Soon, her mother ducked through the opening and motioned for them to follow. Demeter led the way through the village, followed by her attendants, two abreast. Calli and Kore followed them. The big humans chanted things at her mother, but Kore fingered the top in her pocket and watched for Bion and Doris. They were almost out of the village when Kore saw her friends standing next to their mother. Calli kept her moving, but Kore reached out to Bion and Doris. They ran after Kore, waving, and she reached into her pocket for the top. Bion barely managed to catch it before their mother yanked them back, scolding loudly.

Kore turned away, seeing the shimmer in the air ahead of her mother. They were about to Travel, to another village somewhere else. Kore sniffed a little. *Don't cry, don't cry, don't cry.*

In between the planting seasons and the harvest festivals, Demeter would take her court to spend time on Mt Olympus. It was the most beautiful place that Kore had ever seen, shining and bright unlike even the richest of mortal towns. Her mother's palace had a planted garden, but there were plenty of wild woods and streams to play in on its slopes. It seemed that every tree had a dryad, and every stream and pool a naiad. And Kore was allowed to explore all of the mountain's wonders, followed only by one or two of her mother's younger nymphs.

Some nights, her father, Zeus, held feasts for all the Theoi on Mt Olympus. Those nights were Kore's favorite, the great hall lit with bright torches, important Theoi on divans, with children like her on cushions next to them. Everyone was served by nymphs bearing platters of food and drink. Kore was sometimes even invited to sit by her father with some of his other children as he told tales of the beastly Primordials and terrible firstborn Titans. It was at one of these dinners that Kore met her first demigod. Kore hadn't known that someone could be not-Theoi but not-mortal either.

Kore sat on the bright blue cushion as she stared at the demigod boy. He looked like their father, hair bright gold, eyes bright blue, skin tanned. Kore looked at the other children of Zeus gathered on their own blue or grey cushions. The mostly-mortal looked more like their father than the rest of them put together. He was a head taller than she was, even sitting down, and he kept glancing around the hall, eyes wide at all the Theoi. He turned to look at the other end of the hall, where queen Hera lounged surrounded by her attendants.

"Don't," Kore hissed, pulling him back to face their father who was talking of the fall of Uranus. "She doesn't like us, and we have to pay attention while father talks."

The boy nodded and turned back to the sky god, not seeming too disappointed not to be able to explore the hall even with his eyes.

Kore remembered when she was first big enough to be called away from her mother to sit with her father. She had been so excited and proud. "After the story, while they drink we can walk about the hall and try to talk to some of the others, just not Hera. Aunt Hestia will have candy for us and warm rocks when the night gets cold."

II

*T*hese newly thinking creatures lived simple, harsh lives. They worshiped the basic forces found in the world around them. Earth and Sky. Darkness and Light. Air and Water. The Primordials claim that they sprang fully formed from the ground. I think it more likely that they were simply born to the proto-humans that gave them shape. Either explanation breaks every rule that has since been in place for the birth of new Theoi. Although a Theoi may give a mortal a child, or even create a race with marvelous powers, they all wither and die. Theoi come from Theoi. Suffice to say that the Primordials were as brutish and ugly as the creatures that worshiped them, and yet we all trace our descent from those original six.

Eventually, the Warm Growing season returned, and Kore followed her mother through the fields, sowing barley and all the other food crops the mortals depended on. Demeter walked the fields, and Kore walked their edges, coaxing the flowers there to life. It wasn't much of a help to the villages, but they were more beautiful than before. Even Aphrodite said so.

Growing season after growing season, and the hedgerows exploded with color as Kore trailed behind her mother and the Melides. She slowly mastered the garden blooms and would help the richer villages with their plots. Many of the younger mortals would weave her blooms into garlands and crowns. Kore's first tribute that was meant for *her*, not her mother. The smallest ones would simply throw petals at Kore's feet.

But no matter what Kore tried, the important plants still eluded her. None of the grain crops bent to her will, and they remained stubbornly lifeless seeds, but she began to be able to help the fruit trees along, urging them to flower before their season. None of the mortals seemed to care, happy with her contribution of flowers. Although her mother had the nymphs bring crops from all over the world, only the ones with flowers responded to Kore at all, and sprouting any kind of seed was drainingly difficult.

Kore wasn't sure when things began to change during her visits to Mt. Olympus. But as time passed and she grew taller the smiling talk about the new goddess of flowers petered out and then stopped altogether. She wasn't invited to sit on the grey and blue cushions and listen to her father tell stories. Eros and Aunt Hestia were always happy to see her, but everyone else gradually seemed to forget Kore existed.

Kore and Eros walked down the corridor to the library. "Uranus killed Tethys," Kore insisted. "He snapped her neck when she refused to help him!"

"No, she survived and is imprisoned in Tartarus with the rest of the Titans," Eros argued.

The pair stepped into the library, its walls honeycombed with scrolls and trapped memories. An Aurai floated down from one of the higher stacks and walked lightly towards Eros. "What would you like to see, Lord Eros?"

"The start of the war between the Primordials and the Titans," he answered, his feathers buffeted by her wind.

The nymph's brow wrinkled and she looked apologetic. "We don't have any donated memories from that time. I believe we have two examples of that story told by Titans that survive. Would my Lord be interested in those?"

Eros nodded and the Aurai flew off to a high corner of the room, examining the niches on the walls. "This is a waste of time. We should have known better," Kore sighed, slumping down on one of the cushioned benches. "There are a million versions of that story. Why should the library be any different?"

"We can at least see what the older versions are," insisted Eros.

The Aurai returned, setting two crystals on the table, one nearly transparent and the other a deep red. "Lord Lelantus and Lady Leto were kind enough to share their memories." She turned away to help Tyche and Nike who waited in the doorway impatiently. The nymph led them towards the back of the large room, and the goddesses nodded at Eros as they passed.

Kore sat quietly, and Eros greeted them politely. He turned back to peer at the crystals they had been given. "What do you think, red or white first?"

"The red is pretty," Kore said. "No way to tell who they are from without the Aurai."

Eros held out the red crystal in the palm of his hand and Kore folded hers over the top so they could both watch at the same time. She closed her eyes, and the memory began to play. It was very old, and had obviously been watched many times. The colors were starting to bleed, and the voice sounded mushy. It showed a Theoi with crude features and dark hair sitting on the other side of a blazing fire.

She told a story of fear, pain, and death with a haunted look in her eyes. When the memory was over, and the library reappeared before Kore's eyes, she found that Eros had dropped the crystal onto the floor. It glittered by their feet. She gingerly reached down to pick it up and place it on the table for the Aurai. Kore followed Eros silently out of the room that now felt haunted. They didn't speak of Primordials or Titans anymore.

When Eros was busy running errands for his mother or talking to the other Theoi, Kore wandered the mountain. Sometimes one of her mother's nymphs would accompany her, but she often walked alone. Kore would sit where she used to play with Eros and Iris, making their meadow explode with color. Deep in the forests, the dryads would occasionally talk to her. Usually, nymphs and dryads avoided Theoi they did not directly serve. But all of them talked to Kore, even they knew she was harmless.

When Kore walked far enough, the slopes became ringed with mist. If you kept walking you would pop out of the mist somewhere else on the mountain, sometimes in unexpected places. It was an interesting game, and Kore learned hidden nooks and crannies she thought no one else had found. Her favorites she shared with Eros and Iris when they could get away. Iris loved a rock pool deep in the mists of the forest, just before the barrier would pop you somewhere else. Kore decorated it for her with marsh plants. She found Eros a cliff, high and steep. You could jump off and soar for hundreds of hands if you had wings.

Kore walked the hills of the Minoan island, alone except for the wind playing with her hair. It had felt so wonderful the first few times that her mother had let her walk the mortal realm without the nymphs. But now Kore could feel the emptiness of the endless fields and woods.

She had stayed away from the human towns and cities for a long time, unsure of what to do without Demeter and nymphs and crops. The mortals might have a hard time recognizing the occasional demigod in their midst, but a Theoi, even a minor one was hard to miss. When Kore would follow their roads, a rough brown hood pulled over her bright curls, she could still feel their eyes on her as she walked. Unsure of what they saw, but transfixed nonetheless.

Even as Kore got better at dressing in their clothing, and speaking their languages, their eyes followed her. It almost made her miss Olympus, at least there she was unnoticeable. It took her seasons and seasons of wandering to find the trick of pulling her small power into a ball in her chest, away from her skin and eyes, stopping it from reaching out and touching the world around her. It wasn't the way that the other Theoi did it. They could cast glamours to redirect attention, taking the guise of a mortal. But Kore didn't have the power for that. But the one advantage of having so little was she could make herself very, very small.

Things were easier after that. Kore could enter their villages and buy food that she didn't really need at their markets. Occasionally some of them would talk to her, but many times unless she spoke first their eyes seemed to slide over her. A side effect of blending in almost too well. Kore would help the mortals as she passed through, making their gardens bright and helping the vegetables and orchards bloom early.

There was endless countryside to explore, and Kore walked for moons at a time. Between the harvest and planting festivals, no one needed her anywhere. But she learned to be back at the temple when the time came to join her mother for the rites. She only had to be fetched twice for that to sink in. Once Demeter had come for Kore in the middle of the woods which wasn't too bad, but the second time she disappeared from a marketplace which created quite a stir.

But that still left time. Time to walk to many different places, even if she had to leave time to walk at least most of the way back. Once Kore spent two moons in a larger mortal town, growing flowers in the meadows and selling them at the marketplace. Her stall was very popular, and she quickly went from sitting on the edge of a fountain handing out single blooms to a wooden booth with an awning and bouquets. Kore hadn't needed the coin, there was always plenty in the temples to take on her wanderings, but it left her feeling warm inside. Perhaps one day she could be the local goddess of a little town and make it beautiful.

Kore walked over another rise and found a town in the valley on the other side. It was on the larger side with rough cobbled streets and many houses were made of stone instead of wood. She thought it might be a trading town, wealthy and on the edge of a medium-sized river. Kore couldn't sense anyone living in this stretch of the river, so she slowly approached the edge of the houses. They grew bigger as she approached the center of town and the agora marketplace. The weather was starting to turn colder, and she would draw attention to herself in her light chiton before too much longer.

Several of the stalls sold fabric, so Kore wandered over to that side of the street. "A pretty scarf for a pretty girl?" The merchant inquired, holding up a pale grey piece of rough-spun.

Kore smiled and shook her head at him, moving down to the next booth. The woman there was selling warmer wool for winter. She meant to look at the plain brown, white, and grey pieces, but this was a merchant town. Their river must bring them dyes and coin to afford them, because the woman also sold bright blues, deep greens, rich purple, and a beautiful red. Kore couldn't help herself as she reached out to touch the red cloak. It was the kind of thing her mother would never approve of. Demeter favored greens, browns, and golds. Occasionally the lighter colors of new flowers for Kore. Nothing as vibrant as the cloak. And it would be out of place on a girl walking alone, brightly colored and almost as soft as Theoi silks.

Kore turned away from the rainbow of fabrics that reminded her of Iris and back towards the peasant clothes. The grey one wasn't too scratchy, and she would still have enough coins for the occasional meal in a village as she wandered back to the temple.

III

Depending on which version of the tale you believe, Gaia was the first. The earth beneath their feet, from whence food springs. Is it any wonder they spent so much of their energy on her? All Primordials come in pairs, and Uranus soon followed. Or perhaps he was first. Since the first monkeys climbed down from their trees, the humans always had regrets and dreams of the sky. Erebus came next. Worship is something we covet, but fear works just as well. Did those ancients fear the predators that stalked in the darkness, or worship the end of the day? There is no way to know. Even the Primordials told conflicting tales, when they told tales at all. Aether next, for humans in all their forms have always been creatures of the light. Pontus of the waters and then Chaos came last. There is no life without air.

Kore handed over a copper piece to the baker and put her loaf of bread into the bag, to join the cheese and apples. It was a pretty town, and she was glad she had found it early on this trip. *I might stay here until I have to go back for the Warm Harvest and Cold Sowing festivals. I could even sell flowers again.*

Kore wove her way through the market, dodging merchant carts and making her way to where the forest met the houses. Tall pines grew overhead, but the way was soft with ferns growing over the rocks. Her mother would have hated this forest. *There isn't anything here to eat. But it is beautiful. Too bad Apollo has already burned the mist away.* Kore knew the path well, even if a mortal would have been hard-pressed to follow the deer trail. Her feet followed it without having to pause her daydreaming. That was probably why Kore didn't notice that anything was different about her meadow.

When Kore had first found it, this meadow reminded her of the one she shared with Iris and Eros on Olympus. Tree-ringed and grassy, with an outcropping of low rocks in the middle. The only things that were missing were the bright flowers that Kore had grown and the bubbling stream on one end.

Kore didn't miss the stream much, and adding flowers would just draw attention. But the sun warmed the rock just the same.

She scrambled up onto her sunny perch and began to unpack her lunch before she noticed anything at all. Suddenly Kore's head flew up. There was a body in her meadow. *Is it dead?* her first thought rang through her head. The man was so still the thought was only slightly stupid. He hadn't seemed to have moved at all. *Don't be silly. Mortals bleed when they die, unless they are very old. Just asleep.*

Kore considered him for a few moments, watching his slow breathing. He was young and was wearing rich clothing for a mortal. Thick fabrics dyed deep colors. No bag, no horse, but then, they weren't too far from the town. *I could go eat somewhere else...*

His eyes blinked open, and Kore sat back a bit, as he rose onto his elbows, looking up at her. She hadn't realized that he was handsome, but then again, the rich mortals often looked better than the peasants. "I have already claimed this spot. Find another."

Kore's mouth dropped open. *He claimed it! This is my meadow.* "You claimed it! This spot is already mine. *You* can find somewhere else!" Kore retorted. *How dare he?* She might be dressed as a mortal, but most were still polite. Perhaps she should use a little of her power and scare him off.

"Well," the mortal pushed himself up with a groan, squinting against the sun to see her better, surprise written on his face. He seemed to be only a few seasons older than Kore looked, early in his second decade. His expression became slightly more civilized. "Perhaps we can come to an agreement. You remain on your rock, and I will have my little patch of grass," he said magnanimously.

It suddenly occurred to Kore that the mortal probably thought she was scared of him. That was reasonable from his perspective, Kore supposed. But if she scared him off he would no doubt go running off to the town, and then Kore would have to leave. "Fine. But that is your *only* patch of grass. The rest of the meadow is still mine."

The mortal threw back his head and laughed, long and loud. Kore frowned back at him, unamused. His grey eyes continued to dance but the laughter faded away. "You really have no concept of who I am."

Nobleman's son or part of a local merchant family, Kore decided, taking in his easy confidence and slightly strange way of speaking. She would have called it arrogance but he seemed intrigued rather than irritated with her.

"What brings fair young maidens out to the woods?" he continued, raising an eyebrow at her.

"Lunch," Kore replied, going back to spreading out her scarf and taking out the bread, cheese, and apples. She could feel him watching her instead of going back to sleep in the warm sunlight. Normally, she would have used a bit of power to slice the loaf and spread the cheese, but there was the matter of her audience. She sighed a bit, looking at her lunch mournfully.

"You have brought plenty of food for such a little thing," he remarked, still watching her.

"Mmm," Kore considering ripping the bread in half with her fingers and stuffing the cheese inside. A rattle sounded, and Kore looked up to see a small knife spinning slowly at the edge of her scarf. The mortal was smiling again.

"You do not seem to have one of your own."

Kore snatched it up, fighting the urge to glare. *It wasn't a problem until you came.* "And what brings pretty rich youths out to sleep in the woods instead of on soft beds?

For the first time since he had first sat up, the mortal looked away from Kore for a moment. "Sometimes one misses the sunlight even sleeping on a soft bed." But the mortal quickly looked back up at Kore. He watched her slice the bread and spread the cheese.

Kore finished with the knife and tossed it back over the side of the rock. It found its way back to wherever it had been concealed before. She prepared to turn her back to him, and look out over the unspoiled side of her meadow.

"What would the fair maiden say to sharing her lunch?" he asked suddenly, seemingly undeterred by her glare.

"Rich youths should learn to bring their own lunch when sleeping in the woods. Or go hungry like the rest of us."

"Ahh but my journey has been longer than I anticipated. I should not have fallen asleep." He pulled something out of his chiton again and tossed it up to her. "A tribute to the lady of the meadow."

He is still smiling! Kore caught it easily and looked at the shiny rock cupped in her hands. It was a pretty one, but Kore had no idea what it was.

Mortals liked some rocks very much and others were left on the riverbanks. It was all very confusing. "You can have one slice of bread and cheese, and one of my apples." *Maybe he will leave after he eats.*

The mortal climbed slowly up her rock, and sat on the other side of her scarf, picking up his slice of bread and cheese. He took a bite and chewed slowly, nodding in approval. "What would my dining companion like to be called?"

Kore narrowed her eyes before answering. "Kore." They narrowed further when he chuckled again.

"If the fair maiden already liked her name, she could have said so. I will not call you Girl," he chucked again, only louder when he saw her face. "I think Persephone fits you better than Girl."

"Avenging one?!" Kore spluttered at him. *This mortal really is awful.*

"The mighty defender of meadows," he said seriously, nodding.

Despite herself, Kore began to laugh. On her, the choice was definitely very funny. "You can be Pluton then," Kore managed to get out when she caught her breath.

"Rich? I suppose I earned that," he said, smiling. "Pluton and Persephone."

They ate in silence for a while. Kore watched the sparrows fly through the trees and demolished three slices of bread and cheese as Pluton nibbled delicately on his. She got the feeling that he hadn't really been hungry.

The apple was crisp and sweet as it crunched between her teeth. She chewed slowly as Pluton brought out the knife again and began to attack his own apple. It flashed in his fingers as he sliced the apple into eight pieces and began to remove the core. She hadn't noticed how fancy the knife was before—its owner had been annoying her too much. But now it looked slightly ridiculous being used on an apple.

Her eyebrows began to rise as Pluton next began to neatly remove the skin from the flesh of the apple. It would not have been how Kore would have chosen to eat one. Apple skins never tasted like much, and they were better eaten with the flesh, not separately.

By the time Pluton had gotten the apple prepared to his liking, Kore had already eaten most of her second one. He ate the slices slowly, taking his time as he had with the slice of bread and cheese. She had expected him to eat the skins last, but instead he swept them up with all three of the cores and slid off the rock.

Kore must have let out the squawking sound that she had tried to hold back.

Pluton looked up at her and frowned. The apple bits were already on the ground. "I apologize, Persephone. Did you want the skins? I forget some like them."

"I don't like them either," Kore said in shock, "But you can't just waste them like that!" The nymphs would have been scandalized to see edible food treated like that. Maybe rich mortals didn't know any better.

Pluton looked puzzled for a moment. "Next year your meadow will be all the greener for our offering. The peels aren't wasted any more than the cores. Both will help new life."

Kore thought about this for a few moments. Inedible food returned to the earth. Why not apple skins too? She nodded slowly, and Pluton kicked dirt over the forlorn little pile. She was surprised when he climbed back up onto the rock to join her again.

"Didn't you say you had to go somewhere? That you had already spent too long here?" Kore asked pointedly, looking around again for a horse. Rich men traveled on horseback. Even coming from the town.

"Another few hours will not hurt," Pluton said seriously.

Kore looked up at her odd rock-guest. He seemed to switch from laughter to seriousness so quickly. "Maybe I need to go then," Kore said.

He was smiling again. "Does Persephone have family in the village? Would you like an escort back to your home?"

She stayed quiet. Kore couldn't exactly tell him that she slept when she felt tired, usually here in the meadow or by the stream deep in the woods where her blanket currently lay. Theoi didn't need to fear weather or animals.

"I don't need to go home yet. Tell me about your journey?" Kore asked.

"I had business with my brother. He lives in another...town. I do not go often, and it is pleasant to see other woods before I return home."

A merchant family then. Kore couldn't remember what the local family was called. If he wasn't from this town either, it might not even be the right one. "It must have been important for you to travel so far."

"He thought it was," Pluton said. "I am not so sure. It seems nothing is ever decided."

"Maybe next time he should come to see you if your brother thinks it is so urgent." The familiar laugh didn't have as much humor in it, and Kore twisted around to see him.

"That would not be pleasant for anyone," Pluton said wryly. "And if I did not visit him how would I reclaim my patch of meadow?"

"I only said you could sleep there," she muttered. Kore suddenly noticed that the light was slanting down at an angle closer to evening than noon. It had not seemed like so much time had passed. Pluton noticed her glancing at the sun and quickly stood up, offering Kore a hand. He was much taller standing up.

"Persephone, we are losing the light. Can you find your way home before dark?"

"I'll be fine," she muttered before jumping down from her rock and stalking off towards the stream and her blanket. When she turned around just before the tree-line, Kore found that Pluton had already vanished.

IV

*I*t is hard to say whether the lives of the worshippers were made better or worse by the presence of the Primordials. Just as likely to torture as to bless, it is good that there were only six of them. Uranus created the eagle-like rocs, so huge they could take off with a full-grown man in their talons. Pontus's Telchines were the first to create cruel weapons of stone, and unleash them among the proto-humans. Gaia in particular loved to create monsters to terrorize her worshippers—the monstrous Cyclops, who dwelt in live volcanos, and the many-limbed Hecatoncheires who were always hungry.

Kore hadn't expected to see 'Pluton' again. But the little town was pleasant, and the meadow an excellent place to grow wildflowers. She didn't let them take over like the meadow on Olympus, but cultivated a little patch by her rock. This town liked her flowers just as much as the one before, and she soon had a little awning over her stall to keep them from wilting in the light.

The sun was beginning to pass the highest point of the sky, and Kore had already sold all of her flowers. She rolled up the blanket they had rested on and tucked it into her bag. *I should go start growing the flowers for tomorrow.*

Kore could just see the light through the trees when she heard the horse whinny. *Oh not again,* she thought. *Maybe I need to find another spot for the wildflowers. This one is obviously far too easy to find.* She braced herself to shoo off another stranger as she broke through the tree line. Kore blinked in the sudden bright sunlight, looking around for the interloper.

"Good afternoon, fair Persephone," Pluton said.

Kore noticed three things one after another, each more shocking than the last. First, Pluton and his horse were standing exactly on 'his' patch of meadow. Second, the white horse was one of Poseidon's, bread to Travel well and pull Theoi chariots. And the third was that Pluton wasn't mortal at all. He was Theoi.

"Hey!" Kore shouted indignantly, the anger building inside her. "You didn't tell me you were Theoi whatever-your-name-actually-is!"

The smile dropped from Pluton's face. "I apologize, Persephone, and I am happy with the name you chose for me. But you did not tell the 'mortal' you met the full truth either."

Kore considered him for a moment. His gray eyes looked very sad. She walked towards Pluton and his horse, stretching out her hand to its nose. The horse sniffed it delicately before pushing into her palm.

"He is hoping that you have brought a treat. Like you, he eats apples with their skin," Pluton said, tying the reins to the saddle.

"I'm sorry I didn't bring any today. What's his name?" asked Kore. She had never been this close to one of Poseidon's horses. Her mother didn't like them, and neither Iris nor Eros had one.

"Ametheus. He does not need any more apples. He is spoiled enough as it is."

"Ohh poor thing. I bet you haven't had any apples at all this week," Kore stroked her hand down his mane, and he tossed his head, still looking at her hopefully.

"Ammie is lying to you, Persephone. He had an apple only this morning," Pluton looked around the meadow. "The grass would be better for him if you are willing to share."

Ametheus tossed his head arrogantly as if he understood the suggestion and found it insulting. "The horse can share the grass, but you still have only the one patch."

Pluton nodded and released the white horse, who pranced around him, sniffing the ground curiously.

"It looks like he is still hoping for apples," Kore noted. She walked past the dark-haired Theoi to jump up on her rock. The day had been cloudy, and it was not as warm as it should have been in the late afternoon. Still, it was a good place to sit. To sit and watch Pluton. Even knowing he was a Theoi, Kore did not think she had seen him before, nor did he look like any of the Olympians or handful of Neptans she knew either. That didn't mean much. Kore had never spent much time on the mountain, and Theoi families did not look like each other nearly as much as mortal ones did.

Kore leaned down onto the rock, flopping down near her patch of wildflowers. She reached out a hand and ran her fingers through the blooms, encouraging them to grow again for the next day. The stems turned vibrantly green and budded quickly under her attention. She smiled as their leaves turned to her instead of the sun, and brushed them lovingly. She heard the scrape of boots on the rock as Pluton climbed up next to her. He stayed silent as she coaxed each bud to burst into color. Unsure why she did it, Kore paid extra attention to each flower, making sure this batch was especially colorful, vibrant hues not found in natural flowers.

Satisfied, Kore drew her hand back and watched them sway happily in the light breeze. It was a shame she would have to cut them at dawn the next morning. But the mortals were always delighted with her colorful stall. These would be especially popular. They almost didn't look real, even to her eyes.

"You have a marvelous gift, Persephone," Pluton breathed. "This is what you do, yes? Blooms?"

Kore turned away from his smiling eyes. "It's not very useful. Flowers are about all I can do. Maybe plants grow a bit quicker for me. Probably not."

"Ahh well. Shiny rocks are not very useful either," Pluton remarked. "The mortals seem to like them anyway."

Kore had to laugh at that. "Your gift is rocks? At least you can build things with bigger ones."

"The ground favors me," Pluton replied. "Gardens bring joy, and orchards fruit. It is not a bad gift. Many plants would die without flowers."

She smiled back at him and reached out to pick one of the biggest flowers from her bed. It was a wild rose, but its handful of petals were colored as bright a red as the fancy ones in the bigger cities. Kore handed it to Pluton. "A gift in exchange for your shiny rock. Bread and cheese was a bad trade, you know."

Kore loved the way his face lit up when he smiled...as if the flower was a great miracle. "The ground has rocks aplenty. Thank you for the gift." He cupped the wild rose in his hands like it was made of glass instead of the hardy wildflower that it was. Pluton gently tucked it between the folds of his chiton.

Kore tilted her head. The intense color looked at home there, among the dark folds. Somehow the wild rose seemed to belong better against the background of blacks and purples than in the bright meadow. She looked down at her little bed of wildflowers. "You can do bigger rocks too?"

Pluton nodded absently, still looking down at her flowers.

"Well, if you are going to keep bringing that hungry horse I want my flowers protected. Can you summon more rocks like this one to protect them?"

"Ammie would not eat your flowers," he said, looking at Kore like she had wounded him.

"Then to keep the mortals away. My meadow is not as hard to find as I thought if you keep showing up. And horses really don't know any better. Even pretty white ones." Kore gave him a smile.

Pluton frowned seriously and stood up, jumping down off the rock to study her wildflower bed. He reached up to help Kore off the rock and then motioned her to step back. "The earth may be uneven for a moment," he said.

Kore backed off several paces and watched as he reached out to touch her rock, running his fingers across the rough surface. He nodded sharply and raised hands over the soft earth around her flowers. She felt a slight tremble beneath her feet, and Kore squeaked and leapt further back. But it was not nearly as violent as she had feared. The gray rocks rose up around Pluton, stopping at waist height, just like her rock did. When the ground settled back down, Kore rushed over to the ring of rocks, scrambling over one of the new ones.

Pluton stood in the center of the ring. It completely enclosed her untouched wildflowers, in addition to a patch of meadow a few times bigger than her flower bed. The ring was perfectly centered on her new friend. In fact, the only part of the circle that was uneven at all on the inside was her original rock. He smiled softly at her, gesturing to the protective walls that included a ledge that seemed designed to be a bench. "Are you pleased?"

"It's wonderful!" Kore exclaimed. "Even if one of the mortals did find the meadow, they would not be able to see my flowers without climbing over the rocks."

He held out a hand, palm open to reveal another shiny rock, sparkling the same color as the one he had given her a few days ago. "Would you like to walk with me to town, Persephone? We could find some dinner there."

She nodded, but glanced over at Ammie, happily munching on the meadow grass, completely unfazed by what had just happened. "I don't have a horse. I wouldn't know how to ride anyway," Kore frowned slightly.

"Ametheus will be quite happy here while we are gone. And your blooms are out of sight. The town is not far. We could Travel or simply race?" He gave her a wicked grin, pointing at the path Kore was wearing through the trees.

She giggled and took off immediately, forestalling any more talk of Traveling. Kore heard Pluton shout indignantly from behind, but she concentrated on weaving through the trees. The deer path was not the quickest way to town.

Kore kept her lead, but the sounds of Pluton crunching through the underbrush were only a few paces behind her by the time she slowed before the town. A mortal would have been beyond breathless, but Kore laughed brightly for the moments it took for Pluton to find her. He looked a bit disheveled, dark curls just as tangled as her bright ones from the run.

"I believe you cheated, Persephone," he said seriously, but his eyes danced. "Such a little thing should not be so fast. The trees must move their roots away from your feet."

Kore simply stuck out her tongue before reaching out to catch his arm to drag him towards the town. "Sore loser. Let's go find some dinner. I can smell something roasting over the agora fire."

The mortals turned out to be very enamored by Pluton's rocks. All the merchants were quite happy to take them in exchange for juicy meat and hot bread. It was the best meal Kore had eaten since she had left the temple weeks ago. Theoi don't need to eat, and many days Kore didn't bother with anything but a few bites from woodland plants, but this was delicious.

Pluton seemed to agree because he did not try to speak either as they attacked the food. Kore was glad he was not a rich merchant. Rich mortals tended to object to eating with your fingers and licking the drippings off them after. Kore finished first and watched as he finished off the last of his grapes. She noted that he did not bother to peel those like the apple. "Who are you, Pluton?" Kore asked. Most of a day, and she still had not placed his face among the Theoi she knew.

"No one you would know," Pluton answered slowly. "I do not go to Olympus often. It is not a place I enjoy."

Kore nodded absently. Rocks might be more powerful than flowers, but not enough to earn much approval there. There were many Theoi older than Kore, and more who had simply grown more quickly. Pluton could be a disappointment like her, or simply the child of a minor pairing. She was far from the only Theoi that preferred to wander the mortal world. "I don't like Olympus much either," Kore admitted.

"Surely there are some things you like about it," he insisted. "Even I will admit the feasts are delicious."

Kore smiled. "I sometimes go with my mother,"

Kore sat near her mother's divan, on a cushion against the walls. It was easy for her to drift off into a daydream while the Aurai and the conversation bustled around her. The food was delicious, better than anything Kore had found on the earth below, even in the courts of kings. Sometimes the muses sang, and Kore let her thoughts flow with the melody.

"You agree with me about the food, though I do not think I have heard the muses."

"They're very good. Easy to hear from the back of the room."

Other times Poseidon's court would bring the entertainment, and Kore watched them make living sculptures of ice, breathing in the clean smell of salt.

Eros was increasingly busy, many of the younger nymphs seemed enamored with him. They giggled and pulled him off to sit on benches by the fires in the corners of the room. Sometimes they would dance.

"And a friend. It must not be too terrible."

"Eros is nice. Aphrodite too sometimes. She keeps him busy now though," Kore admitted. "But my favorite part is helping Aunt Hestia with the braziers. At the end of every feast she banks them for the next day. Hestia tells stories, nice ones about when they were first building the mountain."

V

Created in opposing pairs, and in pairs they lived and in pairs they fought. Gaia and Uranus may have spawned the most stories, but no less important were Erebus and Aether, or Pontus and Chaos. Capricious and cruel, they delighted in choosing favorites and in destroying what the others had made, jealous of their mates paying attention to anything but them. Nothing can annoy like family, even among Theoi.

And so life continued for a time, the Primordials sustained by the fear and worship of their subjects. But no one can stop the march of time and despite (or perhaps because of) their meddling, new types of humans began to appear, smarter than those who came before them. The new humans told stories about their world, brought new ideas, and the unions of the Primordials bore fruit. The children of the Primordials were smarter than their parents, more sophisticated. Thus came Titans.

Kore sat on the bench carved into the walls of her 'garden fence'. She could feel Pluton's eyes watching her hands dance through the flowers, making them grow. He seemed endlessly fascinated by her work. She sometimes had to fight down a blush.

"You are very skilled," he observed from his perch on the top of the original rock. Kore had long since given him permission to stray from his patch of meadow.

"Thank you," Kore felt that she did blush that time. "I worked hard to earn it. Even baby Persephone was stubborn."

"The hours were well worth it. It is strange that your gift did not come naturally to you," Pluton commented in surprise.

Kore made a face. "I'm just always lucky, aren't I? But I'm not the only one who had to work."

Pluton was still frowning, eyes unfocused. "To increase strength or control, perhaps. For most Theoi that is a matter of use."

Kore paid attention to her flowers once again. She was trying to grow some daffodils that had caught her attention in town. They always took more concentration than the wild varieties. She had heard mortals complain that they were finicky.

"Do you remember when you found your gift?" Pluton asked, sliding down the rock to join her on the bench he had made.

"How could anyone forget that?" Kore laughed. But that story doesn't start with me. Eros was cheating again,"

Kore was chasing Eros through the grass, squawking indignantly when he used his wings to glide faster down the sloping sides of hills. They were mostly alone, Kore's nymph minders talking to the dryads at the edge of the clearing. "Give me back my ribbon!" Kore shouted before she almost slammed into the mortal that had appeared in front of her. She barely swerved in time, skidding to a stop in confusion. Demigods visited Olympus from time to time, but no mortals that Kore had ever seen.

"Mortals on Olympus," Pluton said skeptically.

"Who is telling this story?"

Any Theoi who brought one would keep it safely in their palace. The mountain was beautiful and dangerous for anyone who didn't have even a scrap of power to guide them. But Aphrodite had just Traveled, bringing seven mortal children with her. They looked a season or two away from getting their growth spurts.

Aphrodite smiled down at the children who looked around in wonder. "See, just as beautiful as I promised." She gestured for Kore and Eros to come closer. "And two new friends for you as well. Meet Kore and Eros. You can play with them in the meadow, but stay out of the forest."

The mortals happily spread out, looking at the strangely colored wildflowers and bright grasses. Kore was still standing next to Aphrodite in shock. Mortals on Olympus.

The goddess turned to her son, "Just like we practiced earlier. I promised you could show Kore, and here they are. We can bring others when Iris comes to visit." She ran a fond hand through her son's hair before giving him a little push towards the mortals. "I'm so proud of him!" Aphrodite whispered to Kore.

"Aphrodite should not be set loose among the mortals," Pluton sighed.

"She's not so bad," Kore insisted. "No one got hurt, and they had fun, I think."

Eros skipped across to one of the human girls, whispering in her ear as she giggled. Kore was more puzzled than ever. She followed her friend, who was now sitting on the rock alone, the girl wandering off, blushing towards one of the boys. "She was easy," Eros commented, watching the girl stammer as she tried to talk.

"I'm feeling left out of the joke," Kore whispered back.

"When we were in Crete, I found my gift," Eros said excitedly. "I'm not very good yet, but I can make the mortals love each other. For a few hours anyway."

Kore watched Eros flit among the humans, making the girls flush and the boys show off. Kore turned her attention from his game to a dandelion getting ready to flower. She stretched out her hand to the bloom, willing it to flower. *If Eros is beginning to find his talents, I can too.* The dandelion bud swelled a little bit. Maybe.

"You knew that easily?"

"Hoped. It had to be something to do with plants. There were a lot of flowers there to try with," Kore pointed out.

"We do not all share gifts with our parents," Pluton insisted.

"Mmm."

The games went on until Kore noticed Eros pointing one of the mortals towards her. He braided some of the wildflowers into a crown and approached her slowly. The boy with the soft brown eyes was only brave enough to put the flowers in her lap and smile a little before he scurried off. Kore stroked their soft petals before settling it on her curls. The sunset bathed the meadow in golden light and Aphrodite called the mortals back to her. They traveled back to the mortal realm, and Kore followed the nymphs back to her mother's palace.

Dinner was already laid on the table, and her mother was waiting for her. Kore hadn't realized that the day had lasted so long. "What a lovely garland you made today," Demeter exclaimed when Kore sat down next to her. "I love the warm season flowers you chose!"

Kore looked at her nymph companions who were now beginning to serve them dinner. Neither of them looked confused by the comment. Kore wasn't surprised. When they were not required to play with her, the dryads proved very distracting. "Thank you mother," she said happily.

"This still does not sound like a story about how you found your gift, Persephone."

"I told you I had to work on it. This was why. We all thought Iris would find hers first. I didn't want to be left behind."

Eros and Aphrodite didn't come back for many days, but Kore went to the meadow every day. The nymphs talked to the dryads, and Kore never called them back to attend her. She worked hard, and every day Kore made a little more progress with the wildflowers. When Eros finally came back, she could take the tiniest bud and in a few minutes cause it to open, revealing soft tufts or sweet-smelling petals.

Kore pulled Eros over to their rock and laid down so both were near a plant with three buds the size of her pinky. "Watch," Kore breathed as she reached out to brush the tallest with a finger. Agonizingly slowly it opened, spreading pale blue petals to the morning sun.

Eros clapped, sitting up straight. "Mother! Come see Kore!"

Kore ignored her friend, mesmerized by the second bud growing slowly, fed by nothing but her will. Aphrodite sat down on the rock in time to see the last bud slowly unfurl itself. Kore reached out, satisfied, and plucked the sprig. She offered it to the goddess, who often wove flowers in her hair, smiling shyly.

"How beautiful," Aphrodite exclaimed, tucking them behind her ear.

Kore beamed with pride. It meant something, for her flowers to be declared beautiful by Aphrodite. She chose a different plant and coaxed it to flower. Bright red this time. Kore hadn't yet figured out how to predict what colors her flowers would be. Sometimes they were very different from the others that surrounded them. Eros received the red sprig, and his mother helped him tuck the flowers into his own hair.

"I'm sure Demeter is very proud of you," Aphrodite said as her skilled fingers wove a braid to support the flowers in Eros's fine blonde hair. "It is a wonderful time when a young Theoi discovers their gift."

"I haven't shown her," Kore admitted quietly. "I want to be better first. They bloom so slowly, and I can only do a few at a time."

"A gift should be effortless," Pluton insisted.

Kore laughed hollowly. "I got there in the end."

But Aphrodite could never resist showing off a beautiful present, and Kore's flowers were among the most brightly colored on Olympus. Everyone seemed to know about Kore's first flowers. Demeter brought her flowers from all around the mortal world as well as the mountain. Her mother had the nymphs plant them around her own garden at the palace, and they bloomed thick with color.

Kore wasn't responsible for much of it. Many of the chosen varieties were elegant garden flowers, not the hardy blooms of the slopes. The beautiful flowers the mortals spend so many years shaping, especially the roses with their prickly stems, seemed to dislike Kore. They never bloomed for her.

"But I can't tell you how many hours I spent sitting in a field staring at a mound of earth, trying to make the seeds sprout." Kore could still feel the frustration. Trying to reach deep inside herself, into the place where her power lived. Tugging at it with little success, pushing it into the seeds so they would sprout lush and green. But opening her eyes, to nothing but damp earth. "I was so sure I would get it eventually."

"No one has the same gift as another," Pluton said gently.

"I should be able to do it, even if it takes a lot out of me. Using power within your gift is just easier, and mine does have to do with plants. But I've always been awful at anything else."

VI

The Primordials did not notice these differences, any more than they noticed their children at all. Even Gaia's delight at her new toys waned quickly, as they did not bend to her will as easily as her other creations. Kronos, Titan of time, and Rhea, Titan of the feminine were first and left to their own devices as they grew. Theoi do grow, or we can. Some fast, some slow, some spring fully formed, and others remain forever children. Kronos and Rhea must have grown quickly, for they raised the other firstborn Titans. Their siblings Themis, Iapetus, and Mnemosyne. And their cousins, Oceanus and Tethys born of Pontus and Chaos. Erebus and Aether's Anchiale, Crius, Selene, Helios, and Coeus.

Weeks passed quickly. Pluton came to visit frequently, sometimes every day for three or four days, but always at least once a week. Kore could feel the time slipping through her fingers. Soon she would have to start the walk back to her mother's temple for the Harvest and to help plant for the Cold Growing season. She didn't know what she was going to say to Pluton. He hadn't pushed her about who she was, though she thought he must know. Kore had told him her name the day they first met, and even if he hadn't believed her then, she would not be hard to find out about. He had mentioned Traveling several times, maybe he would take her back near the temple. It would buy them a week or more.

Kore was sitting under the awning of her stall, worrying when a thump made her lookup. A green rock glittered on the blanket by her feet. She looked up grinning, to see Pluton perusing her display. "What would that buy me?" He asked playfully. "One of these bouquets or only a wild rose?"

She laughed happily, jumping into his arms. He always seemed a little surprised every time she saw him. It had puzzled Kore until she noticed that the mortals did not seem to like him much. Their eyes followed him warily, and they leaned away from him even as they took his rocks and gems. Pluton smiled too and pulled a roll of fur out from seemingly nowhere. Kore shot him a glare for using his powers in the middle of her town. The mortals found her strange enough already.

"I thought you might like a better blanket," he said softly, burying his face into her reddish curls. "The nights will be cold soon."

Kore ran her fingers through the soft thick fur. It was far larger than the rabbit furs she had owned before, all one piece instead of stitched together. She thought it must have come from a wild animal, maybe even a wolf or leopard. The entire thing was deliciously forbidden. Demeter hated the wild places and Artemis's hunt. "It's wonderful!" She cried.

Kore rolled up her old blanket and gathered up the remaining wildflowers. There was no point in staying now that Pluton had come. No one would approach her stall with him sitting next to her. She passed the enormous makeshift bouquet to him, and he held it bunched together awkwardly for a moment, before passing it back.

"One moment," Pluton turned his back to the street before summoning a long silky black ribbon from the ether. He quickly tied it around the multitude of stems, turning it into a proper, if bulky, bouquet.

She felt the flowers lifted gently from her arms, leaving her with the fur, and him with the wildflowers, For a second it seemed like such a silly sight she laughed softly before skipping off down the road towards the food vendors. She had several coppers from the morning, and the merchant was happy to give a large lunch in exchange. Kore even included some apples for Ammie. It would help in her ongoing plot to befriend the massive animal.

Pluton followed Kore as they walked slowly along the deer path to the meadow. Neither wanted to race with their burdens. They were light, but bulky and would not take kindly to being dropped on the forest floor. The fur was just the right size to drape over the original part of the rock ring, and Kore found that it was plush enough to make the rock almost soft to sit on. She flopped down onto the furry surface, spreading her arms out and running them over the softness.

"I am glad you like it," Pluton said, climbing up and putting the enormous bouquet into a dip in the rock. He settled onto the fur and helped Kore start opening their lunch.

Kore ran her fingers through the fur, its softness sparking an old memory. "It feels like the kitten I kind of had once."

"How does one 'kind of' have a kitten?" Pluton asked, puzzled.

"My mother and I used to stay at temples, I loved it when we got to stay in one place," Kore began.

Kore played hide and seek among the stone columns, flagstones cool against her bare feet. The mortals that came didn't bring any playmates, but many of them had little bits of sweet fruit for her. They didn't have to move every day, and the younger nymphs sometimes had time to play. The nymphs of the orchards often would chase Kore through their groves, and help her pick fruit from their branches. Even her mother could play sometimes in the evenings when the mortals went back to their tents or the local town. Each temple had a little room in it just for Kore, with a bed built off the floor and woolen blankets for cool weather. She loved not sleeping in a different tent each night.

"You slept in tents when you were small?" Pluton said in shock.

"It wasn't too bad. The mortals would put them up for us. Some of them were actually quite nice."

All six of her mother's temples had a little town near it. Kore wasn't allowed to go into the towns alone, she had to stay in the temples, fields, and orchards. One of the fields even had a little stream running through it. There wasn't a naiad living there, but there were plenty of rocks to play with. But the best part of living in the temples was the two weeks every year when the towns came alive. Once in fall and once in spring after the Warm and Cold Growing seasons the towns coordinated the harvest festivals. They were the best two weeks of Kore's year. People flooded into the towns from outlying villages, and everything smelled almost as delicious as Olympus. And as they each lasted a week, Kore would always make friends with a few of the human children. Once they even came back two festivals in a row!

Kore would watch for the leaves to turn deep red and bright gold, and the fruit to become richly sweet. When the town started to paint walls green and gold, and the grain was harvested, Kore knew it was time. One morning she would wake up, and Calli would have a beautiful chiton for her, light blue, delicate pink, or new leaf green. All had little flowers embroidered on the hem. Kore loved her mother's festival clothes too, dark green with gold sheaves of grain on the hem. It was made by the nymphs and beautiful, the green matched her mother's eyes, and the grain glimmered just like her hair. Kore wished her dresses looked like that. Calli did her best but even the light green chiton wasn't right to match her eyes, and they always made her hair look funny. Calli said Kore's hair was red like her Aunt Hestia's, but all Kore could see was a duller shade of her mother's bright gold.

"Yes, I cannot imagine you in light colors," Pluton commented.

"You're not supposed to say that," Kore spluttered.

"Why? I would not wear them either."

"They were pretty!" Kore insisted. "*And* not what the story is about."

"I apologize."

But the festival clothes were pretty, and not the important part. The mortals brought food and toys, some that Kore only saw at the festival. Pears bathed in crunchy honey, rocks in colors she had never seen before set to be ground into dye, and cheese. Some of them were tasty, but others smelled. Kore would feed those to the stray cats that always seemed to appear for the festival.

The humans were wearing clothes that were even fancier than the rest of their kind, dyed deep purple and blue that fascinated Kore. Calli was talking to them, and one of their servants had handed Kore an offering, a particularly ripe cheese that almost dripped down her fingers. She slipped off down an alleyway looking for one of the many cats to give it to. It would make both the cat and the mortals happy. Kore called out for them in a high sing-song voice, but it was the fifth day of the festival. All of the cats were near the cook fire, trying to catch a piece of the roasting bull. Kore was about to sadly wipe the awful cheese on the wall when she heard a small sound from the corner. It was a tiny thing with dark fur, too young to compete with the larger cats for the good scraps. Kore knelt down and offered the sticky mess to the kitten. It tickled her fingers and Kore laughed as the kitten purred. It looked up at her plaintively when all the cheese was gone.

Kore made her way back to Calli, who was still talking to the brightly colored humans. She kept one hand in her pocket, scratching the kitten's ear. It had curled up in the fold in her chiton, falling asleep instead of wriggling. Kore smiled up at Calli and took her hand without complaint when it was time to go back to the temple.

The kitten looked happy to be on Kore's bed, even though she didn't have any more food for it. It slept in a tight ball as Kore stroked its soft fur. They fell asleep together on top of the blankets. Kore tried not to cry when she woke up, the kitten was gone. She sat on the bed sadly waiting for the sun to finish rising and for

Calli to bring her a new chiton. Kore heard a scraping sound on her windowsill, and when she looked up Kitten had scrambled back into her room. It jumped up on her bed and began to purr. "Good Kitten!"

Kore kept Kitten secret until the last day of the festival, sneaking back little scraps of food in her pocket. Her friend sometimes was gone when she woke up, but always was there when she fell asleep. It was not until Kore had to try to feed Kitten from the kitchen that she was caught by a nymph. Her mother watched in disapproval as Calli tried to pry the little bundle of fur from her arms. Kitten's claws dug through her chiton into her arm. Kore didn't care.

When Calli finally had the cat captured in her hands, mother looked at it disapprovingly. "If you are so attached to the creature, we should find something for it to do," her mother mused. She flicked her fingers and her power reached out, surrounding the struggling kitten with a glittering green and gold shroud.

Kore's lip trembled as she watched the blue leave her kitten's eyes to be replaced by reflective gold. Kitten stopped struggling and hung limply in Calli's hands.

"It can help keep the vermin away from the seed grain," mother decreed.

Kore watched her kitten lope away from her. It didn't look back.

"Your mother should not have stolen your pet. A kitten would only have lived a few seasons, they are harmless," Pluton insisted, looking at her in a strange way.

"They were right, really. It didn't belong inside the temple. And I wouldn't have been able to take it with me when we moved on. It seemed happy prowling the fields." Kore replied.

VII

The Titans tried desperately to keep to themselves, for though they rapidly outnumbered the Primordials, they were far weaker, especially at first. Whenever the Primordials briefly remembered their children, they used them as pawns in cruel games and became angry whenever they were defied. Fiery Anchiale was a great favorite, forced to cause wildfires to burn out of control. Whenever she could, Tethys of freshwater would send rain to quench the burns, but could only do so once Themis distracted their tormentors with fresh ideas, which only started the cycle again in another variation.

They ate in silence for a while, before Kore blurted out, "I wish we could stay here forever," her voice trailed, still a bit sad.

"Is there somewhere you have to go?" asked Pluton. "You have not lived in this village long."

Kore made a face. "Yes, I have to go home soon. For two moons at least. Probably closer to three."

"To go back to Demeter," Pluton said softly. "Surely it is not so bad to go see your mother."

Kore could not bring herself to be surprised, and she closed her eyes as she finished eating her grapes. "I knew you would have figured it out by now. Yes, I love my mother, but I've never really fit in or been useful. I just trail along behind mother and the nymphs, making the hedgerows bloom."

Pluton put his arm around her and pulled her down onto the fur so they could watch the clouds race each other across the gray sky. "When do you need to return, Persephone?"

"Next week, if I walk as usual," Kore sighed. "I could stay a bit longer if you took me back close to the temple. Can you Travel with two, Pluton?" She felt him nod against her shoulder.

"Of course," he turned his head to face her, a wicked grin on his lips. "Or we could ride Ammie. He could carry us both. You do not weigh anything."

Kore laughed nervously. "I don't know about that. We're still getting to know each other after all. And I've never even been on one of the mortal's horses."

"He is devoted to you for life," Pluton pointed out, gesturing to where Ametheus stood near the rocks, crunching happily on the apples Kore had brought. "I would take you wherever you wish to go. Is that Demeter's temple?"

"Where else could I go?" Kore wondered out loud.

"I do not like Mount Olympus much," Pluton said slowly, "but many do. You are a Theoi and have not been banished. You have a home there as well."

Kore laughed bitterly. "No, I've not been banished. I'm simply invisible. Mother would simply collect me from there anyway. No one pays any attention to the daughter of Demeter and Zeus who makes flowers bloom. I'd be a laughing stock if anyone bothered to take notice."

"Surely they are not that cruel," Pluton frowned.

"Cruel, no. I'm simply very forgettable. And embarrassing to think about. I think I frighten them sometimes. I'm what they could have turned out to be, after all." Kore watched a cloud shaped like a bird float across the sky in the cool breeze. Another bright leaf dropped from one of the trees to the ground in the forest.

"The mortal world is vast," Pluton said. "There are many villages and even nymph colonies. Flowers would be appreciated there."

"And that is how I spend my time when my presence is not required at the temples. I might not fit in well, but I get along. I can't hide the fact that I'm Theoi from nymphs, and it makes them nervous."

"But you have chosen no home?" Pluton asked.

It sounded more like a statement than a question. He was annoyingly perceptive sometimes. "I am the daughter of two of the most powerful Theoi, with a gift more befitting a demigod. I'm easily outstripped by the average nymph! If I am unlucky, my father will treat me as one of his demigod daughters and I will be married off to a mortal king who will wither and die, to bear him demigod children who will also wither and die. I suppose I can do *that* better than the demigods. If I am very lucky I will be left alone to find a little town to bless. I could be a local goddess well, I think. Maybe marry a rare male nymph. He would take longer to die at least."

Pluton made a disbelieving sound and ran his fingers through her hair.

Kore forged ahead. "But I've never had any kind of luck at all. I will attend my mother, her only daughter with a conveniently plant-based gift."

They fell silent again as the clouds raced and the leaves fell. Kore could feel him considering something, even as they lay still.

"There are many minor Theoi. You are beautiful, Persephone. You do not have one of them in mind?" Pluton asked softly.

"Even the minor Theoi like you don't bother with me. Maybe once I had that chance before my gift revealed itself, but I have not thought about marriage prospects for a long, time. There are *many* minor Theoi. And all of them are better choices than me."

He let out a soft curse that Kore had not heard before. "They are cruel. You are not worthless even if you are not overly fond of your gift. Persephone, you are intelligent and fierce."

That broke Kore's sour mood. "Oh, you are a romantic, Pluton! Never change, even when you find other fair maidens to befriend. But enough about me. How does 'Pluton' spend his time when he isn't saying pretty things to me? A nice town surrounded by stone walls perhaps?"

He nodded, serious still. "That is not inaccurate."

Kore shook her head, sitting up. "It's not fair. You know everything about me. You haven't even shared your real name," she pressed.

"I have collected several names over the seasons. Aidoneus is one of the ones I like. Or Pluton. There is not overmuch to tell. I watch over my…city. And this season I have a new friend. It does not happen often," he was smiling again.

"I don't have many of those either," Kore admitted. "Will I see you again after the festivals?"

"Of course," Pluton promised. "Perhaps even before then, Persephone. Or do you prefer to be called Kore?" He said suddenly.

She laughed. "I know lots of people find my name funny, but it's always just been a name to me. I like it fine, but I like Persephone too, even if it's a big name for me."

"Kore is a very small name," he pointed out.

"A small name for a small girl," Kore frowned for a moment. "I don't know how well mother will take it if you come to the temple. We don't get many Theoi visitors."

"I can be very polite. And you are long grown. Surely you have other friends."

"A few on Olympus," Kore conceded. "I told you about Eros. We used to chase each other through a meadow like this one."

Aphrodite would often bring Eros and they would pick the wildflowers in the eastern meadow. Kore and Eros would race through the soft short grass, stretching their legs much faster than any of her mortal friends could. When the Neptans visited, Iris would come to play too. Kore raced across the grass, after her friend, tugging at her wing before racing off. Iris squawked and flapped a bit, managing to hover just above the ground for a few heartbeats before her feet landed firmly on the ground once again.

"Why do you have wings when you live underwater?" Kore laughed dancing out of the way of Iris's retaliatory handful of dirt.

Kore watched Pluton smile, holding back laughter. It was funny. There weren't many Neptans with wings.

"You can fly in water too!" Iris yelled gliding down off a rock, landing near where Eros flopped on the grass.

Kore ran closer as Iris laid down on the grass. She dropped down in a heap next to them, stroking one of Eros's fluffy feathers. "I wish I had wings too," she said sadly.

"You're an earth goddess like Demeter," Eros said. "You don't need to fly."

"We can't fly either," Iris pointed out, yawning lazily.

Kore nodded as they lay on the grass.

The food was almost gone, and the shadows were growing long, the patch of wildflowers hidden among them. "You asked me earlier what I wanted, and I'm always the one telling stories. What would *you* want?"

"I am content. I have my work and a new friend. Some others as well, but I am afraid they are not as entertaining as these stories of yours."

The light had almost disappeared from the meadow when Aidoneus mounted Ametheus. They cantered twice around the ring of rocks before he urged the white horse into the twilight sky. Kore watched them until even Theoi eyes could not spot the speck they had turned into anymore. With a sigh, Kore dragged her new fur into the patch of meadow protected by the rocks. The wildflowers had become overgrown, but there was still more than enough room for her to roll herself into the soft fur and stretch out under the first few stars.

VIII

It was Helios of the sun and Selene of the moon who first noticed that things were changing. They, along with Crius and his stars, were most often left alone as their domains and gifts were considered the most useless of the Titans. Their fortune gave them the most time to spend freely among the humans. Selene especially tried to help the nearby tribes, who were often the butt of Primordial, and sometimes even Titan jokes. She used her small power to heal and help them catch food. Her brothers soon followed suit. The humans were grateful, and a cult sprang up to worship their saviors. First Selene and Helios, and then Crius noticed that as their worship increased, so did their powers.

Aidoneus had not meant to fall asleep in the warm sunlight. But when he spotted the clearing on his way back from Mount Olympus, it was the perfect place to let his annoyance with his younger brother fade away. It did not do for a king to return to his court in a sour mood. Aidoneus released Ametheus to wander and graze before lying down in the sweet-smelling grass to enjoy the warmth. It was different than one of the great fireplaces, sunlight penetrated right down to the bones. He might prefer the gray diffuse light of home, but every once in a while it was nice to see the sun or stars.

The shifting sounds on the rock woke him. His bad mood was gone, and he felt lazy in the sunlight. Aidoneus would send the mortal hurrying on their way and enjoy this place. It had been an unconscious habit to put on his glamour in the mortal realm, but somehow they always sensed the presence of death on him. "I have already claimed this place. Find another," Aidoneus called out, fully expecting the mortal to run.

But a girl's voice quickly rang out, indignant. "You claimed it! This spot is already mine. *You* can find somewhere else!"

Caught halfway between an internal groan and being reluctantly impressed with this one, Aidoneus pushed himself to his elbows, squinting against the sun. It was a young woman, not a girl. She was older than she had sounded. And definitely not a mortal. At first, he could not tell what she was. But upon closer inspection, he decided that she had to be a Theoi with a decidedly odd way of glamouring herself.

It was still unusual that she had not run away after a good look at him. Most Theoi did not like him any more than the mortals did. But she continued to berate him. It was endearingly amusing. *Perhaps we can have a civil conversation before she realizes.*

Aidoneus offered to stay sitting below her rock, and then eventually convinced her to share her lunch. It had smelled and tasted of the living world. It was not better than his court's food, but it was different. Even after paying for his share with a diamond, he was forced to believe that the Theoi who had introduced herself as 'girl' of all things still had absolutely no idea who he was. 'Persephone' didn't even have the natural aversion that all Olympian Theoi seemed to have for his entire court.

Ammie was already trying to eat the sweet grass and Aidoneus still was not sure why he had come back. She had been interesting and unfrightened, yes, but he should know better than to push his luck. Persephone probably would not even come back here. The town had no evidence of a resident Theoi. But he had not been waiting long when she reappeared. Persephone froze upon seeing him, first staring at his horse, and then at him. Aidoneus had released his hold on his glamour slightly, she should be able to see what he was. He braced himself for the screaming. Instead, she seemed much angrier that he had hidden his nature. Not that she had told her 'mortal' dining companion the truth either.

Her flowers were beautiful. She still was not frightened. If she had found out who he was she showed no sign of it.

She had given him a true name. Who named their child Girl? Aidoneus had never felt quite so exasperated with his siblings. At least he could not be held responsible for Zeus's involvement. Theoi might not have families quite like the mortals, but he had always felt slightly responsible for his younger siblings. A faint memory plucked at the edges of his mind. He had heard something about Demeter having a child a very long time ago. But Olympians were outside his purview, and nothing else had come to his attention.

Aidoneus found that he could not help himself. The mortal world might be open for all Theoi to visit, but he had not left Hades this often in millennia. The weather grew colder and the leaves fell around them. He kept visiting Persephone. The name Kore did not fit her at all.

It was wrong. He knew it was wrong, this plan to befriend the beautiful Theoi before telling her who he was. Aidoneus tried to tell himself that he was not actually courting her, not yet. He would tell her before then. Hopefully, she would not immediately run when she found out. Olympians tended not to hold still long enough for him to get out a few words, except at Zeus's banquets. And usually not even then. Especially the women, and despite Zeus's offer, Aidoneus would not drag an unwilling Theoi into his court.

Persephone had told him who she was. That she had to go to Demeter's temple for the harvest and planting rites. She did not seem opposed to being courted. If she could find the right match, even if she seemed unwilling to admit her interest to herself. Aidoneus cursed Zeus and his uncouth habits. Persephone had not recognized even his name.

It had been a very long time since Aidoneus had accepted one of his brother's invitations to an Equinox Banquet. Truly, he was not sure if Zeus realized the invitations still arrived like clockwork. But he had taken Persephone to a field near Demeter's temple. The thought of not seeing her for several moons was unbearable. It was time to tell everyone the full truth. If she was not ready or unwilling to be courted, Aidoneus hoped that she would still consider him a friend. Theoi lives were long.

The horses were made ready, and the Lampads polished his chariot until it gleamed. His armor matched it, lacquered black and covered with gold and silver. Aidoneus thought it was a bit much, but the Moirai had designed it, and Zeus loved shiny things. When asking for a Theoi to join another court, it was prudent to be polite.

The horses were excited. They did not get to fly aboveground very often, and the four of them pranced and shook their manes as they neared the mountain. A shudder ran through them as the horses pulled the chariot through the transition from mortal mountain to Mount Olympus.

There were only a few other chariots landed on the marble courtyard. That was good. Aidoneus did not want too much of an audience for this.

Demeter would not be happy with the prospect of her daughter possibly joining the Chthonic court. But she could not possibly object too much to her daughter becoming a queen. Besides, courting an Olympian would require more frequent appearances. Everyone would need to get used to it.

Aidoneus strode into Zeus's throne room, pulling the great plumed helm off his head and tucking it under his arm. His brother was alone except for a few minor attendants. He had been seen in the hall, accompanied by a few muffled gasps, but that could not be helped. The heavy door swung shut behind him. "Greetings, Lord Zeus," he said politely.

"Lord Hades!" Zeus boomed happily, sitting straighter on his throne. "What brings you to my feast?"

"Hades is not a name, but a place," Aidoneus corrected gently, trying to keep the annoyance off his face.

"Of course, of course, Aidoneus," Zeus waved his hand dismissively.

"I would like your permission to court your daughter Kore, and one day offer her a place in the Chthonic court," he answered.

"I told you millennia ago you could have your choice of my daughters," Zeus said magnanimously. "Which girl has caught your eye?"

"Kore, Zeus. Your daughter with Demeter," Aidoneus spoke clearly. *Damn Demeter.*

"Ahh, the flower girl! An excellent choice of mistress. I'm sure she can return with you after the festivities," Zeus gestured at one of his attendants. "Go find the girl." The nymph scurried off.

"No, brother," Aidoneus was relieved at Zeus's response, but his brother had yet to learn to listen when someone else was talking. "I wish to court her, marry her if Kore wishes it."

Zeus stared at Aidoneus for several long moments. "You want to *marry* Kore," Zeus said in surprise. "Aidoneus, are you sure she is the daughter you want?"

He nodded and would have answered when the doors burst open again.

"Lord Zeus!" Demeter screamed. "You will not send my Kore to the underworld! Kore belongs in the sunlight among the gentle breezes and her flowers. She isn't to marry at all, least of all Hades!"

"Aidoneus," he said dully. Demeter did not pay him much attention.

"Demeter," Zeus snapped sharply. "Be reasonable. Hades wishes to court and marry her, make her a queen. It is a far better match than Kore ever had any right to dream of. Send her now before he comes to his senses."

"NO! Kore is sweet, that place would destroy her. She belongs with me, I swore when she was named I would never let anything like that happen," Demeter insisted.

"I am the Lord of the Olympians," Zeus began.

Aidoneus cut him off wincing at himself. "Demeter, Kore is not a girl any longer. She has been grown for a long time. I will court her, not drag Kore away. Give her a chance to decide," he soothed.

Demeter thoroughly ignored the Lord of Hades. "Never, Zeus, never! You may be her father and her lord, but I am her mother. She is *mine* to protect. I will turn her into a crepe tree before I let anyone touch her!"

"Demeter! You will not turn our daughter into a plant. That is a punishment for mortals and nymphs."

"MY daughter!"

Aidoneus watched them argue, growing increasingly alarmed. Demeter was more unreasonable than he had ever seen her. She raved as Zeus became increasingly furious as well. Aidoneus backed slowly towards the heavy doors that were still swung wide. There was something in Demeter's eyes that he did not like at all.

Barely keeping from breaking into a run, Aidoneus jammed his helm back onto his head, cloak flying out behind him. It was incredibly difficult to Travel on Olympus, and he did not want to risk it. He leapt into his chariot and urged the black horses into flight. Cursing himself, Aidoneus promised himself that he would never let them go without time flying in the mortal world again. The mortals and their fear could go hang. Unless Zeus planned on imprisoning Demeter, Aidoneus felt with sinking certainty that she would not be far behind.

Once they were over the mountain again, they Traveled to the field where Persephone had asked him to take her before. He had no idea where she was, but that was as good a place to start searching as any. It was cold comfort that Demeter probably did not know exactly where she was either.

It took three hours to find her, and Aidoneus could feel the cold panic of time passing the whole time. But suddenly there she was. Persephone, sitting in another meadow. He could hear nymphs in the distance. Aidoneus knew he should deliver her to Zeus on Olympus. But he did have a paper-thin justification to take her, and Zeus did not seem to care. And Aidoneus did not want Demeter anywhere near Persephone until she'd had ample time to calm down. The horses dove, pulling the chariot towards the ground.

IX

*D*elighted with the discovery, many of the others soon joined them. Oceanus showed the humans how to catch fish from the salty depths. Iapetus soon had a cult among the men, helping them bond together as brothers. Coeus showed them the rhythms of the seasons, and Mnemosyne helped the humans weave together stories of their pasts. All of the Titans founded cults, and their power waxed. But even the strongest among them was no match for the weakest of the Primordials. Helpless anger simmered under the surface for an age.

It was strange to Kore to be back at her mother's temple, in a way it had never been before. She hadn't even been gone any longer than usual. But the bustle of the preparations for the warm season harvest festival somehow seemed alien. Kore was surprised at how much she felt herself missing her village and the days when Pluton would visit.

She sat under the shade of the old oak tree, watching the temple and Eleusis in the distance, down the sloping hill. She could see mortals and nymphs scurrying like ants. At least no one ever expected Kore to help. Her gifts were much more impressive in the moment, making the hedgerows bloom. The loneliness was becoming oppressive, and Kore shook herself roughly. *It hasn't even been a week,* she told herself. *He said he would visit, and he will. This is far from the longest he's been busy.*

Easy to say, not so easy to believe. Even if it was nice not to have to try to introduce him and explain. Maybe they could just sit in the fields like before and talk. Kore frowned. It was all beginning to seem like a dream. Distant and slightly surreal. Who would take moons just to get to know Kore? And not even to try to meet her mother. Pluton hadn't even known who she was for weeks.

Things were better once the Harvest Festival began in truth. There was less time to think, more use for her abilities. Kore liked to watch the mortals on the first day of the festival from her window. It was the day of fruits, and baskets of all shapes and sizes overflowed. They were spread through the Eleusis's agora and laid on street corners. Kore remembered sneaking out one season when she was small and tasting all of the different basket offerings. The streets had been full of song, and sometimes she could hear them from the window when the wind blew just right. It was the day of gathering, for the mortals who had journeyed far to eat and rejoice. The nymphs and Theoi stayed away.

The second day was Kore's favorite and had been for many seasons. The day of greeting, of flower wreaths and new chitons. Calli always took the time to weave blooms through her hair, creating a living work of art. It was also the only day that Kore was allowed to lead the procession. The road leading to Eleusis was lined with flowering bushes and flowerbeds. In the town potted plants and small plots rested, waiting. It was her job to herald her mother's arrival, flowers bursting to full color out of season. Kore loved turning them unusual colors and watching the mortals marvel. Peasants lined the road into Eleusis, and their clothes became increasingly rich as they drew closer to the agora. There was a large throne waiting for Demeter and a smaller seat for Kore. The nymphs sat at their feet, looking very inhuman in the crowd of mortals. Younger festival-goers were presented to her mother. The mortals shook and bowed.

The third day was fun too if you were a mortal. It honored the beasts and fowl who provided season after season of harvest. Milk and eggs from the local flocks. Merchants sold exotic wares, cloth and cheese from distant lands. All wore white, or a grimy yellow grey if they couldn't afford it. The new cloth was invariably undyed, until sunset when it was dipped in tubs to color it for the first time. Kore was allowed to wear a colored chiton, so there was no point in splashing in the dyes.

Kore woke up on the fourth day to the smell of roasting meat, the smell of an entire bull cooking drifting all the way from Eleusis down the hill. Spices, dripping fat, and smoke. It must have been put over the fire sometime just after midnight if it smelled this good already, slowly cooking over the course of the day. It was a feast for everyone, slices of meat just cool enough to touch eaten with fingers. Even her mother would come and walk the town, talking with the mortals and sometimes granting favors.

At least everyone had full bellies if not a full night's sleep. As Kore didn't really need either one, she thought it must be worse for the mortals to line up at dawn the next day. Men of Eleusis lined the road to the temple, torches glowing in the dim light as a representative from every town and farm in the temple's reach fell in line. The Hierophant and the High Priestess would open the temple doors, as Kore sat at her mother's feet beside the carved stone throne. One by one the mortals filed into the temple and dropped their offerings into the calathus basket. One head of wheat from every field, in each town, for two weeks walk in every direction. More this year in this temple. The goddess was actually in residence. An offering of thanks for the harvest, and a plea that her mother would sow their fields personally this season. Some only had one or two heads of wheat, others nearly a bushel. Somehow the basket never seemed to run out of space. The sun moved across the sky, and the torches burned out and were replaced. Still, mortals came with their offerings. Kore watched the shadows on the floor. The mortals backed out of the Telesterion hall to take seeds from the kiste for the Cold Growing season. Some looked thankful. Others just looked scared. Her mother was always satisfied. Kore couldn't help but think how silly Pluton would find all this.

The morning of the sixth day was another party for the mortals before they began leaving for their homes. The people of Eleusis were busy helping the temple. Kore was enlisted as well, to thresh the wheat for the temple and Eleusis. A tithe to each to help support them along with their own fields. The rest would be seed for Demeter and her retinue for the next Warm Growing season. It was exhausting, even for Kore as a Theoi and the nymphs.

After the frenzy of the festival, the temple and Eleusis settled back into their usual sleepy selves. There would be a week or two of rest before she would have to join her mother sowing the fields for the Cold Growing season. Kore was glad for the rest, even if the festivals were exciting. Her mother had gone to Olympus for a party, but Kore wasn't required to attend. It was nice to be by herself after the frenetic week. She walked out past the empty fields and through a few copses of trees to an empty clearing far enough away from the temple. Even her Theoi ears could hear nothing but the lazy birdsong.

The past few days had been a whirlwind of work and waiting. And still, Pluton had managed to occupy her thoughts. He would have snuck out to see the first night of songs, and loved her flowers. The bright dyes reminded her of him, even if her friend and her mother would probably have agreed on the no splashing with the mortals rule. His clothes were too pretty to stain. And as the long hours of the ceremony had passed, Kore could not help but imagine chattering to him instead of the silence.

Kore allowed the daisy to wind itself around her fingers as it grew. She missed Pluton. More than she had wanted to admit even to herself. And he had been gone a long time now. She shouldn't have believed his promises to visit, but maybe he would still be there next time Kore was free to wander the world. Pluton left an ache in her chest that was altogether different than Eros or Iris when they were gone. Kore plucked the little flower and spun it between her fingers. *Plut...no Aidoneus!* If she was going to admit it, even to herself, she could use his real name instead of childlike nonsense that had somehow grown beyond the original snide insult. *I am falling in love with Aidoneus. If only it didn't hurt so much.*

But Kore was still alone in the clearing, despite the hurt. Unable to Travel, no horse, and no idea where his own town was, though she had a feeling it was not far from where they had spent the summer. The admission hadn't conjured him out of thin air. She sat in the shade of a tree for hours trying not to think so much. Kore knew she should forget him before he forgot her and moved on to another friend. One not tied so firmly to another Theoi and the dance of the seasons.

The sound was and wasn't like thunder. A cacophony streaking across the sky. Kore squinted against the sun to make out the black streak that glittered in places and was so very loud. She almost screamed when it dived down towards her, resolving into a black chariot pulled by four black horses. Everything about it gleamed and glittered, including the Theoi in dark armor and cloak holding the reins. If not for the shock Kore would have been frightened when the whole thing hit the ground heavily, throwing up clods of dirt in the crash.

But the ensemble seemed unharmed, and the Theoi turned a great helmet straight towards her, reaching out a hand across the alarmingly small stretch of grass between them. But it was Aidoneus's voice that came echoing out from the helmet, louder and full of a fear Kore had never heard before. "Persephone, run!"

Kore bolted for him before she had any time to think.

X

All of this passed beneath the notice of the Primordials, too busy with their monsters and their schemes. They were oblivious until the day that Tethys became too enthusiastic while putting out one of Anchiale's fires. Erebus flew into a rage and demanded to know where her new power had come from. Tethys cowered but stayed silent. He held her while Uranus summoned his daughter Mnemosyne to show them the past. Uranus held Mnemosyne about the neck as she showed the Primordials vision after vision. She held out a full day as her sister Themis tried desperately to distract their father. Exhausted, Mnemosyne was finally forced to give one vision of the humans worshipping Tethys before she collapsed. Not only had Tethys encouraged the humans to worship her, she had tied some of their life force to her rivers, purifying the waters and extending their lives. The first Naiads, her priestesses. Enraged, Uranus threw his daughter aside and advanced upon Tethys with his spear drawn. Oceanus jumped in front of his sister, to plead for mercy, but there was none to be had. Robbed of his original prize, Uranus plunged the spear into Oceanus.

Kore slammed into the unyielding metal shoulder of Aidoneus's armor and his arm wrapped around her, cold metal against her shoulder blades. The chariot jerked beneath her and the horses screamed. Dazed, Kore tried to twist her head to see what was going on. But suddenly they were in the air, the ground falling away distressingly quickly. Kore could see the black manes and tails of the horses streaming in the wind. The air was cold as it tried to pluck at her curls. Aidoneus pulled her closer, wrapping his cloak around them both. She could hear his voice rumble through his chest, tone low and soothing as if she were a frightened animal. But the horses and the wind were too loud to make out the words.

Kore could sense his fear as the horses were driven faster and faster, but the ride began to take on a dreamlike quality for her. Exhausted after the days of the festival, Kore squirmed in his arms looking for a more comfortable angle against the unyielding breastplate. A sliver of sunlight was visible through the gap in the cloak and Kore watched the green trees rush by so far below. It was hypnotic, and her eyes began to droop slightly. She had time to sleepily wonder where they were going before the chariot dived once more. It was much more frightening to experience than to watch, and Kore was suddenly wide awake once more.

The ground grew bigger, the horses pulling them down faster than falling. Kore arched her neck, looking for the town or clearing or *something* they were heading for, but all she could see was a rocky cliff face dotted with dark spots. The biggest of the caves yawned in front of them, and Kore let out a soft scream before screwing her eyes shut for the crash. There was no way they would make it, but Aidoneus was holding her too tightly to try to jump. Besides, neither jumping nor crashing would kill them, and probably would be equally unpleasant. The light seeping in through the cloak was suddenly extinguished. Kore blinked against the darkness, but nothing revealed itself. The horses took several turns rapidly and the chariot never so much as scraped the walls. *How big is this cave,* Kore thought and shivered.

Aidoneus started the soothing rumbles again as they went further and further down. Twisting and turning guided by the horses, but always down. Kore very much hoped they knew the way, because at some point he had let go of the reins. They were sitting on the bench at the back of the chariot. In the dark, Kore could only feel the rich fur draped over the seat. Slowly, Aidoneus untangled her from his cloak and armor. Kore made a tiny noise of protest, inaudible against the noises of the chariot and horses echoing from the walls. The fur was suddenly wrapped over her chiton before she realized the air was becoming cold. Cushioned by the fur, being held against the armored shoulder was much more comfortable.

Kore noticed that the walls of the cave seemed to do something strange to distort the sound. Sometimes echoing strongly, sometimes sucking away all sound. It was spooky. If before they were in what Kore was sure was a large, if normal cave the sounds were her first hint that wasn't the case any longer. What before had been ordinary darkness began to push in on Kore, pressing at her skull. The temperature fluctuated wildly, the usual cold punctuated with brief blasts of heat. Her heart began to pound and she focused on his arms around her. They seemed to keep the worst of it away. Kore could sense that the cave...tunnel...whatever it was wasn't used to visitors and did not like the fact that they were here. It felt almost alive, and most definitely did not like guests. Maybe that's what was making the horses so unsettled and loud.

It belatedly occurred to Kore as the path wound down, down, down that she should probably be frightened. In the dark, far underground, with no idea when they would see light again. In this place that seemed so angry and clearly wished they would disappear. But it was hard when all the tension had drained out of Aidoneus as soon as they had entered the cave. He seemed convinced that they were riding away from danger, not towards it. And even in the strange clothes, despite the fact that the cave was awful, Kore trusted him.

"Where are we?" She tried to ask, but the wind still snatched away her voice. The ground dropped sharply again before leveling out. The Olympians hadn't talked much about the underworld and its Theoi who so rarely came to court...only telling horrific tales of its prison for Theoi. And her mother ignored it like she ignored everything that existed outside her domain. Kore realized that was where they must be going with that should-be-scared feeling. The whispers were alarming, but it would explain why Aidoneus never came to Olympus, and he didn't seem scared of his home. Kore mulled it over silently, nodding to herself. It would be hard to make friends when you lived in the underworld. She had a vague awareness that the Chthonic was the smallest of the three courts. *And his gift is rocks,* Kore realized. *I must be stupid.*

Something about the ride changed again. The feeling of wrongness and hatred from the passageway had faded. Kore could sense something ahead, and the omnipresent twists and turns had disappeared. They hadn't gone abruptly down in quite a while. Aidoneus took the reins again, standing them up and moving towards the front of the chariot. No longer protected from some unspoken danger, and with her own fur, she stood on her own feet instead of pressed against his side. Kore gripped the rail, the wood smooth and cool under her fingers but Aidoneus was warm at her back.

The darkness became lighter, and Kore could see the ordinary rough grey walls surrounding them open up as the chariot shot out into a cavern. Much like the night sky above, the ceiling of the vast open space glittered with pinpricks of light, but the moon was absent. Far, far below a river glowed, not with water, but with fire. It moved like the liquid blood of the earth, shifting through bright yellow, orange, and deep red. The chariot had slowed down as soon as they shot out of the passageway, and the wind was not nearly so loud. Kore could make out what Aidoneus was saying. The chariot slowly drifted lower over the largest river. It flowed around most of the cave, leaving only a sliver of a bank outside its bounds. Kore's heart hammered in her chest, but Aidoneus's voice was calm as he pointed. "The Acheron marks the borders of Hades. Charon's river."

The land below was dark and seemed to be...forested? It was not what Kore would have expected. The chariot pulled away from the river and the curving rock walls. Another river split the forest from cleared land. Kore could make out the shapes of fields and small houses among them. "This tributary is the Cocytus. It separates the wilderness from the Asphodel Meadows. Most of the shades live there." The chariot slowed further to give her a clear view of the land beneath before pulling higher once more.

Aidoneus brushed a hand over her shoulder, turning Kore to the right as they flew further from the river of fire she had seen in the distance earlier. "The river Styx has two branches. One separates Elysium from Asphodel. The other surrounds where the Theoi live." The land on the other side of the shining river was smaller but more populated. It also seemed less desolate than before. There were actual towns instead of scattered houses, and much nicer than mortal towns usually were. But it was clear where the Theoi lived. A massive complex of gardens and palaces sprawled on the other bank of the river. Kore hadn't expected there to be gardens in Hades. Things seemed significantly less dead than the underworld would imply in nearly every way. Kore's heart was beginning to slow down the longer they flew over the peaceful lands and serene rivers.

"What was that bit of fire at the other end?" Kore asked, twisting back around and trying to point it out. But that river had fallen below the horizon as they descended. All that was left was a faint glow reflecting against the grey wall.

"The Phlegethon leads down to Tartarus. It is an unpleasant place, designed to entrap souls who will never be allowed back to the mortal world."

Kore shuddered, even though the air was no longer unseasonably cold, and pressed closer.

"Do not be afraid, it is a very effective deterrent. That is the only loop of the river in Hades, and it stays confined to its banks. The last river is the Lethe, though it cannot be seen from here. They are the only two rivers wholly separate from the Acheron."

Kore watched the ground roll underneath them, deceptively normal mortal towns and hills. She yawned and blinked sleepily. Something about the ride had taken a lot out of Kore, even though she had been required to do next to nothing. They passed over the river and Kore felt a wash of relief. She perked up a bit, peering over the edge of the chariot. *I wonder which of the palaces belongs to Aidoneus?* she thought, her half-lidded eyes flicking from one to another. It was hard to get a read on most of the structures, in the dark and only from their rooftops. Courtyards seemed to be common. There was one with a high wall around a garden on the slope near the grand palace. *Perhaps that one,* but they flew over it just like all of the others. Kore had just about decided that they must be heading to the other side of the mountain when she felt the wheels touch the ground with a gentle thump.

Aidoneus stepped out first, and lifted Kore down, still wrapped in her warm fur. She looked around in confusion, unsure how they had passed the mountain. But there was a balcony on the terrace where they landed. Kore shuffled over to it and leaned heavily against the railing. Far below, the river glittered, and the little false stars illuminated the vast sweep of the land spread out below.

She staggered backward, shocked, and spun around. Kore hadn't gotten a good look at Aidoneus's chariot or armor in the meadow or on the ride. But now, it was obvious why they landed on top of the mountain. The dark helm glittered on the bench seat, and Kore felt herself start to slide towards the floor. She was so tired, and it was all too much. A shout sounded from far away, and Kore barely felt the arms that caught her just before she hit the ground.

XI

As the Primordials raged against the humans, the Titans watched Oceanus struggle and bleed golden ichor onto the ground. When Selene tried to remove the spear, he seized and died, dissolving until only the golden spots on the grass were left. The Titans stood surrounding the pool in shock, staring at the spearpoint in Selene's hand. The third rule of Theoi existence cruelly demonstrated for the first time. A weapon crafted and held by Theoi hands can kill another Theoi.

Kore dreamed, one of the good dreams.

One rare day Eros and Iris both came with Kore on her explorations. She took them to Eros's cliff and watched them glide for what seemed like most of the morning. They were far enough into the mist that time was an uncertain concept.

Kore was startled when Iris ran back to her perch on the ledge, legs dangling off the drop. Iris reached out for Kore's hand and pulled her up, dragging her along the edge until they reached Eros, standing in the middle of one of the rare large flat spots.

"We're going to take you with us," Iris said excitedly.

Kore peered nervously at the drop. "In case you haven't noticed, I don't have wings. I promise I'm not hiding them or anything."

Eros laughed, walking around Kore, contemplatively. "Yes, but we both do, and you're not very big. We should be able to take you gliding with us."

"You two can't even fly properly! Just flutter a bit!" Kore squawked.

"I think one of us should take the front and the other the back," Iris said, ignoring her. "Besides, what's the worse that could happen? You're not exactly going to break your legs like a mortal."

Kore didn't protest too much. They had always made flying—gliding—look like so much fun. Iris summoned some ribbons and tied one under her arms and the other around her ankles. Kore thought they would talk some more. She real-

ly did. But while she was still debating how best to launch, Iris and Eros picked up a ribbon each and dumped her over the edge, and jumped after her.

Kore screeched before their wings caught her and stole her breath away. They were still falling faster than Kore had ever seen Eros or Iris lose height on their own, but nonetheless, Kore was flying. Kore hadn't thought that she would ever fly. Not for many, many seasons, not since she was very small. Theoi could fly in many ways. Some were lucky enough to be born with wings. If you were powerful enough you could make the air support you, sometimes with the aid of a chariot pulled by Poseidon's horses. Her mother never bothered, as Traveling was easier and faster if you knew where you were going. You could make your glamoured wings real enough to push at the air. All those ways were closed to Kore. But today *I'm flying.*

The ground came up out of nowhere, and they skidded and tumbled in a way that would have killed anything but a Theoi. It did kill Kore's chiton. Iris had to summon her a new one. But it was worth it for the few brief seconds in the air and many minutes laughing in a heap on the rocks at the base of the cliff.

Kore woke slowly into a soft, warm cocoon. The light coming in from her window was still hazy, it was early. She smiled to herself. It was not often that she could luxuriate in the warmth of her temple bed. Usually, there was something to do, or nymphs to remind her to get up at the proper time. She could sleep in on her travels through the mortal world of course, but it wasn't the same. *But no one will be looking for me today,* Kore thought in satisfaction. *They are still threshing the festival grain.*

Kore drifted in and out of sleep for an age, deliciously warm although she could feel the cool autumn air pricking at her scalp. She curled tighter, waiting for the glow of daylight to change from predawn but Apollo didn't seem to want to get up either. *Maybe there is a storm coming in,* Kore wondered, but it was the wrong time of year for storms. She yawned and stretched, finally deigning to poke her nose out from under the covers. Her heart stuttered.

The day of threshing had already passed, and her memories unspooled quickly. *The meadow. The chariot. The cave. The underworld. Hades.* Kore sat up slowly, drawing her legs under her. She couldn't decide how to feel, so many emotions tangled together like a ball of yarn in her chest. Aidoneus had been scared, they were running from something. Kore was still absolutely sure of that, even through her anger. Anger at him for not telling her the truth. Anger at herself too. Everyone always called the ruler of the underworld Hades, but she was sure Aidoneus was a true name. She could have found out, but she hadn't wanted to. The fear bubbled up in her. *What could make one of the most powerful Theoi so scared? Her mother, the nymphs, even the poor mortals in the town!*

Kore shook herself. Kore might be helpless, but her mother was not. And nymphs and mortals were almost always ignored in Theoi conflicts. She slid out of bed, suddenly wanting to get out of her chiton. It wasn't too grimy, but it felt dirty. Too much had happened while wearing it. There was a wooden cabinet standing against the wall near the bed, which had turned out to be enormous. Kore walked over to it, the stone floor warm beneath her bare feet. The door swung open easily to reveal an array of chitons and cloaks not too different from her own clothes. Kore ran her fingers down a light gray one, marveling at the softness. *They only look the same. And a fur cloak!* Kore pulled them on before noticing the heavy shoes at the bottom. They looked like they were designed for deep mountain snows of the cold season. There weren't any sandals. After a moment's hesitation, she slipped them on, remembering that Aidoneus had never worn sandals at all.

Feeling better, Kore looked around the room. It was large, even for a Theoi palace. There was the ridiculously huge bed she had woken on, piled with furs. A wooden trunk at the foot held woven blankets. The walls and floors gleamed like those on Olympus. But the floor was smoky gray instead of white. The walls were lighter, with patterns worked into them, but smooth to the touch. The decorations were somehow inside the stone. Kore stepped towards the windows. They were high and wide, allowing the diffuse light into the room. *No wonder I thought it was dawn earlier.* A door led out onto a balcony, and Kore saw that the mountain did not slope down into more palaces as she had thought. Instead, gardens flourished blending into wild-looking woods at the back. Kore couldn't see any buildings at all, even though she was high in the palace.

Kore discovered she had not been given a bedroom like at the temple or her mother's palace on Olympus but an entire suite of rooms. The terrace led into a sitting room, low divans in pearlescent gray and light blue, wicker baskets filled with more fur throws. A few game boards and memory crystals. Another door led to a more formal room with a great wooden door and several chairs. Wandering back into the bedroom, Kore discovered a basket of fruit she had missed, apples and grapes next to a set of bowls. She ignored the bowls but picked up a handful of grapes. Another door led to a washroom, a large stone tub sunk into the floor. The walls swirled with all kinds of color, sometimes forming into patterns before breaking up again, interrupted only by the large mirror, which also seemed to grow from the rock walls.

She walked back to the large wooden door, the only one which had been closed, and slid back the dark iron bar. Screwing up her courage, she pushed it open and walked confidently out. Kore wasn't sure what she had expected, but she didn't find it. Her rooms didn't even open onto a corridor, but a large chamber filled with more couches and throws. A few dark-haired nymphs looked up in surprise from where they had been changing out a low table filled with food. They scampered away and didn't even have the courtesy to wake Aidoneus. He sat in one of the blue chairs, slumped against the back. Kore thought he looked more like himself without the intimidating armor. She crept closer, and picked up one of the rolls from the basket, sliding down onto a divan near the breakfast table. Nibbling on it, she watched him, trying to stir up the anger from before. It was hard. Kore hadn't caught him sleeping since the first day.

She ate her roll as he slept, then another, then a slice of some kind of roast. It was a strange breakfast table. If it was breakfast at all. It had been hard to tell anything through the thick mist, if there was even a sun at all. She had seen stars last night but that did not mean there was a sun. Kore picked up another roll and stared at Aidoneus. She knew he must also be Hades, but he looked far too much like her friend Pluton. And acted like him too. Kore threw the roll at his head. It skidded off through his curls and he grumbled a bit. The next one hit squarely and tumbled down to stick in a fold of cloth. He shifted again, groaning, and Kore readied another missile. His gray eyes opened when she was halfway through her arc. He blinked sleepily before glancing down at the roll sticking to him and back up at her hand.

"Hey!" He squawked, covering his head. "Mercy, please. My head still aches from that terrible passage yesterday."

The anger was back. "Very funny, I'm so so sorry that dragging me down here has inconvenienced you. We can go back now, *Hades*." Kore demanded.

Something incomprehensible flitted across his face. "I apologize, Kore. You were not meant to find out this way, I never... Please, listen to the whole story. I will take you wherever you want to go."

"Fine," Kore spat out, still annoyed. She had never really thought that he would strand her here.

"When I met you in your meadow," he began, words tumbling out of him. "I had wanted to tell you everything, and ask if you would allow me to court you, but instead I found myself forced to try to protect you from the problem I had caused," Aidoneus finished.

"My mother threatened to turn me into a tree," Kore buried her face in her hands. It was the truth. He had held her hands to share the memory. Her mother had looked so angry.

He stroked her hair soothingly. "In truth, I do not know that she meant it. But how she said it. I could not bear to risk what she would do. I thought we could give her a few days to calm down, whatever your decision. Demeter has never been so unreasonable before."

Kore curled into herself on the divan, picking at another roll. It fell to pieces in her hands. It was hard to think about everything that had happened so quickly. But Kore would make one decision just for herself. "I'm not going back today. Your memory scared me. I don't have an answer for anything else, but Mother needs to accept it is *my* choice."

Aidoneus nodded, relief playing across his face. "I am glad. It will be easier to return to the mortal world than your journey here, I swear it. We were forced to use the closest passage, instead of one of the true entrances."

He had to leave then, but he gave her a pendant made of the same material of the floors. "Wander anywhere you wish and this will be able to lead you back here. Just leave the Phlegethon alone, it is just as unpleasant as it looks."

XII

The Titans huddled and hid, fearing death for the first time. Helios, who had the oldest and strongest cult spoke first. "We hide here while everything we have built is destroyed! Together we are stronger than they are, or shall we wait until we have all met the same fate as Oceanus?"

"Why should they rule us, simply because they were first! We are smarter and more beloved!" cried Iapetus.

Kronos picked up the spearhead still caked with Oceanus's blood and bound it to a new staff.

"Whatever we do to them will one day be done to us!" Themis cried after the other Titans. Themis always knew things she shouldn't.

"Then we will not kill them," Rhea decreed.

That there were gardens in the underworld was hard for Kore to accept. It was much easier to accept the glowing gray mist as the sky and the sparkling dome at night. The plants that grew in Aidoneus's gardens were different from those she knew in the mortal world or Olympus. They grew despite the lack of direct sunlight, and never had to worry about drought. Thick mist every morning and evening as well as occasional drizzle kept the soil damp. Kore rubbed the rich dirt between her fingers, marveling. It was richer than almost any soil she had ever seen, dark and lush. The flowers fascinated her too, more akin to her own than any others she had seen. The underworld plants bloomed with vibrant colors that rivaled even the most cultured rose or deepest anemone. Others bloomed brown, black, or even grey.

The gardens were wild, clumps of bushes and flower beds growing in a lazy sprawl. Low ferns and moss grew in the open places. They were soft, and Kore lay down to watch the low mist roil above. Beyond the gardens, the forest spread over the rest of the plateau and continued down the sloping hill towards the Styx. The afternoon of the first day she stayed in the gardens, only darting through the first few sparse trees. A few times she glanced back towards the palace and saw Aidoneus watching her through one of the windows. She giggled when he turned away to face whatever was keeping him cooped up inside. But her pendant brought her safely back, so the morning of the second day she walked further down the hill.

The forest was lush, like those of the far north in the mortal world, or by Olympus's rivers. But the dense underbrush was broken by craggy rocks and the forest itself seemed to open up paths for Kore. It was deep in the trees that she realized that she really didn't understand the rules of Hades. The gardens didn't seem to have any insects at all, but the forest echoed with birdsong, and Kore got into a staring contest with a small doe. She wondered what the birds ate. As she walked through the trees, Kore carefully dug up several plants, placing them, roots, leaves, blooms, and all into a bag she had found.

She ate lunch down by the river, on a rock that jutted out over the waves. Plants grew under the water too, and she could see larger fish darting between their waving fronds. A dolphin played in the deep water, sometimes surfacing to chitter at her. Kore tried to feed a few pieces of bread to the minnows, but none came. Eventually, the crumbs were swept downstream. The trees on the top of the rise grew tall enough to brush the mist, but down in the valley she could see the tips of the pines. They were very old, taller than most she had seen outside of Olympus. *I wonder if dryads live in them?*

There was an art to keeping time in the underworld that she hadn't mastered yet, but Kore thought there were still several hours of light left when she began making her way back to the gardens. Her pendant unerringly lit up on the side closest to her rooms, and the rise of the slope was easy to follow. Kore climbed, careful of her bundle of plants. She was grateful that the light was still strong when she reached the gardens. Kore frowned to herself. With no orderly layout, she was uncertain where best to add her own plants. She was sure Aidoneus would not mind wherever she picked, but someone must take care of the garden. Kore did not want to upset the gardener either.

The plants were not heavy, but she was beginning to be concerned about them being in the bag for so long. Kore was just about to give up and put them on the edge of the woods when she came across three of the strange nymphs. For such a large palace, there were not many people in the few rooms and passages she had found. And Kore had yet to come across anyone at all in the gardens and woods. They watched her approach curiously, sitting in a little knot on the soft ferns.

"Hello, my name is Kore," she said, smiling at the nymphs. One of the ones with black hair nodded back at her.

"Would you like something?" asked the one with hair so pale and fine it was almost transparent. "We can guide you anywhere you wish."

"I'm looking for a place to plant some things I found in the forest. Is there a section still being finished?" Kore asked.

The second dark-haired nymph looked confused. She gestured around at the open ground. "Is this not a good place for new flowers?"

"I need a bed for new flowers, they don't match the ones already here," Kore tried again. "Can you take me to the gardener?"

"One who tends the plants?" The pale one tilted her head. "I don't think we have those here. All the plants anyone has ever added seem happy enough here. We do keep the trees away from the open spaces."

Kore opened her mouth and then closed it. It was a big garden, but the soil was so rich. Maybe plants really would just grow anywhere here. "No, here is fine." She knelt near them and began turning over soft dirt, enlarging the bed that held bushy purple flowers. After a few moments they joined her, easily breaking up the shallow roots of the current inhabitants. Kore turned her attention to her bag and its cargo. Carefully she removed them one at a time, each one nestled into a depression in the ground. Even after the jouncing they had endured, the underworld plants were healthy. They stood straight once dirt had been packed tightly around their rootball.

Kore sat back and surveyed their work. It was a blobby, patchwork addition to the flowerbed, each plant different from its neighbors, no pattern other than her interest. She thought it matched the esthetic of the garden perfectly. Their eyes were on her, three pairs of strange nymph eyes. Despite their hair, they could have been sisters, and all their tawny eyes seemed to glow.

She glanced back at the palace, at the window where Aidoneus had been the day before. It was empty and dark. "Do you know where my rooms are?" Kore asked, gesturing to the rock around her neck. "The fancy rock will take me back, but it's not always so smart about walls."

The nymph nodded and rose to her feet. "This way, lady."

Her confident step reassured Kore. She might be always a little lost, but the nymph lived here. "I'm not really a lady, just Kore. What's your name?"

"Orphne, Lady Kore. These are my sisters Gyra," the other dark haired one nodded, "and Akhea."

Despite their refusal to call her Kore, the sisters (if they really were sisters...nymph families were nebulous) were unlike any nymphs she had ever met. Most were very uncomfortable with strange Theoi, or even with any and all Theoi up to and including their patron. These sisters seemed to know no fear at all. It was nice to have someone to talk to. She hadn't seen anyone since Aidoneus had shared breakfast with her.

Kore followed Orphne through the unfamiliar stairways and corridors. She only saw a few others, and they flitted out of their way without a word. They reached the large circular room with the table and divans much more quickly than Kore would have been able to using her pendant. Covered in dirt, she beelined for her suite and the washroom inside. Warm water poured out of the sluice into the deep tub, and Kore luxuriated in the heat. There wasn't much she could do about the dirt and grime on her chiton, but there were plenty more in the wardrobe.

Out in the lounge room, the table had been cleared of snacks, and Kore sensed that dinner would soon replace them. There were doors other than her own and an archway into the hall that she hadn't paid much attention to before. The closest one was carved with a pattern of clouds and swung open easily with a gentle push. It was a suite much like her own, but the wardrobe was empty, and there were no signs that anyone had slept there for a long, long time. It even had its own balcony, but the view of the gardens wasn't quite as nice as her own. Kore explored six other suites as she waited for the table to be full again. Some of them were slightly smaller than her own, but they all shared the grey-blue silks and carved walls. It was obvious they were a set, and it dawned on Kore that this was some kind of guest wing. It was less apparent who they were for. Kore rarely heard of anyone visiting the underworld, and the other Chthonic Theoi lived in their own palaces. She had seen them on the wild night ride down from the mortal world.

Kore left the final suite, its door carved with sunbeams through scattered clouds, and found Aidoneus and a full table waiting for her. She smiled and hurried over to her divan. The food smelled delicious, although she didn't recognize some of the dishes, or even their ingredients. It was much better food than they had ever shared in their little town, and Kore was slightly put out that he had never brought any for their picnics.

Aidoneus only smiled and said that new food always tasted better. "It will not be as interesting after a while. I am sorry I was a terrible host today. I had to make time for tomorrow. What have you done with your day?"

Kore told him about wandering the chaotic garden, and then the deep, misty woods. "I made it down to the river at the foot of the hill, the Styx? I saw a dolphin playing in it. I've never seen a dolphin in a river before."

"The animals in the underworld are different than those in the mortal world above," Aidoneus explained after he had stifled his laughter. "To begin with, they are all dead even if they seem lively enough. They simply appear here when they die. They do not strictly need to eat or drink, the freshwater will not harm your dolphin."

Kore thought about that for a while, chewing on a tasty bite of stew. "It seems like you would soon be overrun with them."

"I do not believe all animals need to come when they die. We have no insects or lizards. Few small animals at all."

Kore thought back to the ancient trees and her new plants. "What about everything else here? The forest and the plants in the garden? I planted some new ones. What will happen to their spirits, now that I moved them?"

He didn't manage to hold back the laugh this time, and Kore glared at him. "I apologize, it must seem very strange to you. As far as anyone can tell the plants here are quite ordinary, if sometimes distinct from the common variety. I am sure your flowers are both beautiful and unharmed."

Kore uncrossed her arms and nodded, relieved. That might mean her gift would work on her new collection.

"Would you like to see Elysium tomorrow, Kore?" Aidoneus asked as they finished eating.

"Of course! I haven't seen any humans at all yet. What is a visit to the underworld without a few shades," Kore thought about all the people who had come to the temple over the seasons. *Most of them must be here now.*

The gray light was fading, but still bright, when Kore made her way back to the gardens. She could barely see her blooms from her balcony, and she wanted to make sure they were all right, despite Aidoneus's assurances. They were easy to find, but Kore could hardly believe her eyes. Transplants, even carefully done, always took days to take hold. These were vibrant and healthy, blooming where they hadn't before. Kore stared in disbelief. *Underworld plants are strange no matter what he says.*

XIII

Helios and Selene, who felt responsible for everything that had happened, led the way as the Titans searched for Chaos. Tethys, still crying for her brother trailed behind them. It was not hard to find Chaos as she lounged among the ruined campsite of a tribe that had worshiped Coeus. "Mother, Uranus has killed Oceanus. Help us find him, he wishes to kill me as well," Tethys pleaded.

Chaos did not reply, simply plunging her own spear into Tethys's belly. "Traitorous brats!" She cried before advancing on Helios, swiping her spear across his chest.

Helios stumbled back with a cry, but Chaos had turned her back on Selene, who cracked her across the head with her staff. When Chaos collapsed to the ground, the Titans looked around to discover that Tethys too had vanished. Helios's ichor mixed with hers on the ground.

It was the second time that Kore woke up in the underworld and she was beginning to get used to the diffuse gray light. Dawn, such as it was, was much slower, transitioning from glittering cavern roof to gray mist. In some ways it was easier to mark the start of the day as when the mist rolled back in, the brightening was so slow. And it was the mist that woke her, the scent changing in the air so high up on the hill. Aidoneus had promised to breakfast with her again and show her Elysium, but she sensed it was not time yet. Kore had gotten better at finding her way down to the gardens after following the nymphs and her steps were more confident than before. She wanted to see what the night had done to her plants.

She had found them easily the night before, but in the new day, she walked past them twice before realizing it. The forest plants had been blooming and content in their new home the evening before, but what Kore saw then was just too much. They were an explosion of color, rioting leaves and vines tangled together. Her plants had overtaken the poor bush with the purple flowers that had seemed so large before. Kore reached out to touch a petal gently, and it seemed as if the flower stretched towards her of their own accord. She backed away slowly, unsure of what she should do. But the sky was getting brighter, and she turned and ran back towards the palace.

The stables were large, Kore recognized them from her first night in the underworld. The terrace where the chariot had landed stretched wide between the grand palace and the smaller stables that were hewn from the same black rock. Aidoneus led her through a door large enough for a full team of horses and a chariot into a central space with high ceilings. There was a row of stalls on one side, and Kore caught sight of a flash of white fur.

"Ametheus!" She gasped and hurried over to her friend. The horse poked its nose over the door and nuzzled at Kore, whickering plaintively. Kore saw a basket of small apples on the floor and offered one to him. Mollified, the animal delicately picked the offering off her palm and crunched noisily. She laughed and ran her hand down his mane.

"Ammie apologizes for not coming to meet you the other day, but he does not play well with others, and cannot pull the chariot alone," Aidoneus said, offering the horse a handful of grain in his feed trough. It was ignored.

"He looks bigger than the others," Kore noticed. "And white. It's hard to be different."

"We do not know why he was born so pale. The other lines of horses from the Neptans are deep gray or black. But Ammie is gentle. I thought we might ride down to Elysium," Aidoneus suggested.

The horse suddenly looked very big to Kore. "You know I've never ridden before. I'd fall off."

"I will not let you fall," he promised. "It is a long walk down, even if we run."

"We can Travel?" Kore asked, still staring at the horse.

"It is possible to Travel within the underworld," Aidoneus admitted. "But it is unpleasant." He reached out to open the stable door and Ametheus happily followed. "We can take a little ride on the ground. If you are still nervous I will have the chariot brought out. But that will draw attention and you are not fond of that, Kore."

Kore followed along behind, the horse getting bigger with every step. She was paying so much attention to Ammie that she did not notice when

Aidoneus crept up behind her and quickly lifted her onto his back. Kore was stunned for the moment it took him to swing up behind her and begin a gentle walk.

They circled around the broad terrace, passing the entrance to the palace and turning back to the stables. Kore had to grudgingly admit that she felt fairly secure. Part of the saddle and Ammie's head in front, and Aidoneus's arm circled around her to hold the reins. It did seem like it would be hard to fall. He kept up a gentle one-sided conversation as she struggled to find her voice again. "Nice and even, that is a good boy. Look, Kore. Down the slope is where Hypnus lives. You will like him..."

When they finally finished their slow circuit Kore had recovered enough to wrap her hands around the pommel and actually ask a few questions about the palaces she could not see from her balcony. It was not nearly as bad as she had feared, but that was while they were still on the ground. But Aidoneus had ridden Ammie many times and was still in one piece. Kore didn't think that even a long fall in the underworld would permanently harm her. They stopped at the stable door once again.

"What is your choice, Kore? Has Ammie met with your approval, or shall the nymphs ready the chariot?" Aidoneus asked.

Kore took a deep breath. "Let's go before I lose my nerve. But I'm keeping my eyes closed!" She felt the horse ease into a canter beneath them, and it seemed to go on for longer than she would have expected to reach the end of the terrace. It dawned on Kore that they had to be in the air already, and she hadn't felt the change. It made her cling tighter to the pommel with one hand and Ammie's mane with the other. Now that she was paying attention, the wind was whipping through her curls, though not as fast as the chariot ride.

Her eyes were still closed but she was thinking of opening them when she did feel the gait change beneath her, and she could hear hooves on solid stone again. "It is safe again," Aidoneus teased. "We are on the road near Elysium."

Kore blinked and looked around. Not much had changed, they could have been riding through the forest behind the grand palace, though this one did have a road. She had expected something different, on the mortal side of the river. Aidoneus dismounted behind her and lifted Kore down. Her knees only shook a little as she took her first steps. He caught her hand and began walking confidently down the road, although both directions looked the same to Kore. She supposed it was much easier to find your way when you could fly with your eyes open.

Even though they had landed in an area that seemed to be deeply forested, it was not a long walk until Kore saw the vast city. She had a dim memory of seeing it from the air, and realizing that it was larger than any she had ever seen before, but it was different standing at its entrance. Elysium had no gates or walls, the houses simply started ten paces from the edge of the woods. They were beautiful houses, even the smallest would be at home in a mortal king's city, made from stone of all colors. Some of the houses were built in styles that Kore had never seen before and they were all mixed together without a care. It was rare to see more than a dozen similar houses next to each other.

But it was not the houses that held Kore's attention, but the people. At first glance, it was hard to accept that they were mortals. While there were plenty of children, running about without a care Kore could not see anyone who was in more than their second decade of life. All seemed healthy and well cared for. Looking closer, she saw that they seemed to glow, it wasn't just that their colors were brighter like many things in the underworld. Light actually seemed to shine from their hair and skin. And the array of colors and shapes of the mortals was more than she had ever seen. Some Theoi like Apollo told tales of many kinds of mortals, but most never went too far afield. There was considered to be no point. No one had ever found any Theoi in other lands. But in the underworld they all mingled together. As Kore drew closer she realized that they could all understand each other as if they were Theoi or nymph.

Kore followed Aidoneus deeper into the city, watching everything with round eyes. The mortals—shades—around them seemed not to notice or care about the Theoi in their midst. They must be very used to Theoi or Aidoneus must be shielding them somehow. As they walked Kore begun to spot other differences in the city of the dead. Canals and fountains were common, but it was only occasionally that she could smell food cooking. Wandering the many agoras revealed wondrous crafts from art to jewelry to clothes, but little fruit or pottery. Leather seemed to be common, and meat and fish roasted over fires instead of bread. Some of the stalls sold wares all of a kind and others had many different things spread out on blankets or tables. But what was absolutely everywhere was gold, silver, and many kinds of shiny rocks.

"Your city isn't like any I've ever seen before," Kore said, staring at the bits of gold children were playing with before abandoning them on the cobbles.

Aidoneus shrugged. "The underworld is different. The earth is rich with many things this deep and the shades enjoy them. Though this may be the only city that has no currency."

"Elysium is a rich city. There is art and other things I've never seen before. But you said the animals eat? Do the shades?"

"Sometimes. It is not necessary for them anymore, and food can be difficult to come across, most of the land here is wild," Aidoneus explained.

It is a beautiful city, even if it is a bit different, Kore decided. Although it struck her as sad that there were so many children. In places, it seemed like there was one for every adult she came across. They played freely in the streets, seeming to have no fear of anything at all. The city was vast and Kore wasn't sure if they had crossed the entire thing or only a district when they came to the river. A large complex of docks stretched out almost halfway across, and there were many boats. Most of them were small, built to hold no more than a few people, and none of them bore the sails Kore had seen in the mortal world.

Aidoneus walked down one of the longer docks to one of the medium sized boats. A Theoi was waiting for them, leaning on a long oar in the back of the boat. He smiled at Kore, his long brown hair pulled back with a tie, similar to how Aidoneus wore it sometimes. In fact, Kore noted, there were a lot of similarities in their clothes, although this new Theoi's were simpler. She was certain that this was another member of the Chthonic court.

Stepping into the boat expertly, Aidoneus reached up to help Kore down. It bobbed lightly under her feet. She was grateful for the steadying. The floor of the boat was filled with cushions, and Kore sank down gratefully. It didn't seem to move so much when she was sitting down.

"You must be the famous Persephone," the boat-master said, pushing them away from the dock smoothly. He grinned easily. "I am Charon, ferryman, shade-wrangler, and apparently giver of tours. Because there is nothing else I should be taking care of today. I live to serve our dear Lord Aidon's whims." He poked Aidoneus with the end of his pole.

Kore realized that no one other than Pluton had ever called her that as she watched them. Not even Aidoneus, since they arrived in Hades he usually used her real name. She found that it wasn't unpleasant. Aidoneus watched her, ignoring the jape as Charon continued to talk, describing different parts of the city and the palaces of Theoi on the other bank, barely visible through the trees.

"I'm afraid I still don't understand what you do," Kore said after a while. "Charon, what is shade-wrangling?"

"You will get a better idea when we join the Acheron and see them. The newly dead shades appear on the far bank of the river. About half of them don't take it well. I have to get them on boats and to the halls of judgment."

Aidoneus leaned back to grin up at the other Theoi. "And what else, Charon?"

"Menial tasks. Fetch and carry," he said stiffly. Charon turned to Kore. "Aidon uses us terribly you know. Always leaving us to do all his work for him."

Kore looked at them curiously, and Aidoneus twisted back to answer her unspoken question. "He does the orientation, in his bigger boat. Explains to the new shades where they are and the way things work here."

The boat ride took most of the afternoon. Kore saw new shades reaching out for the ferryman from the banks, the endless gray meadows of Asphodel, and in the distance the river of fire. The three interconnected rivers of the underworld wound through the forest and against the rock walls. Her two guides had something interesting to say about almost everything they passed. When at last the dock reappeared, she found that Ammie was waiting patiently for them.

"Ammie is intelligent," was all that Aidoneus would say about it.

She even managed to open her eyes a few times on the way back to the palace. Kore found that the mostly empty room where she and Aidoneus had eaten before was transformed. Charon was back, somehow beating them there with his brother Thanatos, who was not as frightening as his role would suggest. Others filtered in until the table was full. Hypnos, a legendary Titan sat on her left and happily told tales of a land long gone. His daughter

Makaria, who was responsible for the marvelous Elysium city, and her sister Gorgya of Asphodel. Their brother Ascalaphus took care of the wilderness. It was the most interesting dinner Kore had ever had.

XIV

*A*nchiale stood over the bound Chaos, poking her with a spear. "And now Tethys! Why should we not kill them, they are cruel to all they see."

"I know we must not," said Themis softly.

The ten Titans hunted the Primordials, never again trying to make peace. They ambushed Pontus, then Aether easily enough, for Primordials rarely cared what the others were doing. But Gaia felt them coming through the earth and was more ready than her siblings. She shook the earth and tripped Helios, falling upon her prey before she could be restrained by the others. As she was bound Gaia let out one last cry to warn her remaining brothers. Nine Titans shuddered to face the two remaining Primordials.

She had spent less than a week in the underworld and already Kore realized she was becoming more at home there. At first, she had only stayed because of Aidoneus and her mother's temper tantrum, but the other Chthonic Theoi were kind and wonderful to talk to. She explored further every day and although she still would not ride a horse alone, not even Ammie, many places in Hades could be reached by the rivers. Charon had brought her a boat, a little one just for Kore the morning after their feast. It was easy to use, with only a little pole at the back and it was very hard to get lost. If she allowed the current to carry her for long enough she was back by the palace.

Kore found that she loved Asca's wild places, deep forests thick with mist and creatures she new to her. As she wandered, Kore collected seeds for her garden from all kinds of plants she had never seen before. Some even more exotic than those in the little patch of forest beyond the garden. She had wandered the Asphodel meadow, but only once. Unlike the shades of Elysium, they would crowd around any Theoi they could find, begging in many different languages. Kore learned to leave them and the new shades on the outer banks alone.

Even her gift seemed to respond better in the underworld with their strange flora. Some seeds were beginning to sprout under her care and her original flowerbed looked like a jungle. She thought she might start a garden entirely of her own from seeds for the first time.

The time slipped by without much notice from Kore until one day when Aidon met her for breakfast. He was not there every day, and each time he was it was a treat. Kore ate her rolls while he toyed with a bunch of grapes. "It has been ten days since you came here, Kore," he said slowly. "Thanatos has kept a watchful eye and Demeter has not raged since the sixth day, although she has not been seen at her temples either. Would you like to go back to the mortal world?"

Kore stared down at her plate and thought. There wasn't much for her to do with her mother and the nymphs. It was not surprising they were gone. It was past time for them to begin sowing for the Cold Growing season. When Kore had not reappeared, things must have continued without her. A flower goddess was not needed for any of that. And, with a deeper realization, she liked it in the underworld. "I want to think about it today, Aidon. It sounds as if she's already started sowing without me."

Aidoneus nodded and the strain at the table eased somewhat. It was a strange, subdued day for Kore. The sights that had begun to be familiar seemed distant. She wasn't sure if she wanted to return to the mortal world yet. There was still so much of the strange land yet to learn about. And despite what Aidon thought, her mother would look on her ever returning with a dim view. Oh, she could ignore that, but it would be easier if her mother got used to having her gone. Kore might go back after the sowing season and spend some time with her before exploring more of the mortal world. The things she had seen in Hades had taught her there was much that Theoi ignored.

Kore walked through the halls of the palace. She had slowly realized that there were more and more nymphs populating it, and sometimes even shades. It made her wonder if in the beginning it had been cleared for her. But she knew the route well even though she dragged her feet. Kore knew that Aidon would be waiting for her, the light was almost gone and she had promised him an answer.

She found him sitting in the chair that had slowly become his even though it looked no different than any number of others in the room. The dinner, as always, smelled delicious. She sat down and filled a plate, but she could feel his eyes on her. He watched as she slowly ate, not taking anything for himself.

"Night has fallen," Aidon said slowly after a while.

"It has," Kore acknowledged, twisting the cloth in her lap. She didn't want to let her mother worry that she was all right, but she didn't want to go back either. Not yet. Not really. "You said Thanatos went to the temples."

"He is the only one of us who goes to the mortal world regularly. As the god of dying it is one of his duties."

Kore took a deep breath, "Could he leave a message there for me? She must know where I am but I don't want her to worry. And I want to stay if you'll have me." Kore said in a rush.

For a moment she thought she must have imagined the relief on his face. "You are not a prisoner *here*, Pe...Kore. Once you let one of us teach you to ride you will be able to go where you wish. I swear it is much easier on horseback. But you can stay as long as you would like."

"I want to stay," Kore said, suddenly certain. "I'll write to Mother and Thanatos can put it in one of the temples. They can always find her if the Hierophant and High Priestess want to."

Kore had nearly finished, but Aidon finally took a few bites for himself. It was good to share food. Kore knew why the shades missed it. At least fish and game were easier for them to come by. The strange stars were out when they had finished, only a few wisps of mist left sticking to the treetops. Kore had moved a few of the cushions from her bed onto her balcony, creating an easy nest. She liked looking up at the not-stars, and someone had somehow replaced the pillows on the bed. Aidon lay down beside her and looked up at the twinkling lights far above. She knew that if she watched long enough one would wink off or another would sparkle to life.

"Look there's one," Kore exclaimed, pointing nearly straight above them. One of the not-stars was fading, once bright now merely a glimmer.

"Mmmm," Aidoneus replied. "I do not know that one, but someone has gone to sleep."

Kore pushed herself up on her elbows. "What do you mean 'gone to sleep' what lives on the ceiling?"

"Didn't your maids tell you?" He grinned at her. "You know all nymphs are bound to something. In the mortal world and the other courts, it may be the wind, or trees, or a stream. Here most are Lampads. Their rock glows until they go to sleep. Although we do have a few dryads."

Kore looked up in awe. She had no idea how many nymphs lived in the world above, but nowhere could one see so many at once. Even sacred groves would only have a handful of dryads. She slowly laid back down, gazing up at the glittering, glowing diamonds above. Aidon shifted beside her, and Kore settled her head on his shoulder. "I didn't realize that there were dryads here. I don't think I've seen any in the forests."

"There aren't many. Most have their trees on the slopes near the Theoi who brought them here."

Kore gazed up at the glittering light that weren't stars as Aidon played with a curl that had fallen across his chest. "They are beautiful. I think some of them even have little bits of colors in them."

"You are beautiful, Kore," he breathed into her ear.

She turned her head towards him. "I like it when you call me Persephone. You were right the day we met in the meadow. Kore doesn't really fit anymore." She met his gray eyes as he pulled her closer and closer, snuggling onto his chest. His cloak was warm, and his fingers soft as they tangled in her hair. Persephone leaned down, finally closing her eyes when his lips met hers.

XV

Uranus and Erebus made their stand on a steep cliff overlooking the angry sea. They taunted the Titans who slowly advanced upon them. Uranus called down terrible storms to make the heavens tremble, and Erebus turned the day to darkness, blinding the Titans. But Anchiale hemmed them in with fire, Coeus blasted them with winter winds, and Themis called out warnings before their strikes. Iapetus, and Mnemosyne advanced upon Erebus led by Selene, who was unafraid of the seething darkness. Iapetus tripped Erebus with a handful of vines, but he pulled Selene down to the ground before Mnemosyne could tie him tightly enough. Selene joined her brother as moonset followed sunset.

The world was vast, even to a Theoi. Demeter walked and walked, Traveling to places she had never seen, and then never even heard of. She was sure that Kore was somewhere to be found. Such a bright flower could not live in the dark underworld for long. No. Just as she had every growing season, Kore was living somewhere among the mortals. Demeter could not start the Cold Growing season without her. She had not for an age. It was hard to remember how that had been, without her daughter to brighten the way. So Demeter walked, searching each mortal village and city, calling through the woodlands. Her nymphs were far behind, confused when they did not sow the seeds to make the cold crops grow. It was their duty, just as naiads could not choose to stop the waters nor lampads could choose not to shine. But it was Demeter who blessed the seeds and turned furrows into fields. Without her, the seeds withered in the cold, and only a few plants clung to life.

In the towns closest to Demeter's temples, the mortals planted their cold-weather crops, wondering why no one had seen the goddess and her attendants. But she was not seen in every region, every year, and life continued as it always had. They ate the harvest from the warm seasons and waited for the new plants to sprout, plants that would sustain them until the earth warmed once again.

Demeter left no stone unturned. The world was vast, but she was Theoi. Distance was no object, and neither was the blowing wind or new falls of snow. She found signs of Kore in a mortal village far away from any of her temples. A patch of wildflowers still blooming in the first snows. A few blankets. But the place was old, and Demeter reluctantly left it be. There were no nymphs in the town and the mortals, although properly respectful of a goddess, knew nothing.

The world was wider than the cult of Demeter, although some mortals even far away had heard whisperings of beings unlike any other, and a beautiful woman of the crops. They planted for the cold season without any concept that anything was wrong. Those mortals felt no relief when the first green shoots put down roots in the cold ground. Everything was as it always was.

The nights grew longer and the days colder, and there was nowhere left for Demeter to search. She had scoured the earth. Every village, every corner of every forest. Kore was nowhere to be found. Only the scarce patches of her flowers remained to show that she had ever existed at all. Demeter knew not what to do. Kore had sometimes been late returning, but she had never before been nowhere to be found. The thought that she really was gone from the mortal world altogether was too much for Demeter. She returned to the temple where she had last seen her daughter.

The mortals, those of Demeter's cult and the rest spread out over the world watched the ground with trepidation. The cold season crops had been slow to sprout, and the fields were a patchwork of sparseness and dead spots. The harvest would be poorer than any in living memory. Some put their faith in the bounty of the wilderness as their distant ancestors had done before them, hunting game and collecting wild plants. Others prayed and made sacrifices to the bountiful goddess. Lucky mortals made desperate entreaties to local Theoi and nymphs. Most Theoi did not notice the changes in the earth or even the mortal's begging.

Demeter's attendants had waited for her at the temple for many moons, growing more anxious with every day that had passed. Soon the only ones left were her nymphs, the Hierophant, and the High Priestess. The others had all returned to Eleusis, fearing they had earned her disfavor. Demeter was almost unrecognizable when she first appeared at the bottom of the temple steps. Theoi are all naturally strong and beautiful, untouched by age or mortal illness. But Theoi bodies are reflections of their inner state. In her despair,

Demeter's skin had become sallow and her hair lank. She looked almost mortal. The high priestess stood at the temple doors, twisting the crystal in her hands. She knew not what it contained, none of the mortals could read a memory crystal and the nymphs refused to. But it had been delivered by the god of dying himself. It could not be welcome news. Demeter was the one to read it, desperate for any word of her daughter. She rejoiced to hear Kore's own voice, but her joy soon turned to anger. Her daughter was no longer in the mortal world, on Mt. Olympus, or even with the Neptans. She planned to stay in the underworld as an invited guest at least until the seasons turned again. The letter fell to pieces in Demeter's hands as she strode to her throne. She screamed so loudly the people of the town cowered as their buildings shook. The goddess swore that the earth would have none of her gifts until Kore was returned to her.

On the longest night of the year what crops that had managed to cling to the cold ground withered and died before the sun returned. The chickens laid no eggs and the cow's milk dried up. Even the wool on the sheep became thin. The mortals had never seen such a thing before, and many despaired. The cold and snow were forbidding in a way that no one could remember. But their prayers to the goddess went unanswered, no matter what was sacrificed or how many priests and priestesses did the beseeching. Those mortals that lived too far away from Demeter's cult to have any understanding of what was going on watched the snowfall and shivered. Desperate villagers hunted even more in the woodlands and foraged for what was to be found. For they seemed untouched by the curse. Even the most powerful and benevolent of local gods and goddesses barely managed to make the farms and fields produce anything at all. The world starved.

Demeter sat uncaring on her throne, the doors of her temple closed even to the Hierophant and High Priestess. Why should she walk the world when her daughter could not? Kore must return, no matter what her daughter thought the underworld was no place for a Theoi born to the earth. With the doors of her temple closed, Demeter was left alone for a moon.

It took a while for the other Theoi to notice that things had gone wrong in the mortal world. Most were not given to paying attention to humans beyond their own confined interests. It would not have occurred to any of the ruling Theoi to ask their minor brethren or nymphs even if they had been aware of a problem. It was not until the mortals were so desperate for survival that they no longer had the time or energy for worship or sacrifices that the Olympians and Neptans began paying attention. Of course, by that point things had gone almost too far for recovery.

In the larger cities thousands starved. They had too many people living in a place with no resources to turn to in an emergency. Some kings sent soldiers out into the countryside to appropriate any food they found. There was not much to find. Smaller towns lost the very young and very old. It was easier for the farming communities to stretch the warm season's harvest and fish the rivers and hunt in the hills. Isolated farms and hamlets became ghost towns as people left to search for gentler lands that were nowhere to be found.

Zeus sat uneasily on his throne. Something had gone badly wrong with Demeter, and he had the sinking sensation that it had something to do with the Kore problem he had almost forgotten about. But Demeter refused to appear on Olympus. She ignored his requests, threats, and bluster. Zeus and Poseidon sent Apollo down to talk to her in desperation.

The warm sunlight followed the sun god wherever he went, even in the height of winter Demeter's temple warmed before him. "Hello, Lady Demeter!" he said merrily. "Lord Zeus sent me to ask about the mortals' crops. They seem to be having an unusual amount of trouble this season. I haven't seen any green fields from my chariot for a long time!"

Almost all the Theoi got along with easy-going Apollo. But Demeter barely raised her head to look at him. "I have wondered when Zeus would send someone," she said listlessly. "My daughter Kore has been kidnapped by Hades and taken to the dark underworld. I will not share my gift while she is not here to rejoice in the green growing things."

Despite what the mortals thought, Apollo could not see the entirety of the earth from his chariot. But he had noticed the sweet goddess of flowers and the serious god of the dead. Apollo loved love, and falling in love. It had been a story he had been watching avidly as his bright sunlight shone on their meadow. He had been quite put out when he had seen Kore run to Hades before they both disappeared under the earth. He hadn't been able to watch them anymore. "Lady Demeter," Apollo said delicately. "I do not think your daughter has been kidnapped. Zeus gave Hades permission to court her, and she did not seem opposed to the idea."

At his words, Demeter showed more life than she had the entire time Apollo had been watching her sitting slumped on her throne. Her green eyes crackled with power and she stood up straight. Demeter waived her hand and Apollo felt her power slam into his chest and he sailed out of her temple and down the steps. The sun god had forgotten she had that kind of power concealed in the husk on her throne.

"Kore does not belong trapped beneath the earth. It was not Zeus's place to give her away! She is my daughter and until she is returned to me the earth can wither and die," Demeter's voice echoed from the temple and shook the ground. The doors swung shut with a resounding boom.

Apollo stared at the building in shock before he leapt onto his chariot and flew back to Olympus. He left the ground so quickly the wheels of his chariot and the hooves of his horses left burning patches on the ground that melted through the snow and smoked the dead grass below.

Poseidon sent Iris to talk sense into Demeter. Despite their easy relationship, Demeter refused to even allow her daughter's friend entry to her temple. The high priestess relaid her only message: the world would not grow and Demeter's temple would be closed until Kore had been returned to her proper place.

Zeus was reluctant to try to extricate Kore from the Chthonic court. He hated dealing with Hades any more than strictly necessary. But what Zeus loathed more than anything was changing his mind once it had been made up, especially when it would look like his hand had been forced. He had given his brother permission to take her, and it had not seemed like the girl had been too opposed, not that it would have mattered.

When the threats and bluster did not work, Zeus and Poseidon tried other methods. Bribes crafted by the hands of Theoi and nymphs piled up as unnoticed on her temple's steps as the mortal's sacrifices had. Finally reduced to sweet entreaties and carefully veiled begging, the world only withered further. When finally Aires, Poseidon, and finally Zeus failed to forcefully pry Demeter from her temple, the king of the Olympians sent a messenger down to the underworld.

XVI

Only Uranus still fought on the cliff, surrounded by battered Titans bleeding ichor. Kronos and Rhea faced off against their father as Anchiale continued to distract him with fire. When all seemed lost, Kronos slowed time enough to trip the Primordial, sending him sprawling across the precipice. The Titans had learned from their failures. All the rest had twisted ropes in their hands, ready to swarm—two to each arm and three for the legs.

Crius, Themis, Iapetus, Mnemosyne, Coeus, Rhea, and Anchiale bound Uranus as Kronos stood above threatening with his spear. But before Themis could call out a last warning Kronos struck in revenge, castrating Uranus and tossing the bits of flesh into the raging sea below.

Emboldened by her decision, Persephone embraced the underworld. It was still strange, but it was beautiful and always had some new secret to explore. Even her power seemed stronger than they ever had before and she was forced to admit that she had changed, not that the underworld flora was so very different. The palace gardens responded to her touch eagerly, each bed reaching towards the pearly gray mist with joy. It became like nothing she had ever seen before, the open paths hemmed in by flowers and bushes on every side, almost maze-like. Some of the plants even blended into each other forming sweet-smelling arches. Persephone and her maids ran through them, chasing each other as she had once done with Iris and Eros. Sometimes she wished that she could show her friends what she had done. But it would be difficult to convince them to come to the dark underworld.

Persephone spent her mornings playing in the gardens with the nymphs or in the forests, but Aidon never failed to meet her for lunch. He was still her friend, playful and happy to listen to what she had to say, but Persephone could sense that things had changed there too. He joined her more often than not on the divan, sitting next to her and offering her bites from the dishes he chose. Sometimes Aidon even stole from her plate, the smug smile on his face when he managed it made him look like one of the mortal boys she had watched playing with the mortal girls. When they walked together one often caught the other's hand.

She spent the long afternoons with him too. Sometimes she watched as he went about the business of ruling Hades, working with the Theoi, nymphs, and occasional shade that made up the court. The inhabitants of the realm created far less trouble than Persephone remembered from her visits to Olympus. Most often it was a new shade that was beyond the capacity of the judges to sort. She listened as they were compelled to tell the truth and Aidoneus wrung their story out of them. Many who were brought before him were sentenced to punishment in Tartarus for some amount of time and sometimes cast into the pit never to return. She pretended not to notice as the chair she was given to sit on at court steadily grew larger and closer to Aidoneus's own. Until it seemed natural that one day he turned to her and asked her opinion on the shade of a mortal King.

Tantalus had been forced to admit to a fairly gruesome life story. Persephone hated that they shared a parent, but almost all demigods ended up in front of Aidoneus, for good or ill. Tantalus had managed to keep the attention of their father Zeus quite well for a demigod, she was forced to admit, but she was thankful to have been out of favor by the time he had been born. Tantalus had a son Pelopes by one of his concubines, a disfavored son, made worse by his mother naming him after Tantalus's oldest legitimate son. Zeus had taken interest in Pelopes II instead of his older brother, infuriating Tantalus. The next time the Theoi had visited his city, Tantalus cooked and served them Pelopes II. Zeus had struck him down, and now he was the underworld's problem.

"Such a shade is always punished in Tartarus," Aidoneus told her. "You are more familiar with the Olympians and their demigods than I am. What would you do with him?"

Persephone looked down at the shade standing before them. He managed to keep some of his kingly pride even as the Theoi discussed his fate. He didn't cry or beg as they sometimes did. Instead, he looked up at them in hatred. "Tantalus profaned food by serving guests human meat as well as killing his own son. Perhaps we should seat him at a feast he could never eat?"

Aidoneus nodded, and two nymphs dragged the king away. "He shall have a pool of water that will never cross his lips. A fruit tree can be placed just out of his reach. A shade will become hungry after a time, even if he will not quite starve."

But even days spent in the throne room were not usually so dark. She helped Aidoneus send far more shades to Elysium and the isles of the blessed than Tartarus. And most were only given a short time in the punishment realm. Other days there were more pleasant tasks. Petitions were heard and answered from Theoi and nymphs, and entertainment from the best of nymph and mortal talent was to be had. One memorable day Persephone accompanied Aidon on his chariot as they flew to the far reaches of the underworld's cavern. She watched as he enlarged the cavern, making the great wall of rock part in front of them. Twice they flew above the gray mist into the bright realm of the lampands to check the roof of the cavern. Persephone plucked several large diamonds from the roof, larger even than those commonly found on the ground below.

The evenings stretched long and lazy beneath the cool gray mist, light lingering long after it would have been gone in the mortal world. This was the time that Aidon could spend exploring with Persephone. Looking at his realm through her eyes, everything was new and fresh. She would often drag him down the hill through the forest to swim in the river below. The fast current was no trouble for Theoi, and often dolphins would come to play.

Persephone had pulled herself out of the river to sit on one of the rocks. It was one of the few times when she missed the sunlight. The diffuse light was soft and beautiful, but it wouldn't dry her off, even if she sat on the rock for an hour. Her control of her power had gotten better, but she still hadn't gotten the hang of delicate things like that. Suddenly a wave of water rose out of the river and crashed over her rock. She sat up spluttering, and Aidon was floating by, laughing uproariously as she dripped.

"The rock cannot hide you from me!" he shouted.

She jumped back into the water, splashing for a second before the current began pulling her back towards him. Persephone took a deep breath and ducked under the surface. The water was clear, but he was not watching her closely. It was easy for her to stay under the water. It also felt good when they were in the deepest part of the river to take ahold of his feet and pull him down to join her.

Aidoneus came below without a fight, and she swam around him, blowing bubbles at him until all her air was gone. Persephone laughed silently below the roiling surface, trying to wriggle out of the way of Aidon's bubbles. She wasn't sure where he got the air, but the bubbles tickled as they raced for the surface. They floated near each other and Persephone reached out to run her fingers through his curls. They were wild under the water, but still soft. He pulled her towards him, and her hair, waterlogged and almost properly red tangled with his. Suddenly Aidon kicked off the bottom and pulled her to the surface. They had been swept far down the river, and the rock she had jumped off was almost out of sight. He pulled her through the water and she relaxed making him do all the work as she watched the shapes in the mist.

She didn't notice at first when they reached the rock until she was suddenly floating free in the water again. Persephone floundered for a moment, twisting around to find him. Aidon stood on top of the rock, holding out a hand to help her out. She accepted before she was swept away again. The rock was well and truly soaked now, river water accumulating on its pitted surface. He kissed her hand before letting go and drying them with a gesture.

Even with his attempt at cleaning, Persephone looked down at her chiton in disgust. Bits of mud had been ground into it, and there were several small tears in the fabric. "I think this one is dead too. It's the last one in the closet too."

Aidoneus laughed and pulled her closer, pushing her dry and now tangled hair off her face. "You look magnificent. But if your handmaids cannot fix it, you will just have to wear those furs you like so much."

Persephone laughed and tried to push him off the rock, but he held firm. She stopped squirming when he kissed her but their laughter kept bubbling up and they broke apart.

Persephone was used to waking up to little gifts waiting with her breakfast. Sometimes she found them scattered about in the garden or in the forest. But she had never woken up to anything like the sight that greeted her. She had almost finished eating, wondering where Orphne and her sisters were when she heard a rustling out in the corridor. She turned to see a veritable procession of nymphs and shades. They all carried baskets of fabric, leather, and furs.

She watched them unload their burdens with her mouth open, a rainbow of colors suddenly exploding across the circular room. Orphne walked over to the breakfast table. "Lord Aidoneus sent for the tailors, as you found your wardrobe unsatisfactory. They can replace the chitons or make anything else you would like."

Persephone walked among the chairs and divans looking at all of the different fabrics. They were all soft and well made and looked to her like they might hold up better than her light chitons ever had. She had never seen such colors, even in the biggest mortal markets. Most of the Olympians preferred white and the blues and greens of the fabrics rivaled the Neptans. She picked up a bolt of vivid red wool, remembering the cloak from so long ago. "Can we make something out of this?"

If the tailors, two nymphs and a shade, were surprised or displeased that she hadn't chosen something more like the clothes she had worn before they did not show it. Before they left she had several new chitons, as well as clothes in the Chthonic fashion. They almost made her look like she truly belonged there. She loved the soft boots that were perfectly shaped to her feet. A few days later when the rest of the work arrived, Persephone found intricate embroidery as well as plain. Leaves and flowers danced across them but so did other things. She saw a dolphin, several gemstones, and lapping waves. And a rich cape made out of plush fur.

XVII

The victorious Titans left the Primordials bound in the deepest cave they could find, trapped on a tiny rock island surrounded by the hottest fires Anchiale could summon. When the Titans returned, they found a young Theoi clinging to the rocks beneath their cliff. Themis fished the beautiful young woman out of the water, but she ran off before they could ask her where she came from. Undeterred, they celebrated their victory as Themis brooded. But not even Themis could stay somber long. The Titans had deposed all six Primordials, and lost only four of their number! It was a great victory, and their grief did not last long. New cults were soon formed, and any worship of the Primordials was punished harshly, lest they rise again. Soon only Mnemosyne would speak openly about their parents and lost siblings.

Persephone did not notice the time passing. It was easy to do in the underworld. There was no change to the seasons, no moon to watch cycle, and one day was much like another. Instead, she marked time based on her projects. The days she had spent exploring the palace and the gardens, her days in the little boat, when she had begun to focus on her gift, finally growing pears she brought to dinner with the other Theoi. The days of joining Aidoneus on his duties, and now learning to ride the little gray mare. She had explored so many of the places you could get to from the interwoven waters of the rivers, but the underworld was vast.

Aidon had been almost sickeningly excited when she asked to go to the stable for the first time. "There are several gentle beasts to choose from," he said. "Unless you would rather learn on Ametheus. Perhaps it would be best to start with a horse you trust."

Persephone thought about how big Ammie was, towering over even Aidon, and shuddered. She had never really been scared of him until then. But she just could not imagine trying to ride him alone. "Maybe there is something a bit more my size?"

All in a rush, before Persephone could change her mind, she was on the back of a small gray mare, all alone. She rode in circles outside the stable and after her heart slowed down it was not nearly as difficult as she had feared. The animal was indeed gentle and eager to please. In fact, it was all quite anticlimactic. Even learning to fly went well, somehow her horse seemed to know what to do even when she did not. They followed Aidon and Ammie in great wheeling circles above the hill of the palace, darting in and out of the mist layer. It was how Aura got her name, swift and gentle as a breeze.

And so without quite realizing it, Persephone had become a denizen of the underworld. She wore their clothes, navigated their rivers, and flew on horseback instead of Traveling as they did. She explored the inner reaches of Elysium, taking her fruit to trade for trinkets and art that caught her eye. It was amazing how readily they accepted her gifts. Even the scraggly grain she managed in one of the Asphodel Meadows was met with joy. The Isles of the Blessed were even better. Nearly half of the inhabitants were demigods, some she even vaguely remembered meeting on Olympus. They could tell that she was Theoi, unlike the other shades, and most magical of all did not seem to care. Occasionally one would even ask her to hear a petition or settle a dispute instead of backing away in fear or awe. They liked her even better when she used her gift to improve their gardens and fields.

As she grew more skilled at riding Aura, Persephone spent her mornings further and further away from the palace. It was novel that no one seemed to care where she went, other than Aidon once more warning her away from the river of fire and Tartarus. That was no hardship, the Phlegethon was beautiful from the air, but the intense heat could be felt even from high above. And Tartarus did not sound like a pleasant place to explore, especially as the tales of the captive Titans and Primordials filtered down to Persephone. Lunch had even been slowly shifted back a little to the early afternoon as she went further and far afield.

Several times she met the other Theoi on her travels. She shadowed Charon from high above, and once tried to land Aura on one of his bigger boats, sending them all into the water. Charon sent up water spouts at her after that. Ascalaphus showed her the hidden trails of the wilderness, and she saw spirits of animals she had never seen before. One was a white spotted cat, that seemed to disappear into a boulder field. She had wondered where the fur for her cloak had come from. Persephone learned arts of the woods she had never imagined in her wanderings in the mortal world. Perhaps she could have learned from Artemis, but her mother had never approved of the wild places in the world. Not when there were fields, orchards, and domestic animals to take care of.

She followed Asca down a slim trail, glimpses of tan fur just visible through the underbrush. Persephone held a small throwing knife the way he did, their Theoi muscles keeping easy pace with the deer. "Why doesn't it run off into the forest?" she asked.

"Animals are not used to being hunted by Theoi, all their instincts are for running from mortals and earthly predators. It thinks it can outrun us on good footing," Asca explained. He fell back a step, allowing Persephone to dart ahead of him. "Remember to aim! I bet my sister you would bring home the roast tonight, and I'm a sore loser."

Persephone laughed under her breath. Growing up among her mother's temples she was not unfamiliar with butchering animals, but pigs did not try to run from the nymphs and priestesses. Still, it was similar, and her knife hit in the same spot Calli would have chosen for a goat. The deer went down slowly, unsure of quite what had happened. The Theoi slowed as they approached, allowing the deer to sit down, looking around quizzically. Persephone felt bad for a second. It had been wild and free.

"They do not feel pain in the underworld," Asca commented. "That's why it looks confused. It knows something is wrong, but without the pain it cannot figure out what to do."

Persephone waited by her guide for another minute as the deer laid down its head. She started forward, but Asca's hand caught her arm. "Wait just a moment longer."

She turned back to the deer, but there were suddenly two deer. The body of the original deer, still curled up on the trail, and another deer, stepping away from it and shaking itself. The second deer was translucent and glowed in a way subtly different from how she had grown used to shades glowing. Persephone hadn't even really noticed the glowing in a long time. The body of the deer did not glow at all where it lay on the ground. Suddenly the glowing deer turned and bounded away through the trees. "There it goes," Asca breathed. "It is amazing to see each time. It's too bad the shades can't watch."

Persephone was confused. This was not what she had expected when Asca had helped her learn to throw a knife and then offered to take her hunting. "We seem to have doubled the number of deer by killing one?"

Asca laughed. "No, we're still down a deer. The spirit just left the body behind for us, it's gone to find its way back to a new life in the mortal world."

"That makes no sense," Persephone insisted. "Everything down here is already dead. The shades can't die again!"

"The mortal shades stay until they're ready to return," he agreed. "But the animals don't need to be here. They just appear, and when you damage their 'bodies' too much they leave. The underworld isn't obligated to make sense."

Persephone helped him, the deer similar to the tame animals she had helped with before. Although Asca's explanation reminded her of something Aidon had said long ago, it was unsatisfying. Her mind worried at it, trying to make the pieces fit together. Aidon complemented her as well as the kitchens as they feasted with her new friends that night. It made Persephone feel warm inside. The kisses felt even warmer.

The next time Persephone killed one of the spirit-deer she did it from the Aura's back. She felt bad about leaving the solid half of the deer behind, but maybe the snow leopard would want it. Persephone only wanted the translucent spirit half. When it peeled itself away from its skin and started to run, she was ready for it, directing the horse to follow from just above the treetops. She lost that deer, and the next one. Aura could not run through the trees like the insubstantial deer could, and the spirit leapt quickly under the cover of the dense foliage. It was the third deer that led Persephone to the foaming banks of the river.

"Look, Aura," Persephone breathed watching the roiling water. The other rivers of the underworld might be swift in places, but she had never seen them violent like this. "I wonder if it's the Lethe," she mused. "No wonder everyone avoids this river if it's always like this."

They flew above the river, watching it bubble over rocks and pull branches and other debris with it. The violent water hugged the wall of the cavern, carving out the wall so it almost disappeared in places. Persephone had chosen to go left, against the current. Following the river, she saw other insubstantial spirit animals jump into its depths without fear and disappear. The churning water hid whatever happened to them. It took most of that morning to reach the headwaters, flowing out of a crack in the wall of the cavern. The water shot out bright and clear but quickly became muddy as it fought its way along. Persephone urged Aura as close as she dared to the crack, but although there was a peculiar smell coming from the mist rising from the spout, there was nothing else unusual about it. The smell was not unpleasant, she could simply not place it.

The next day she returned, drawn back to the puzzle of the river. She turned right and followed the flow of the water. As they flew, she saw more and more of the animal shades leaping into it. In places they wriggled through tiny gaps in the rock overhang to get to the water, singleminded in their determination. The waters only grew more turbulent as the morning wore on.

It was almost time to turn back when she saw the first mortal shade on the bank of the river. She slowed down, calling out to them. It was like the shade did not even hear her. It—Persephone could not tell if it was a man or woman—too had a single-minded focus like the animals. The shade drank handfuls of river water, uncaring of its muddy state. She watched it drink, growing ever more indistinct and insubstantial as it did so. When finally Persephone could not even make out the color of its hair, the shade sighed and slipped into the water.

That was somehow even more disturbing than what had happened before. But something drove Persephone to continue down the river. More and more shades lined the banks, all looking lost. She tried not to watch as they slipped into the water. It was only a few minutes before the slim bank opened up onto a wide beach scattered with shades. The ones at the back were normal shades. Some glanced curiously at the river before turning away. Others were drawn down to the water, watching it with fascination.

But at the end of the beach where the river tried to return to a crack in the wall the way was blocked by a huge accumulation of debris. Dead branches, rocks, and a smattering of mud were all overgrown over with ivy. The river still managed to run, squeezing between the pieces of the obstruction to disappear back into the wall of the cavern but Persephone was no longer mystified as to why the river was so turbulent. Most of the way was blocked here at the end. The water was backing up and eroding its banks.

Persephone and Aura flew over the river. It was no longer strange to see the shades disappearing into the water. They seemed content, and the smell coming from this crack in the cavern wall was that of the mortal world. Persephone could not have said how she knew that. She hadn't been aware of that having a smell and had not missed it in the underworld. But it was recognizable nonetheless.

The obstruction was another matter. Despite how insubstantial the shades seemed, it could not be a pleasant trip wherever they were going. Asca and Aidon had both said that shades returned to the mortal world, and Persephone sensed that this was true. She watched another branch crash into the dam and tangle in the ivy. Aura carefully alighted on the top of the dam, water rushing around their feet. Persephone could feel that it had power like the other rivers of the underworld, but the water did not seem to bother with her or the horse. The compact mud and rocks shifted slightly under them and Aura took off again, nervous.

The shifting gave Persephone an idea, the obstruction, though large did not appear to be completely solid. Without the roots of the ivy they might be able to break it up. Flying low, Persephone leaned off Aura's back and reached out to pluck a leaf off the climbing ivy plant. She cupped it in her hands. Persephone had never tried to make a plant wither before, but her mother removed weeds from the fields that way. It was possible. The leaf slowly shriveled in her hands, drying like it would in the cold season in the world above. Before she had come to the underworld Persephone would have never bothered to try something so large and complicated. But here her gift had grown by leaps and bounds. Perhaps even enough for this.

She flew just above the top of the dam, and Persephone held her hands over it, reaching out to feel the life in the ivy. It was easier than she expected. Not only could she feel every leaf and root of the ivy, but the branches trapped in the mud and the water and souls rushing through the gaps. Concentrating on the ivy, she felt its roots shrivel, loosening their grip on the mud and rocks. She could feel some of the rocks and mud shift, but it wasn't enough. The branches responded to her as well, and finally the water started to find bigger gaps in the dam, pushing at them and enlarging what was once barely there. Without consciously thinking about it, she urged the water faster, pushing it along its rightful course. The mud washed away and the stones began to crumble under the onslaught.

Persephone watched the river begin to smooth out with satisfaction. Even the souls seemed happier with the clearer water and widened bank. She could catch glimpses of them traveling beneath the water, floating with the current. Persephone waited until the crush of souls on the bank had lessened before she allowed Aura to take her back to the palace.

XVIII

The ages passed, and Anchiale and Crius were the first to bear children. Themis and Mnemosyne held their breath, but Leto, of childbirth, and Hyperion of day and night turned out just like their parents. Mollified, Iapetus and Mnemosyne bore strong Atlas and the twins Epimetheus of regret and Prometheus of waking. The Titan age continued unabated with Coeus and Themis's sleepy Hypnos, breezy Lelantus, and crafty Metis. It was an age full of wonders. Prometheus taught the humans to harness fire, Lelantus dabbled in hunting, and Atlas made spears fly farther than ever before. The humans slowly changed again, and once again, no one noticed until it was too late. At last, even wary Kronos gave in and Rhea gave birth to Hestia.

The riotous river that Aidon had called the Lethe slowed and shrunk away from its banks. What had only a few days ago been a roiling monster transformed into what was little more than a large stream. Crystal clear and not more than waist-deep in its pools, rocks that had once created fearsome rapids stuck out of the surface creating stepping stones. Persephone could see the souls drifting slowly downstream in a current not much faster than walking speed. The large sandy beach at the end of the river only became wider, but in other places soft, dark earth was revealed where water once ran. It dried out slowly without the sun, but it was the largest patch of unused earth she had yet seen in the underworld. Remembering the seeds and cuttings she had been collecting, Persephone claimed one of the wider stretches for her own. The plants had just broken the surface in a haze of green when the messenger arrived.

They were in the throne room. Aidoneus hearing petitions from the nymphs and Persephone sitting in her chair that had begun looking uncomfortably throne-like. She did not recognize the Theoi who was led before Aidoneus, but her clothes marked her out as an Olympian. Persephone leaned forward, watching her approach with interest. Despite her love for the underworld, it had quickly become clear to her that other Theoi did not visit lightly. In fact, this was the first Olympian or Neptan she had seen since she arrived. The white drape of her chiton with the yellow accent looked jarring to Persephone now.

Aidoneus also was very interested in the new arrival, although he concealed it better. Persephone could feel his curiosity through his mask as Lord of the Underworld. It was clear that he did recognize the Theoi before them. The goddess's eyes flickered from one to the other before becoming fixed on the floor.

"Greetings Lady Arce," Aidoneus called. "What brings you to my hall this day?"

Her golden curls covered most of her face as she looked at the ground, but her voice was clear and steady. "Lord Aidoneus, my Lord Zeus sends a message about Lady Kore." She held out a sky blue crystal, waiting for one of the nymph attendants to retrieve it from her instead of giving it directly to Aidoneus.

Persephone sat up. She had not expected the messenger to be for—about—her. After her mother had not answered her letter she had thought she was being ignored. When she returned to the surface she fully expected her mother to pretend that nothing had happened. The other choice was to try to order her back, which had not happened. She was mystified as to why her father was involved. He had not taken an interest in her in seasons upon seasons. Approving Aidoneus's suit was probably the most he had thought about her in an age, and he had seemed pleased in Aidoneus's memory. "What about me?" Persephone asked.

Arce shuffled her feet a bit and looked miserable. "Lord Zeus has reconsidered his approval of your potential match with Lord Aidoneus in the light of Lady Demeter's disapproval," she replied evasively.

A look of dawning horror briefly crossed Aidoneus's face before it disappeared behind the mask again. Persephone caught it out of the corner of her eye, but she was too busy staring at the unfamiliar Theoi to puzzle over it too much. Whatever Aidoneus had just put together was not good. But her mother hadn't so much as sent a strongly worded message.

The nymph who had taken the crystal from Arce mounted the dais and offered it to Aidoneus. His eyes went briefly unfocused before causing it to disappear, presumably to the library. "Lady Kore," he began formally.

Persephone started a bit. He hadn't called her that since she had said she liked it when he called her Persephone. In fact, no one had called her that for what had to be moons.

"You are a welcome guest in my halls, however with Aura, returning to the mortal realm would not be a hardship. Would you like to return to Lady Demeter or Mount Olympus? Lord Thanatos can escort you if you would prefer."

Persephone thought a moment, but only a moment. She wasn't sure exactly how much time had passed. But it wasn't quite time for the warm season planting when she had planned to return to the mortal world and her mother for a time at least. Aidoneus, the underworld, and her new garden were too fascinating to leave early. "No, Lord Aidoneus," she replied equally formally. "I am still happy to stay until the next planting season, as I have said before."

The expression on his face hardened as he returned to the messenger. "Very well, the Lady Kore has spoken. Lady Arce, please remind Lord Zeus that I do not tolerate the blackmailing of anyone under my protection, and advise my brother to control the members of his court."

If the blonde Theoi had looked nervous before, she then looked completely petrified. She nodded, wordlessly turning to leave the hall.

Persephone felt Aidoneus shift a bit before he spoke again. "Lady Arce, the journey back to Olympus can be difficult for those not accustomed to it. Lord Thanatos can accompany you and the message."

Arce paused for a moment, looking over her shoulder at the lord of the dead before shaking her head and squaring her shoulders. "I am a messenger, my lord, I can find my way. My Lord Zeus is fully occupied with other problems without adding a Chthonic."

Persephone had the odd feeling that the words said had little to do with the meaning, but exactly what had occurred stayed just beyond her grasp. She waited until the doors had closed firmly before turning to Aidoneus. "What did Zeus want?"

"Demeter is finally throwing a temper tantrum large enough to annoy him," Aidoneus replied. "He wants others to solve his problems, as always. Do not worry, Persephone."

She thought for a moment as most of the other nymphs, shades, and Theoi returned to what they were doing before. *Mother is not ignoring my disobedience. Aidon knew something was happening but did not put it together until today. What could Mother possibly do to make Zeus, Lord of all Theoi reverse himself?*

Persephone thought of all the new shades lining the banks of the Archeron. Were there more than just a few moons ago? She wasn't sure. But her mother wasn't a war goddess. She did not play political games, rarely even went to Olympus at all. Just watched over the crops and livestock. There were a few members of the council in the chamber, but Thanatos and Charon both refused to meet her eyes.

There were only a few people left in the throne room, four council members and a handful of nymphs when Persephone finally asked the question. "What did she do?" There was really only one thing her mother could have done.

Aidoneus still sounded calm and kind. "I will protect you as I protect all who dwell here. Zeus is simply trying to avoid difficult decisions."

But the next day when Arce returned her message wasn't for Aidoneus, but for Persephone. His expression was stormy as he strode down the steps of the dais to intercept the message.

"I'm sorry Lord Aidoneus," she insisted miserably. "But I cannot deliver it to anyone other than Lady Kore!"

"And as I informed you yesterday, I do not stand for the blackmail of anyone in Hades. Lady Kore will not be cornered into doing something she does not wish."

Persephone darted around the distracted god easily and snatched the blue crystal away from Arce. The memory was short and unspooled before Aidoneus could interfere. The blue crystal shattered on the obsidian floor, spraying shards like tiny pieces of ice. She couldn't breathe. It was worse than anything she had considered. The cold season was always less vibrant than the warm season, but the fields she had seen in the memory looked dead.

The wilderness still stood tall, but mortals do not eat pine trees. Arce quickly backed out of the throne room, slipping out of the heavy doors.

"We have to go to Olympus!" Persephone said. "My mother is killing them. She is killing them and you three knew. You and Charon and Thanatos knew!"

Aidoneus winced a bit. "No matter what Zeus thinks, he gave permission for you to leave the Olympian court. I will defend you as I would any other Chthonic or guest. We may have noticed an increase in mortal deaths, but that is not uncommon. No one thought much of it until yesterday."

"I can handle facing my parents. Take me back to Olympus today before this gets any worse. Maybe if she can see I'm all right things will grow again!" Persephone insisted.

"Demeter has taken leave of her senses. She knows you left of your own accord and has made no attempt to send you a message or find out if you are safe or happy. Her response to you leaving for a season was to starve the world. Persephone if you return you may never be free again!"

Persephone opened her mouth to respond, but Aidon continued ranting.

"Even if I did not love you I would be honor-bound to protect you as a guest of my court. But I *am* in love with you and I am beginning to believe her threat to turn you into a tree, or somehow bind you to her temple permanently. Is that what you want Persephone? To have your will, your very mind taken from you? Because it will mean war. A war I will win, but only Demeter could release you from such an enchantment." He seemed to deflate as he looked at her.

Persephone stepped into his arms. She could feel him shaking against her. Aidon had never told her that he loved her, not in as many words. She tipped her face up to catch his kiss. The shaking slowly evened out and he pressed his lips to her forehead.

Aidon's voice turned steely. "Perhaps I will stop accepting shades into my kingdom until Zeus cleans up his mess. Demeter is not the only Theoi who can cause havoc in the mortal world."

Persephone's blood froze for a moment at the thought of all those lost shades wandering the world. "You wouldn't do that. It would be cruel."

"Maybe not, but there are other things I *can* do. And the Olympians will have a hard time entering Hades without my permission."

XIX

The Titans were smarter than the Primordials had been and noticed that Hestia was different immediately. Kronos, remembering what he had done to Uranus and Themis's warning, swallowed Hestia whole as Rhea wept. But she dried her eyes quickly. All the others had borne normal children, why couldn't she? Kronos was convinced, and Aidoneus soon arrived. He too was different, and Kronos disposed of him as well. Rhea wailed and cried, but Kronos was wary of what Themis had said so long ago. Poseidon, Demeter, and Hera went the way of their elder siblings. But when Zeus arrived, Rhea could bear it no longer. She gave Kronos a rock to swallow, and spirited away her youngest child.

The stalemate lasted for three days. Aidon would not hear of Persephone forcing herself to return and risking Demeter's rages. Persephone could not stand the thought of the mortal world withering and dying. There seemed to be an oppressive number of shades on the banks of the Acheron now that her eyes were opened. She thought that even if her mother would not set the earth to rights, her gift had gotten stronger. Persephone could help a little.

It was by far the longest argument she had ever had with him. And the worst part was she couldn't even counter his arguments. Everything he said was true. Persephone was happy in Hades and she hadn't been ready to go back to her life in the mortal realm. Her mother was being unreasonable and even Persephone had to admit that anything could happen once she returned. But she was willing to take the risk. She was no longer completely defenseless and above all, she did not want there to be a war. Persephone didn't remember the war with the giants, but Eros did, a little. She didn't want anything like that happening again.

Their argument culminated with Persephone refusing to speak to Aidon for over a day while the King of Hades flew off to circle the great cavern on Ametheus. He returned with his shoulders slumped, looking older than

Persephone had ever seen him. Theoi were always beautiful, and it was rare to see one look so tired. He knelt before her. "I must apologize for my words," he looked up at her with sad eyes as she pulled him to his feet. It was as if all the fight had been blown out of him by the winds on his ride. "It would be wrong to keep you here in Hades, even if you could leave yourself if you truly wished to," he said slowly.

Persephone relaxed a bit. She had not wanted to try to ride Aura back to the surface, even if everyone insisted most crossings were more pleasant than her own journey had been. "I know I have to go back. But I don't want to never see you again or be turned into a tree," she acknowledged.

"There are a few protections I can give you," Aidoneus said, pulling a deep red fruit from the folds of his robes. "Even if on a technicality, Zeus gave his permission for you to leave the Olympians and join the Chthonic court. Completing the ceremony will make it harder for him to reclaim you."

Persephone took the fruit, turning the firm flesh in her hands. "I've never seen this before. What is it?"

"We call it a pomegranate, I have only ever seen it grow here in the underworld. Our ceremony for joining the court is to offer the fruit. Only the seeds are eaten."

"Eating seeds?" Persephone asked dubiously.

"They are different from apple seeds," He smiled tiredly, obviously remembering their first meeting. "Peas and corn are seeds too."

The skin of the pomegranate fell to pieces easily, if a bit messily in her hands. The seeds looked a little like gemstones, packed together tightly inside. They shimmered red in the juices. She scooped out a handful, crunching them between her teeth. They were sweet even if they didn't taste like much.

The ride back to Olympus was the first time that she had been on the chariot since she had fled from the mortal world. The horses, chariot, and Aidon looked exactly as she remembered. The black chrome and gold and silver accents gleamed. Even the harnesses on the horses were quite decorative. Deep red and dark purple accents in the forms of gemstones subtly winked as they caught the light. Aidoneus's armor was just as impressive, although Persephone wasn't nearly as scared of the helmet as she had been before. The red and purple plumes on it were actually quite soft, although she couldn't imagine the bird they had come from.

It was only Persephone who was different. She had ridden down the first time a scared girl in a dirty white chiton. She was returning dressed as a powerful Chthonic Theoi. From her boots to her leopard-skin cloak, she was transformed. Akhea had chosen her tunic and pants to match Aidon although hers remained mostly in shades of red with hints of purple and gold. Unlike most of the Chthonic clothes she had collected, the ensemble wasn't very comfortable.

Thanatos and Nyx rode ahead in another gaudy chariot, and Hypnos and Ascalaphus followed behind. It was a much shorter and more pleasant ride than the one many moons before, even though they had to travel all the way to the mountain. The sunlight seemed almost painfully bright when it first hit Persephone's eyes. It was beautiful, but a different beauty than she had gotten used to in Hades, where the mist gave everything soft edges. They flew high over several mortal villages as the mountain approached on the horizon and mortals below them gawked. She had forgotten that too. How unused the living were to Theoi.

It was always interesting to Persephone to approach Olympus from the mortal world. It was strange to see it look like a normal mountain. But one by one the chariots got close enough to the barrier to Travel away from the mortal realm and to Olympus proper. The trees and meadows of the mountain suddenly became more vibrant and the peak was covered with palaces and gardens. The gleaming white marble was no longer familiar to her.

They landed on one of the terraces fairly far from Zeus's court, but there were already many chariots and horses. Persephone had never seen so many, even on feast days. It sent a shudder of foreboding down her spine. No matter the evidence, she hadn't quite believed that her mother had created such a furor over her.

They strode through the halls in a tight little knot of six, the other Theoi scattering out of their way as nymphs did. That didn't surprise Persephone. She had grown up on all the stories about the underworld, the Chthonic Theoi, and their role in the giant wars and the defeat of the Titans. She thought that some of them didn't even recognize her, although that wasn't exactly a surprise either.

The throne room was packed with Theoi, expanded to hold the entirety of the Olympus and many of the Neptans as well. She could see Poseidon on an elevated dais to the left of Zeus's throne. Even Hera was sitting on a throne, something Persephone couldn't remember seeing before. The Olympian queen seldom bothered with audiences. All were wearing their best, gleaming white chitons for the Olympians edged with their colors or symbols in gold, and bright blues and greens for the Neptans. All except Demeter, who was wrapped in mortal homespun. She couldn't tell if her mother's clothes were stained in mud or intentionally dyed that way. Her hair was streaked with grey. It was a shocking sight and there was a small hole in the crowd around her. As much due to her appearance as to what she had stirred up in the mortal world.

Even Zeus looked uncomfortable as they approached, glancing from the corner of his eye at Demeter and then back at the Chthonics as they approached. It was interesting to Persephone to see her father, King of the Olympians look so out of his element and unsure. He did not do nearly as good a job at hiding it as Aidon had done. *My father really has no idea how to diffuse the situation he created,* Persephone thought.

"Welcome to my hall, Lord Hades," Zeus boomed. "And welcome back home to Lady Kore as well."

Persephone could feel Aidoneus internally sigh at her father's clueless rudeness. "Hades remains a place, Lord Zeus, and Lady Kore's home. She accepted your permission to join the Chthonic court."

The fact that Persephone hadn't answered his other offer probably only hung in the air for the two of them. But the Theoi and nymphs in the room still shuffled in shock. Some were there to watch the chaos among the major Theoi. It wasn't often that Demeter and Aidoneus became caught in Zeus's trouble. And even Poseidon had been dragged into this fight. Demeter's actions had threatened everyone. Other Theoi, wiser Theoi, watched anxiously. It felt like war between the courts, or at the very least a power struggle between major Theoi that would leave vast scars across the mortal world they all depended on. What no one had expected was for the 'kidnapped' girl few remembered to return having willingly changed courts. Persephone could feel their curious stares skittering across her skin. Gasps and whispers filled the room.

Zeus glanced back at Demeter nervously and then back at Aidoneus. "That was not finalized, Lord Aidoneus. And in light of new events, Lady Kore will return to the Olympian court and her mother."

"The members of my court are not toys to be given to end a temper tantrum. She is under my protection as a member of the Chthonic court. Lady Kore agreed to come to Olympus only to reassure her mother."

Zeus was about to reply when Demeter interrupted. "The fields will remain fallow, the livestock barren, and the trees fruitless until my Kore returns to me. I only agreed to leave my temple because you promised she would be here, Zeus. Give me back my daughter," Demeter said in a lifeless monotone.

Zeus and Aidoneus glared at each other for nearly a minute before Poseidon intervened. "Brother, be reasonable. If the girl does not return Demeter will refuse to feed the mortals. Many will die, and our cults will suffer. No one wants that, however distasteful the situation is."

"Lord Poseidon, I will remind you that as her Lord, Zeus is responsible for keeping Lady Demeter in line and handling situations like this one. I can also create havoc in the mortal world when angered."

The crowd shuffled nervously. Even immortal Theoi did not like the idea of the underworld in disarray. "Yes, Lady Demeter is my responsibility, as is Lady Kore. The solution is simple. You must release the girl, Aidoneus. Everyone knows your rights to take her were slim. Surely one of my other daughters will do if you still desire a consort."

Aidoneus's eyes flashed. "I will remind you that I offered Lady Kore sanctuary after her mother threatened to turn her into a tree, a punishment fit only for mortals and nymphs for the great crime of considering my suit. I will not release a Theoi to a fate worse than a mortal slave."

Zeus stood up, lightning crackling through his blonde beard. "Lady Kore is an Olympian, and on this mountain I hold sway!"

Aidoneus did not back down. "She ate of the pomegranate after receiving permission from you to leave Olympus. That makes her Chthonic, unless you feel the need to renegotiate the terms of cooperation between the courts?"

The Olympian King deflated a bit in the face of his older brother. "Very well, but this does not solve the issue at hand. We all need Lady Demeter's crops, even you, Lord Hades. Would you like to take responsibility for the mother as well as the daughter?"

Persephone watched as even Aidoneus blanched a bit at that idea. "I do not force anyone to join my court, or hold them there against their will, Lord Zeus. Not even Lady Demeter."

Zeus crossed his arms and glared down from his throne. "Sending Lady Demeter to Tartarus would still not awaken the earth. There is no guarantee executing her would either, as it's unknowable what another incarnation would do," he continued, as murmurs swept around the hall. Theoi did not like being reminded of what had only been known to happen during the wars. "Lady Kore must return to the mortal earth at least long enough for a harvest. Will you allow her to return for half the year on the condition Lady Demeter will not be allowed to harm her?"

Aidoneus glanced over his shoulder to where Persephone stood, watching. She gave him a little nod. She had known she had to return. Half the year was a better bargain than she had been expecting.

"That is acceptable, Lord Zeus. But she is still a member of my court. If I return to find her as anything but a Theoi it will mean war."

Zeus nodded, and before anything else could be said, Persephone felt a hand on her arm. The grip was like iron, and colors whirled as they Traveled.

XX

Rhea raised Zeus in secret away from the other Titans, afraid they would take away her son. Zeus was a lonely child, as his mother could not often stay with him and refused to explain why. It was not until he met a beautiful Theoi among the humans that Zeus began to understand. The girl was like him, not like his mother, and when he finally convinced her he meant no harm, he learned that her name was Aphrodite. Zeus and Aphrodite lived and loved among the humans for a time, hidden from the other Theoi, as Aphrodite admitted she had always been scared of the Titans. They named themselves Olympians after their favorite mountain. And so things might have remained if it weren't for Metis, the youngest of the second generation of Titans.

The temple was familiar, but Persephone had never seen it look so dead before. What had once been rolling fields and verdant fruit trees had been replaced by a light dusting of the last snow and withered branches. The only things left untouched were her flowering hedges, although most of their flowers were curled up for the cold season. She almost didn't recognize Calli as she stood on the marble steps to greet them. The nymph was gaunt and her hair hung limply. The rest of the attendants hovered behind her hesitantly, wrapped in thick woolen cloaks.

"My Lady and Lady Kore, welcome home," Calli said, the desperation shining out of her eyes. She looked at Persephone like she was salvation.

Persephone looked over her shoulder at her mother. In contrast to the defeated thing she had been on Olympus and the poor condition of the nymphs, Demeter was already looking better. Her steps were once again confident and her hair had begun to shine again. "Please take Kore to her room and help her find something appropriate to wear," Demeter ordered, disappearing to her own rooms at the back of the temple.

Calli turned and waved Persephone to follow her. The rest of the nymphs sank down onto the floor, already looking exhausted. It was only then that she noticed that there were only Melides. There were no Epimelides of the fields among them. "Calli, are you all right?" Persephone asked, catching her as they turned a corner.

The nymph smiled tightly. "We will be. It is easier for those of us tied to the trees. Deep roots have helped. But now that you have returned things should go back to the way they were."

Persephone followed her in shock. It hadn't occurred to her that the nymphs would be hit so hard. She had been so focused on the memory of the thousands of shades lining the riverbank.

The room looked so tiny when they reached it. Persephone stood in the doorway, it seemed barely more than an alcove with a tiny bed pushed in the corner. She wasn't very big, but she had gotten used to the underworld palace. She spread her fur cloak over the woolen blankets. It didn't quite cover the whole thing, but it would be much warmer while the frost lay on the ground. Persephone carefully folded her Chthonic ceremonial clothes on the bed. They were not as comfortable as her daily wear, but they were designed for warmth. She might not need them, but it would be nice to have.

Calli had found her a fresh chiton and a pair of sandals. Persephone let the plain white fabric run through her fingers sadly. It was thick enough, even if it wasn't soft. She pulled it on with a sigh before lacing up her sandals. Calli followed closely behind her as she wandered through the temple. It seemed very small and Persephone missed the etchings and geometric carvings that were omnipresent in the underworld.

Demeter was still absent when they returned to the audience chamber. Persephone looked around at the other nymphs slumped on cushions. Her mother had several temples, but there were still four nymphs who were tied to the nearby trees. Three absent others belonged to these fields. Persephone only hoped that they were simply sleeping. She turned and marched towards the door. Calli and two of the others followed on her heels, but they said nothing as she marched towards the nearest tree.

Even linked to a nymph, it looked awful. It only had a few leaves clinging to it and fallen branches littered the ground. Persephone pressed her hands to its bark, feeling the life thrumming inside it. She tried to remember the feeling of using her gift in the underworld. It had grown by leaps and bounds, and she should have been confident of reviving a single apple tree. But it was the first time she had tried to use her new strength in the mortal world. *What if I am still weak here?* she thought.

Persephone reached deep inside herself for her gift, pushing it into the bark through her hands. If it did not respond quite as it had in the underworld, it still flowed much more easily than it ever had before. Slowly the tree perked up as if it was a tiny seedling given water after a drought. Its' nymph ran out from the temple with a shout, but Persephone ignored her. She didn't stop until the life ran through the tree as it should have in the cold season. Ligeia clutched her tree, blinking tears out of her eyes as she stared at Persephone. The nymph was already looking much better and she started to stutter out thanks. But Persephone was on a mission. Calli's tree was at another temple, but another of her assigned attendants was close to begging.

She was bound to an orange tree on the other side of the temple. Persephone's gift leapt inside her like it never had except for when she tended to the river, and it bolstered her determination. Peisinoë's tree too returned to life under her hands and the light-haired nymph dropped to her knees at Persephone's feet. "My Lady Kore, thank you," she sobbed, one hand still clutching one of her roots.

Persephone finished the fruit trees and gazed over the dead fields. The nymphs of the trees had been in a terrible state and insisted that their sisters were even worse off. Persephone felt numb. The shock had worn off and nothing was left. She had spent seasons beyond count with the loyal nymphs. They had cared for her, attended her mother, and faithfully done their duty. And her mother had abandoned them to a slow death. It was unthinkable. Worse, without Aura, she could not reach the other temples and she wasn't sure she could even help the rest of those who were within her reach. Persephone had learned to help the flowering fruit trees, but never the grains of the fields.

She took a deep breath and walked out onto the bare ground. Tiny bits of snow crunched under her sandals. Persephone wished she had kept her Chthonic boots. Remembering what she had done to the ivy, she reached out with her gift, searching for the nymph's power under the earth. She wasn't sure exactly what to look for, but she walked slowly over the ground, the lines of the furrows falling beneath her feet. There was a pulsing, a heartbeat beneath the earth, and Persephone knew she had found the right place. She had no clear idea how to grow wheat as she had done to the tree, but perhaps she could pass energy to the sleeper instead.

Persephone buried her hands in the soft dirt, pushing past the snow and icy bits. The heart of the nymph pulsed with weak life beneath her. She closed her eyes and imagined that the nymph was one of her flowers. She just needed to give it a little push to bloom. Her energy spiraled around the nymph for what seemed like an agonizingly long time. But it did sink in, faster and faster once it started. She did not hear the gasps of her companions or see the soft frosting of green across the field. Persephone kept her focus until she could sense the nymph become restless.

When she stepped back and opened her eyes, the green was all around her. It was a tiny fuzz, unlikely to survive in this weather even under a nymphs's care, but it was more than Persephone had ever had anything to do with before. The nymph was lying on her back in the field breathing heavily, looking up at the sky. It was easy to see how terrible the last few moons had been for her, but she was alive. Disheveled, but alive.

With new confidence, Persephone walked the other two fields. By the end her gift was beginning to drag in her chest, the way mortals described feeling after running too far. But the last nymph was awake again, even if Persephone was sitting in the dirt beside her.

Calli and Peisinoë had to half drag Persephone back to the temple. By the time they got there, her sandals were caked in mud, cold dirt oozing through her toes, and she had ruined another white chiton. She wouldn't even bother trying to fix it. Her control over her power might have improved, but not that much. The nymphs gently helped her clean off and delivered her back to her room. She flopped down onto her bed, ready to curl up and sleep when she noticed that something was missing. She was lying on her own sheets again, exactly how they had always been. "Calli, where are my things?"

XXI

Younger than any of the other Titans, Metis had been delighted at the prospect of a new playmate when Rhea had fallen pregnant and horrified at what Kronos had done. When she stumbled upon Zeus and Aphrodite in a human village, she was ecstatic. Two of Rhea's children had survived! Metis was puzzled when Aphrodite said she wasn't one of Rhea's children, but Metis wasn't picky. Though skittish at first after Rhea's warning, Zeus and Aphrodite soon accepted Metis. Away from the other Titans, they played with the humans until Metis had an idea.

Persephone quickly gave up her questioning of Calli, resolving to retrieve her new clothes the next day. She fell into a dreamless sleep, even her Theoi constitution strained by the exercise of new power. The newly refreshed nymphs went about their duties while their less fortunate companions watched in envy. Demeter did not reappear that night, but something changed in the world, undetectable to mortal senses. Sap began to run strongly in the trees. Deep beneath the earth seeds began to reawaken. Perennials prepared to send out new growth. The starved nymphs felt this change as an ease in the strain they had been carrying for many moons.

Her senses newly attuned, Persephone too felt the change when she woke with the sun. It seemed as if the entire mortal world was experiencing a slower version of what she had done for the nymphs the night before. Even in the face of her annoyance over her mother's behavior and her disappearing things, it gave her deep satisfaction. The world would be right again.

Peisinoë had provided a breakfast, although Persephone looked at it with veiled distaste before sighing to herself. *I am not in Hades anymore.* She did not notice that it was sparser than the temple's table had ever been before. The nymphs ate with her as they waited for her mother to reappear from her chambers.

"Where is my cloak? I missed it last night, it is still cold here," Persephone asked Calli.

"I do not have it, My Lady," Calli replied, refusing to meet her eyes.

Persephone was rested enough to notice her new title but doggedly pursued her original goal. "And the rest of my things? My boots, tunic, and pants?"

Calli only shook her head, staring down at the table. Peisinoë interceded. "We do not have your things," she insisted passing Persephone another dried apple.

They had nearly finished breakfast when Demeter walked into the room. She had undergone nearly as much of a transformation as her nymphs. Gone was the wretched creature of the night before. Persephone stared at her mother. There was nothing to indicate that anything had happened to her at all. It was as if the past season had not happened. She was as healthy and beautiful as any Theoi ever was. Even her clothes had been replaced. Persephone recognized one of the many earth-colored chitons with grain along the hem, its pleats falling as they always had.

"Good morning mother," Persephone began diplomatically. "Some of my things seem to have been misplaced. It is still cool outside and I would like them back. Do you know where they are?"

"You already have such beautiful chitons, Kore darling," Demeter replied. "And it will soon be quite warm again. We need to start preparing for the warm season's plantings." The goddess turned away from her daughter to speak to Calli.

"It is cold *now*, and even if it wasn't I like those clothes. I want them back," Persephone said evenly.

"They are completely inappropriate for the goddess of spring," Demeter replied. "I disposed of them for you. You didn't need any reminders of that awful place!"

Persephone wasn't sure where to start. "What is a spring? You didn't get rid of them, mother, you didn't leave your rooms at all last night!"

"I had the nymphs burn them while you went for your walk," Demeter said airily. "And of course you are the goddess of spring, you have brought life back to the earth. It's what I've decided to call the warm planting season in honor of your rescue."

Persephone stood up, her chair screeching across the stone floor. "First of all, my walk, my walk?! I came back from *visiting* a *friend*, of my own *free will*, and Melides are half dead, and the Epimelides are gone. They raised me, my friends, your attendants and you abandoned them! Killing them along with the mortals. You don't get to do that and just decide what my gift is. It doesn't work like that. My gifts are *mine*, not something you can choose for me! And while I was trying to save them you burned my clothes? They were warm and soft and never did anything to hurt you, just like the nymphs!"

Demeter stared at her like she couldn't hear a word she had said. "I felt what you did last night, you are finally discovering who you are, helping in the fields. The mortals will love you so much and you've already found your nice new clothes."

Persephone turned away, disgusted. It had never been like this before. Her mother had never really tried to understand her, but she hadn't willfully ignored her either. Zeus may have sentenced her to six moons on the earth, but he didn't chain her here. She had taken only three steps when she felt something wrap around her waist and drag her back to the table. She struggled against the power that held her, but nothing she had practiced in the underworld had prepared her for this. Persephone suddenly wished she had used her newly strengthened power for something besides gardening.

The expression on Demeter's face hadn't changed despite Persephone's fury. The nymphs faces may have shown their shock but her mother only talked to Calli about the preparations for planting. Persephone felt as if invisible iron bands held her to her seat. She had always known, in a distant intellectual way that her mother was Demeter, Goddess of Agriculture. A powerful Olympian on par with Hera, Zeus, or even her Aidon, but she had never felt it before. Her mother did her duties and protected her people and the nymphs. But the invisible bands had no give and her mother had abandoned both her duties and the gentle nymphs to drag Persephone home.

Persephone struggled and shouted at her mother. Demeter seemed not to hear her. Calli was studiously engrossed in talk of the plantings. The other nymphs refused to meet her eyes. Persephone's anger simmered. *I'm the one who helped them, I tried my best.* Peisinoë tried to give her apples and even a handful of raisins, but Persephone refused to touch them. She let the forcefully normal conversation wash over her.

When her mother and Calli stood up, Persephone felt the iron bands release her. She prepared to bolt but felt a tug. Trailing behind them, she was dragged through the temple as they checked on the seeds and blankets for the plantings. Calli kept glancing at her surreptitiously when her mother wasn't looking. Her mother looked right through her whenever she talked but sometimes addressed meaningless comments to her. As if Persephone cared how much barley they brought.

Persephone tallied the number of days until she would be released from Zeus's sentence. *One hundred and eighty-one. Sixty days of planting. Seven festival days. One hundred and fourteen days to wander in between. I can do this.* Persephone held her tongue.

The world came back to life seemingly by the hour. By the third day Persephone could see the difference even in the fields she hadn't helped. An invisible tether connected her to the temple. She could walk the fields, the orchard, and even a section of the woods and the town. But the further she walked the harder the tug became. Persephone took to hiding in the woods most of the day. When she ventured into Eleusis, a town that had always been prosperous and well-fed, some mortals hid in the houses. They warily watched her and the temple through the windows. Others fell on their knees before her, begging even the weakest Theoi they knew to help them.

"My daughters are starving!"

"Nothing has sprouted in my garden in the whole cold season. Bless it, please!"

"The fields are barren. Why has Lady Demeter abandoned us?"

"I lost my grandfather. Will the warm season bring food again?"

"There is nothing left in the woods!"

Persephone tried to refresh the soil and help the seeds sprouting under the ground grow faster. Without a guardian nymph, it was much harder. She vacillated between shame at herself for abandoning the world and seething anger at her mother for doing so on purpose. But too many mortals began to come out from the buildings, surrounding her and begging for help.

Persephone backed away, pushing her way away from the crush. "It will not be this way forever. The fields will grow again as the world warms. Plant as much as you can." She fled before them.

No one bothered her in the woods. No dryads or naiads in sight and her mother's nymphs stayed out of her way. She could sense them watching her, but they never came close enough to see. In a clearing, she lay in the sparse grass and stared at the clouds. The memory of another clearing far away and long ago was too painful and she pushed herself back up. Persephone thought about the sensation of Traveling. She had done it thousands of times. Gathering up her power, she focused on the feeling, but the air did not ripple in front of her and the scenery stayed the same. She thought that she had the power to do it, but her mother would never teach her and the nymphs couldn't. She wasn't even sure if she was doing something wrong, or if the tether held her back somehow. Persephone wondered if the sprouts in her underworld garden had grown proper leaves yet in the half-light. *I wonder if things would be different if I had given him an answer before I left.*

She walked at the back of the procession, further back than she had ever been before, as far as the tugging would let her. But even her mother could not force her gift. The mortals would have to muddle along without flowers. They didn't notice. The towns and villages were too hungry to be thinking about such trivial things. Unlike the ones nearest the temple, they seemed to have no concept that their misery was Demeter's fault. They were simply pathetically grateful to see them. She counted footsteps and days.

Every night she laid on the hard ground and remembered another night. Lying on her balcony on the soft furs, listening to Aidon tell her stories of the glittering not-stars. She missed her maids and Asca, and even Charon splashing her. Persephone pressed her face to her blanket and cried silently. She imagined the flowing river and her garden, untouched by the ravages of the mortal cold. Persephone thought she must be a terrible person for wishing she had never left.

Every day it was harder. She stared listlessly at the nymphs going through the motions of planting. The earth was back to life in full and they all looked healthy again. Many of them seemed to have already forgotten what had happened, pushing it out of their mind. Peisinoë still tried to walk with her every day and so did Calli when Demeter released her from her duties. It didn't help.

But Persephone managed to keep her head down and her mouth closed until her mother called her forward in one of the sprawling orchards of the rolling hill country. "Kore, come see if you can make these trees flower early!"

Persephone trudged forward. Her mother was examining a branch, just as she would every year. Something in her boiled over. "Why did you name me Kore?"

Her mother looked over, startled, most of her attention still on the tree. "It's your name. Why shouldn't the springtime maid be called Kore?"

"Girl is not a name," Persephone ground out.

"Kore, what kind of ideas did Hades put in your head? You love your name, you love our work. We need to forget this terrible year and move on."

"Hades isn't a name either, and stop calling me that! I'm not a springtime anything, and I haven't been a girl for a very long time now," Persephone insisted.

"It is a horrid place," Demeter retorted, releasing the branch. "No life, no sunlight, a place for the dead!"

"Have you ever even been there? It's full of light and life, it's beautiful! My name is Persephone. You didn't give me a real name, so I found one of my own."

Demeter's face suddenly became paler than it had been even on Olympus. "Never. Never that, and never the land of the dead."

Kore felt her tether tug awkwardly, and Calli's footsteps quick behind her. Calli and Ligeia shadowed her footsteps. That was the first day that Persephone found one of the baskets.

XXII

Metis had seen each of her cousins swallowed by Kronos and she had never forgotten. "It is very hard to kill a Theoi," she remarked one day. "If we could only get Zeus's siblings out, they would probably be fine."

Zeus and Aphrodite agreed and soon Metis hatched a plan. She would slip mustard seeds into Kronos's wine. Zeus and Aphrodite would be ready to run and hide with the other Olympians when Kronos coughed them up. It never occurred to Metis that the other Titans wouldn't calm down after a week or two. After all, there was nothing wrong with Zeus or Aphrodite and Metis had no memory of the Primordials.

The woven basket was filled with furs, warm and plush and thick. Persephone grinned as she thought about sleeping on them instead of the cold ground. Deeper, she found a new pair of boots and warm clothes from her wardrobe in the underworld. But most precious of all, nestled protectively in the furs there were memory crystals. She picked one at random and found a memory from Makaria of Elysium. Children played and laughed in the city street. The flavors of an underworld deer burst in her mouth. It was short but it felt delightfully of home. She could not wait to find out what the others held. Calli and Ligeia wouldn't touch the basket, but Persephone carried it back to their tent on her own. She was careful not to spill any of her new treasures.

The furs looked nice spread across her sleeping space. Persephone split her time between glancing eagerly between the crystals and the furs. She would save the crystals for when she was falling asleep. A message from home every night for a week. She was busy looking for a fur to turn into another cloak when her mother returned. She was never sure which of the nymphs had found her mother so fast.

"Kore!" She snapped. "Get rid of those nasty things now. Hunter's goods do not belong at planting, and they smell like death!"

Persephone buried her face in one of the furs, savoring it for as long as it lasted. She couldn't smell anything bad about it. Just the mist and the thick soil of the forest she had run through with Asca. She wondered if he had caught these for her. Calli and Ligeia hadn't scrunched up their faces on the walk back like they smelled something bad either. She was braced for the disintegration, the fur in her hands and beneath her knees fading away to nothing. The crystals glittered one last time before disappearing. "My name isn't Kore," she whispered.

It wasn't the last basket. Persephone suspected that the nymphs found and burned some of them before she saw them. But they could not find them all. In the end it didn't matter. Her mother took them all in the end. But she never made the mistake of saving the crystals again. Aidon sent her memories of Aura and Ammie playing together in the stables, the Styx flowing past their home, and once a glimpse of her garden and the river Lethe, still flowing and clear. Asca showed her a memory of a baby leopard leaping clumsily from rock to rock. Hypnos an old memory of Charon tipping Adon from his boat into the river. The planting seemed to stretch forever in front of her.

"Kore, what would you like to do for the cold planting season? You could work on new flowers that love the snow." Demeter was pruning a pear tree, shaping it to take the best advantage of the light.

Persephone took a deep, calming breath. So the cold planting season didn't merit a new name, did it? "I'm not going to be here for the cold planting season, remember Mother? I decided to join the Chthonic court and I'm going home."

Demeter's eyes seemed to blaze with inner fire. "You have to forget that horrible place. I don't know where I went wrong that you want to go back, but I will never give up on you."

"The people there listen to me, took the time to get to know me, and like me for *me*. I have friends. Aidon loves me!"

"I listen to you!" Demeter screamed. "You love playing with Calli and the other nymphs. Are you going to abandon Eros and Iris as well?"

Persephone couldn't keep the disbelief off her face. "You haven't listened to me about anything, let alone how I want to spend my time. Playing with Calli? I'm not a child anymore. And I barely see Eros or Iris as it is! I may be bad at Traveling to see them, but you never bothered to help me, and Iris doesn't even live on Olympus."

"Neither do we!" Demeter insisted in triumph. The goddess knew where she belonged, among the fields of the earth.

"Do we? I was an Olympian Theoi, I should have had a home there," Persephone sighed and buried her face in her hands. Maybe things would have been different if they had lived on Olympus. Or even returned to the same temple for each growing season. "But you never asked me where I wanted to live or hosted my friends. In Hades, I have one of Poseidon's horses and no one Travels anyway. I can come and go as I please and invite guests. That's more than I've ever had here!"

"And that is enough for you to live with Hades and the dead?" Demeter snarled, the tree branch snapping under her hands.

"In Hades, *in* Hades mother! He was your brother. Use his name! And the shades are pleasant people. All the mortals were shades once and will be again." It was unbelievable. Persephone hadn't noticed how everyone spoke of the Chthonic court until she had met them for herself. If anything the Olympians and Neptans should have treated them with *more* respect. The Chthonics guarded the gates of Tartarus that confined the Titans and Primordials.

"You would abandon your mother for that? You are right, you need to spend more time with your real friends, Eros and Iris. They will help you make more friends, you do not need the Chthonics!"

Persephone sucked in a breath in disbelief. *Now, now of all times mother is suggesting I spend time with friends?* It was ironic. "I didn't want to abandon you, but I'm not going to spend my every waking moment worshipping you. I'm your daughter, not *girl*, not an accessory, not even one of your nymphs! And you've never wanted me to meet anyone at all. I might have met someone I liked more than I liked you!"

"Your sweet gift of flowers was a true blessing. We were to meant work together, not for you to get married. No Theoi would have asked for you," Demeter insisted, sure in her conviction.

"How would I know, you never let me find out! Aidon loved me before I learned how to use my gift better." Persephone remembered their meetings in the meadow in a different light now. He had been interested in her, bringing her gifts and giving her his time. If Aidon had told her who he was from the first, it would have been she who would have run.

"He must have somehow known the extent of your gift beforehand," Demeter said with a nasty smile.

"I'm going to say yes," Persephone hadn't been sure of that before. She wasn't even sure at that moment, but it felt like the right thing to say.

Demeter's hand shot out to slap her. "Never!"

Persephone collapsed to her knees. It hadn't hurt, not really, but her mother had never struck her. She had never even considered such a thing, not in her childhood, not when Aidon had shown her the memory of her mother threatening to transform her into a tree. Not even when she had been chained to the temple. Persephone looked up at her mother with a little bit of fear.

Demeter sank down to her knees next to her daughter. There was regret in her eyes as she brought her hand back to Persephone's cheek, chilled and healing. "Oh Kore, I won't let them take you. I'm sorry, but you must let go of these ideas. I promised I will protect you, and I will. Forever."

Demeter refused to talk about their argument or the upcoming cold season. Her focus was back on the planting, moving from village to village. It was exhausting, but Persephone found it better than the alternative. She was still not allowed to keep anything in her gift baskets and neither Eros nor Iris appeared.

It was with relief that after sixty-seven days Persephone finally stumbled back into the Eleusis temple. They should have gone to one of the other temples, but perhaps her mother had actually taken some of what she had said to heart. Persephone curled up on the bed. It seemed much larger and softer after over two moons of travel. She looked forward to being able to leave for her wanderings the next day. There was no way she would stay at the temple longer than she needed to and maybe Aidon would find a way to visit her. She drifted off to sleep imagining her upcoming freedom. At least she might see Thanatos on his regular visits to the mortal world.

Persephone was up before the sun, quickly gathering her things. She didn't have much. Her feet felt light as she walked the forest path. The temple was nearly out of sight when she felt the tether yank her suddenly backward. Her mother was waiting for her on the temple steps.

"Kore!" Demeter said worriedly. "Where are you going so early?"

Persephone wasn't prepared to face her mother again. "You don't need me for the growing season," she replied evenly. "I'm going to go visit the mortal world, just like I always do."

Demeter frowned. "Of course you're not going, Kore. Just think of what happened last time."

The tether dragged her back inside to breakfast.

It was the longest season Persephone could remember. Most of the days dragged on endlessly. She was once again free to walk the nearby woods and town without a nymph on her heels, but no further. True to her mother's word, Eros and Iris visited several times. It was stifling. They both shot nervous glances at her mother. Iris refused to talk about anything that had happened in the last season at all, even once they had escaped the temple. Her stories of the Neptans were still entertaining, but Persephone longed for the freedom they had enjoyed on Olympus.

Eros bore up better under Demeter's watchful eyes. He talked around what had happened, careful and oblique. Persephone learned that Olympus had been in complete disarray for three moons before her summons. Even Aphrodite had been concerned. Zeus had nearly had a riot on his hands.

They both had grinned when they heard her new name. It was music to her ears to be called Persephone again.

The boredom was almost worse than her mother. She found some underworld seeds that had rolled under her bed when the nymphs had confiscated her things. They reminded her of her plan to try to bring a little bit of Hades to the mortal world. Persephone planted her seeds and gave serious thought to what she should say to Aidon. The seeds refused to grow.

Persephone poured her power into a tiny patch of shaded earth in the forest. She loved Aidon. It was clearer to her every day she wished to return home. But they were Theoi and had time. Unlike her mother, Aidon would wait for her to come to her own decision in her own time. Nothing grew in her makeshift plot.

Halfway through the growing season, Persephone broke down and begged her mother to let her go early. She seemed to hear nothing, not even when Persephone asked just for a visit. Demeter only smiled sadly and told a story from when she was small and always cried when they had to leave another temple or village. The moral of the story seemed to be that she always got over it. "It's wonderful you connect deeply with all the places we visit. But we always have to leave and go home."

XXIII

Cunning Metis's plan worked, and Zeus and Aphrodite safely spirited the other five away as Kronos lay unconscious. Metis stayed innocently behind and was horrified by the firstborn Titan's reactions. She and the other younger Titans cowered in shock as their parents first searched frantically for the missing Theoi and then began to shout angrily. Even Rhea seemed unhappy. Metis had thought she would be pleased. When Metis tried to point out that nothing terrible had happened yet, Themis called her a little fool. Metis ran for Olympus in fright.

The memories of the mortals seemed very short to Persephone. Eleusis was preparing for the harvest festival, as they did every year. *Those mortals at the very least should understand what happened,* thought Persephone. But after their bellies had been reliably filled for a few weeks they stopped begging Persephone for help and the priests and priestesses had returned to the temple. *Either they are very good actors or have actually convinced themselves it was some other Theoi who ruined their harvest.*

Persephone watched the preparations with enthusiasm and for the first time in moons was willing and eager to help the nymphs and mortals around the temple. She had slipped from counting the days to hours. Sunset on the last day of the festival, and Aidon would come for her. She knew that deep down to her bones, falling asleep every night to dream of the look in his eyes and the sound of his laughter. Her mother alternatively threatened terrible things and confidently pronounced that he would have forgotten about her. Calli was beginning to look vaguely nervous. The other nymphs seemed to have gone the same route as the mortals. Nothing was to be different about this harvest festival. *If everyone pretends hard enough it will be true.*

But sometimes Persephone could see something else in the nymph's eyes. Calli came to her room every morning for a moon to brush her hair and braid her hair in her favorite style. Persephone loved the feeling of the brush running through her hair. She could feel the words her old nursemaid was holding back but wasn't sure what they were. On the first day of the festival, Calli twisted her hair tightly around her forehead, making a crown of red gold. "Remember us as well as the mortals," she whispered into Persephone's ear before she left.

Leucosia brought her a fig fresh from her tree every day, slicing it for Persephone's breakfast. Aglaope and the other nymphs of the field baked for her rolls appearing like offerings, always fresh from the ovens. They never dared to say anything at all, but as the last few days before she would leave melted away, she could see the fear in their eyes.

Persephone was walking around the corner towards the main hall when she heard it. Soft breaths, catching in a throat. Another voice, too low to make out over the harsh breathing. Her first thought was one of the priestesses had injured themselves. Persephone walked closer, only to see two nymphs huddled in an alcove. One was holding the other, who was half-collapsed against the wall. Their long hair hid their faces from her. "I can't survive that again," one sobbed. "Kore is going to leave, and our Lady will abandon us again. I've never been so cold before."

"It will not be so bad again," the other one soothed, but her voice wobbled too. "We will be prepared this time and maybe our Lady Kore will stay, or not go quite so long. Maybe she will visit to help as she did when she returned."

Persephone slunk back down the corridor, silent on her bare feet. Part of her insisted that her mother would not take it so hard this time. She was assured of having Persephone back. A season was nothing in the life of a Theoi. Another part insisted loudly that everything would happen exactly as it had before. Her mother hadn't exactly become more reasonable as the moons had gone by. If anything, in the past few weeks she had seemed increasingly desperate.

The festival distracted everyone, even the nymphs. Persephone listened to the music from her window. All her flowers bloomed deep purple, red as pomegranates, or glittered golden in the sun. She stole away from the temple, dressed in the most humble white roughspun she could find, her hair bound under a kerchief. Persephone splashed through the colors until there wasn't anything white left on her at all. It made the bull the next day taste especially sweet. Every supplicant that came to her mother's temple represented another second of her time slipping through her mother's fingers. Persephone could almost hear the thunder of Aidon's chariot. His armor would glitter in the sun, and the four black horses would stamp their feet, and the wheels would leave deep ruts in the temple's road.

She woke with the sun. Peisinoë greeted her at her door. Unlike many of the others, the nymph hadn't given her anything all festival. But now in her hands she held a chiton, cut in the style and patterned with flowers as all the clothes Kore had ever worn were. But this one started in a purple so dark it was almost black at the neck and faded to fiery red at the hem. It was still embroidered with flowers, but instead of pastel on white, these were as golden as the grains that decorated her mother's own. It was something between Kore and Persephone.

"It's beautiful," Persephone breathed, taking it into her own arms. It was heavier than it looked.

"I had to thank you after what you did for us," Peisinoë said quietly. "No matter what happens today, I know My Lady will not forget us. You deserve to have something of your own."

And for the first time since she was very small, Persephone joyfully joined the townspeople in threshing the grain. Her mother frowned down at her from her throne, unsettled that she was having so much joy on the day she would leave. But what could Demeter say? For the first time all season, her daughter was fully and willingly participating in the temple's business. The petty revenge felt so good.

As they began storing the grain in baskets to return to the town, Persephone could hear her mother begin to lecture passionately. She watched the sun slowly descend towards the treetops and wished that Apollo would hurry. The day and night were completely balanced during the harvest festivals, but she knew that soon the days would shorten and the earth would cool. Persephone bit her lip as she thought about the mortals. Maybe some of them would have planted and stored additional food, but most of them would be relying on their second harvest. Even the nymphs who had a season to prepare were nervous. She looked down and ran her hands over the flowers embroidered on her chiton. *Can I stay here to protect them?* It would have been a foreign thought to most Olympian Theoi, but Persephone wasn't Kore anymore, and even Kore had spent many hours with the mortals. Persephone had spent a season in the underworld with the Chthonics. They actually cared about the shades under their care, far beyond the worship they received. Many of them would say it would be right for her to stay to protect them. The sun kissed the treetops.

Persephone was jerked out of her thoughts by the sound of hooves on the road outside the temple. She ran to push open the doors, even though there was no thunder of a chariot or clatter of the wheels. The tether dissolved in her chest as she burst out of the doors.

Aidon was waiting for her, not as the strange savior on the glittering chariot from the meadow, or even the King who went head to head with Zeus and her mother for her rights to at least half of her own destiny. It was her friend Pluton who sat on Ametheus, wearing the rich mortal's garb she had first seen him in so long ago. Aura pranced next to her friend, underworld flowers braided through her mane. It was then that Persephone knew she wasn't Kore at all anymore. Neither was she the perfect Theoi the nymphs hoped she was, and the mortals needed.

She flew down the steps, knocking Aidon back into Ammie as he dismounted. Her arms wrapped around his neck, and he pulled her up into a hungry kiss. He smelled like the underworld mists. Calli's careful hairstyle which had held up to threshing for hours disintegrated under his fingers.

Dimly, Persephone heard her mother shouting something from the top of the temple's steps. Aidon broke away and quickly swung her up onto Aura's back. The grey horse put on a burst of speed, and she was airborne above the mortal world for her third time, and the first under her own power. She screamed her freedom into the evening air, spiraling up into the sunset. Ammie was larger and faster and soon Aidon overtook her, gesturing to the south. Persephone followed with a laugh, urging Aura to chase their heels. The setting sun turned the trees below them to gold.

They were wheeling lower to a gap in the trees before Persephone realized where they were. Their meadow was decked with tiny sparkling lights hung in the surrounding trees and skimming across the tops of the grass. A black fur was spread across her rock, and a small feast rested upon it. Even her little garden had overgrown its bounds and the entire hollow was lit with tiny lights.

Aura landed behind Ammie in the tall grass, and immediately tossed her head and leaned down to taste the grass. Persephone leapt down a beat behind Aidon, clapping her hands in delight. "What are the little lights? They look just like the Lampads in the underworld!" She cupped one of the little lights in her hands. It wasn't a firefly. Its' light was cool and floated freely through the air.

He took her hand and led her towards the picnic, grinning sheepishly. "Orphne may have helped a bit. Chiron said glowing quartz would not be as beautiful. Seeing it now, I have to agree."

Biting into the first taste of the feast, Persephone savored the flavors of the underworld, subtly and wonderfully different. She let Aidoneus peel their apples and flung the peel as far as she could. The core trailed seeds as it hit the soft earth. Perhaps next season her meadow would have an apple seedling or two.

"You were hidden from our sight this season," Aidoneus begun slowly. "Thanatos could tell you did not receive my gifts." He gestured to her new chiton. "But your new clothes fit you more than they did before. Perhaps this season was not as difficult as I feared?"

Persephone thought about all the things that had happened. She could tell him of how she found the nymphs or the mortals. Of being bound to the temple to keep her from running away, his gifts being burned, or her mother's awful words. "I helped a nymph when I first returned. This chiton was a gift from her today. All the other ones were the same as they always were." She looked down at her fingers digging into the black bearskin. "My mother kept me with her the whole year."

The look on Aidoneus's face as he pulled her into his arms told her she did not need to tell the rest. Not tonight. Maybe not ever, if she wanted her mother to keep her hand. "Persephone," he whispered, "you will not have to return at the end of the season."

She knew it was a lie. But it was a pretty lie and nice to hear. "I'm ready to say yes, when you're ready to ask me again," Persephone whispered back into his soft dark curls. That kiss was soft and slow and sweet beneath the true stars.

XXIV

Zeus happily reunited with his siblings as Aphrodite watched. They had prepared a cave full of food and clothes and Hestia lit a fire for them to cook over. The Olympians feasted happily until Metis burst in. "They are so so angry!" She gasped. "I do not know what they will do to us. We must hide." Metis sat down at the fire with her head in her hands.

Unknown to Metis she had been followed by Prometheus, Hypnos, Lelantus, and Leto. They had been frightened by their parent's rage and did not know what else to do. "They do not look so terrible," remarked Leto as she stepped out of the shadows.

Persephone would have happily returned to the underworld by the horrible route a thousand times, but their ride home was only as rough as the average mortal road. She had forgotten how long twilight in Hades lasted and there was still light reflecting off the scattered mist when they entered the cavern.

But it was the lights of the palace that caught her attention. They glowed in the semi-darkness, every window alive with it. Even the smaller palaces on the slope were brightly lit, but nothing compared to Aidon's home. Sensing a warm stall and grain in her future, Aura pulled slightly ahead of Ammie, dashing downwards towards the stables. Persephone flattened herself against the horse's back as the wind tugged at her hair.

The warm glow of light puddled from the palace and the stable across the terrace, like honey on the stones. Persephone slid off the gray mare's back and Aura happily galloped away, one of the stable hands chasing after her. Persephone leaned over the railing, suddenly assaulted by the memory of the first time she had seen the underworld at night. It had been beautiful, but so strange. Now all she saw was home.

Persephone was so engrossed in the land spread out below her that she didn't notice when Aidon came up behind her, taking her hand in his. "The others are waiting for us, whenever you are ready," he said softly, brushing her hair behind her ear.

She took one last look at the peaceful land and turned back to the door that would lead her back to the life she had been forced to abandon what felt like so long ago. "I'm ready."

Persephone walked forward confidently, and the door opened before her, revealing Orphne and her sisters. They smiled widely at her, replacing her sandals with soft boots and giving her a warm cloak to keep out the chill of Hades. It looked just like the one her mother hand burned so long ago. The dark spots shimmered against the white fur, like rocks on a frozen river. "The chiton is lovely," breathed Gyra. "The colors suit you even if it is not quite as fine as our weave."

Persephone looked at the dark red tunic her maids offered her before shaking her head. She had spent the last season trapped in her mother's temple. It would feel odd to meet her friends looking like she had never left. She was stuck somewhere between Hades and Olympus. Let everyone see that.

Her maids scurried off and Aidon offered her his arm as he led her down the long hall to the throne room. The light and music hit Persephone like a wave. The chairs that usually lined the walls for the court and advisors had been replaced with feast tables, the center of the floor left clear for dancing. Couples whirled about, light on their feet to music played by talented shades. The smell of the feast and the sound of the music drew a burst of laughter from her. She had forgotten how good it felt to laugh. The door they had emerged from was small and hidden in the shadows of a far wall. Aidon leaned against the frame and Persephone took a few steps into the party. No one noticed them in the cacophony. She laughed again.

Aidon moved from his place by the door and bowed low before her. "Would the Lady Persephone care to dance?"

Her lips pulled into a smile as she took his hand. "I would be honored, Lord Aidoneus." They had never danced like this before. Not with music flowing full and thick and other people whirling around them. They had mock danced once, long ago on top of her rock. She had barely kept up with him. She hadn't danced with a partner since she was small. Persephone didn't think she was hitting the steps quite right, but Theoi were graceful and Aidon wouldn't let her fall.

They danced in the shadowed corner until the song wound down, but the next brought them into a wide arc onto the proper dance floor. Persephone found herself partnered with first Chiron and then Thanatos before the women split off into their own line. Sandwiched between Makaria and Orphne, Persephone tried to copy their movements. She might have failed abysmally, but everyone was laughing merrily.

There were only tiny snatches of conversation on the dance floor. "It's good to have you back, Olympian girl." "Did you like the furs I sent you?"

"There were not nearly as many souls to guide," this from Thanatos and he leaned down. "They owe you their lives, even if they do not know it."

It struck Persephone how different this day was than when she had first returned to her mother's temple. Dances with friends, and memories of exhausting herself in the fields. Joy or desperation.

Aidon hovered the next day, waiting for her at breakfast, the table filled with all the things she had missed. Hypnos was slumped in another chair, nodding absently at the list of duties Aidoneus was reeling off at him. Orphne brought in new dishes and tried not to giggle when Persephone caught her eye. He was acting like Hypnos hadn't been helping to run Hades since before there was a Hades.

Persephone had to half drag him out of the room, light already brightening to full day outside the windows. Ammie and Aura were waiting for them, but Persephone stood by Ammie. Aidon lifted her up in front of him, and Ammie whickered happily. She hadn't ridden him for a long time even before she was exiled. Persephone had missed her fourth friend.

Aura wheeled freely about them as they soared over the city below. It was a beautiful day, cool and crisp. Persephone was glad of it after the heat of the mortal world, and glad to have her cape back. Ammie chased Aura through the forest through the edge of the city. She was winning until they dismounted, freeing the larger stallion from his burden. Aura darted off through the trees in alarm as he thundered after her.

Aidon laughed quietly at their antics and pulled Persephone towards the city. She looked around at the clean streets and wild architecture. "I know I shouldn't be surprised, but everything looks exactly the same as before I left. Even a season can change the cities in the mortal world," she mused.

"Things change slowly here. The buildings do not burn down, and Makaria rarely allows them to be torn down. You would see more differences on the far side where it is still expanding."

Persephone found a silver bracelet and a red ruby orb polished to a high shine. She thought it would look pretty catching the light in her window, even though she had a sneaking suspicion it had started life as a toy. Even Aidoneus found a wooden lyre he thought Hypnos would like. "I do not usually abandon all duties to him for an entire day."

They came across Makaria as they wandered. She was sitting on the edge of a fountain, listening to a handful of shades. It reminded Persephone of a tiny version of Zeus holding court. Persephone had never seen Makaria in her city. She looked at home there. Even her clothes which had seemed vaguely odd before fit in among the many styles of the shades.

It took her nearly ten minutes to notice them standing at the edge of the square. She untangled herself from her court and wandered with them for the later part of the morning. Persephone had been satisfied with Aidon's version of a tour of the city, but Makaria actually knew who dwelt in many of the buildings. Persephone asked the taller Theoi about some of the stranger buildings. Some of them puzzled even Makaria, but she knew when many of them had been built, and what kind of shade had built them. One group of buildings looked like they had been carved from solid rock. "I don't think there are any of those shades still dwelling there. They came from a land far across the sea, a land of canyons and rivers. Thanatos said that their rocks were red like the sunset. I haven't seen any of them for a long time."

Persephone learned more about the city in the better part of a morning than she had in the season she had lived in Hades. She thanked Makaria before she pushed Aidon into the river and jumped in after him. Makaria squawked and jumped away from the spray of water, waving at them from a safe place on the dock.

She splashed in the river, ducking under the surface when Aidon threatened to splash back. Persephone had missed this. There was always something to do at her mother's temple. Planting, growing, harvesting. It seemed like work was sometimes even invented. There was no time or inclination for being silly or simply enjoying another's company.

The water fight ended and they allowed the current to carry them along the river, watching first the buildings and then the wilderness go by. Once they even passed Chiron in his boat, and Aidon threatened to steal his oar until he held it high in the air and threatened to smack them with it. "You are a terrible influence, Olympian girl!" He shouted. "Aidon was not this bad until he brought you here."

Persephone tried to splash him, but the sides of the boat were too high. They had well and truly floated out of the bounds of Elysium then and had long since stopped seeing fishing boats. She floated on her back, watching the silvery mist roil above. *I wonder how my garden is doing? Perhaps all the seeds were bad, I couldn't get any of them to grow in the mortal realm. But they seemed to like the ground beside my river. When did I start to think of it as mine?* Persephone wondered. But at the same time, it felt right. The river had been blocked, and she had helped it. In return, it had given her wonderful black soil for a special place all her own. She had thought about it often for the first few moons with her mother but she hadn't for a while.

All through the smaller party that night, just for the court, Persephone thought about her river and the sliver of land beside it. She missed the knowing glances that passed between the guests as they looked at her and Aidon.

It was good that Aura remembered the way because Persephone would not have been able to find her way back to the spot she had chosen for her garden, not in one day. Elysium might change slowly, but the wilderness of Hades was not under the same obligation. Aura confidently touched down on a rocky patch of ground by the Lethe. Persephone breathed in the spray from the river. This time she recognized it, the taste of the mortal world. It was much more recognizable after only a few days in the underworld.

But when she looked up from the waters, she almost thought Aura had been wrong. What had been a somewhat muddy stretch of empty dirt beside the rushing water was now something else entirely. Several young fruit trees had sprung up, along with low underbrush and a carpet of sweet-smelling herbs and grasses. Persephone picked her way through it gingerly, careful not to step on the young growth. There were some berries on the bushes, but more marvelous was the red-gold fruit hanging from the branches. She spun around in wonder. *But they refused to grow at all before.*

Suddenly, the spirit of a deer rushed through the grove, barely missing Persephone on its headlong plunge to the waters and to life. She reached out to cradle the nearest fruit, cool and firm in her hands. Something unwound itself from deep inside Persephone as the lap of the water filled her ears. The river led back to the mortal world, carrying its cargo to life. It was the water of the river that watered her garden. *A gift should be effortless,* the ghost of Aidoneus's voice whispered in her ears. Persephone threw back her head and laughed. The power of the river thrummed in her veins. She could feel the pulse of life on the surface high above her and the tiny sparks of shades ready to return home.

XXV

Zeus made to drive the other Titans away, but Metis stopped him. "They deserve the chance to make up their own minds. Perhaps they can help convince our parents to be reasonable."

The Olympians and the younger Titans hid in the cave for three moons, protected by Aidoneus's power over the earth and Demeter's hanging vines. They could feel the rage of the firstborn Titans shake the earth and sky.

At last, Prometheus stood. "I will go find my brother Epimetheus. He will be able to tell us what is happening."

The world above grew colder. Persephone was aware of it through her new sense, but there were not quite as many shades waiting for Charon's boat as there had been last season. Apparently, the mortals were smarter than she had given them credit for. The palace was busier than she had ever seen it before and for the first time she had duties of her own to attend to. Not her mother's, not Aidoneus's, hers. Persephone tended her strange garden, and rode Aura up and down the banks of the river, keeping its waters clear for the shades. The same water pulsed in her wherever she went in Hades.

Persephone tended the garden lovingly, nurturing the trees with their golden fruit and running her hands through the dense underbrush on unfamiliar herbs. After half a moon she felt comfortable enough with her new discovery to invite Aidon to the bank of her river. The satisfaction of it was bone-deep. Persephone knew she belonged in Hades. Ammie followed Aura over the treetops to land in the clearing near the river. Aidon didn't comment as she took his hand and led him through the thin strip of trees.

Her garden stretched before them, running along the riverbank that had been so recently flooded. The river was loud in their ears and its water could be easily glimpsed through the sparse fruit trees.

Aidon turned to Persephone. "This is a beautiful place you have built here," he said wonderingly. "I do not recognize any of these plants. Did you create them?"

Persephone shrugged. "I found the river last season when I followed one of the deer spirits Asca and I hunted. When I found it the Lethe was choked and blocked with debris. Aura and I cleared it. The garden I planted on the bank when the water went down. I just used seeds I had collected from the forest."

Aidon ran a hand through the herbs, picking a sprig and smelling the spicy scent. "I do not think these grow in the forest."

Persephone leaned back against one of the slim tree trunks. "A long time ago you told me that gifts were supposed to be effortless."

He looked at her sharply and then nodded. "A gift is part of who a Theoi is."

Persephone felt his power reaching out to her, and allowed the river to rush fully through her blood again. The garden shivered around them, and she could hear both Asca's forest and the world above calling to her. "You were right. I am not the goddess of flowers, or 'spring' no matter what my mother says. I found my place here without realizing it."

Aidon smiled back at her, reaching out with his own gift. Their power entwined and Persephone shivered a bit. "Life and death," she whispered into the sound of the rushing river.

To her surprise, the look on Aidon's face became troubled. "You never discussed your gift with Poseidon, Apollo, or Artemis, did you?" He questioned, although it sounded more like a statement to Persephone.

She shook her head. "Why would I?"

Aidon took a deep breath. "Did any of the Olympians ever explain to you what a Titan fundamentally is?"

"First there were Primordials, and their children were Titans. The Titans gave birth to Olympians," Persephone replied in confusion, before making a face. "And Chthonics and Neptans too, I suppose."

"Then why are some of the children of the Titans still considered Titans?" Aidon asked carefully.

Persephone's forehead wrinkled as she stared at first the ground and then the shifting canopy of leaves above. "That doesn't make sense."

"No, and most Theoi do not think about it too much," Aidon agreed.

Persephone felt his power flex through the cavern. It made all the rocks, the soil, the rivers, the trees, and the shades pulse with it in the sight of her power. The only things unaffected were the river flowing beside them and the garden. She suppressed a grin. Those were *hers*.

"There is, in truth, not as much of a difference between a Primordial and Titan. Both kinds of Theoi have powers anchored in the constants of the world. Hypnos's gift is sleep and his power comes from that. The same way Artemis's comes from the moon sailing across the sky." He glanced away from her. "As mine comes from the death of all things in the mortal world to come to this realm. As long as we stay connected to that gift our power flows."

Persephone's heart began to race. "Before I found the Lethe, and tried to be the goddess of flowers, my gift didn't work right. Now I'm connected to the river, but you're saying something more. I don't understand."

"Most of the Theoi you know draw their power from concepts created by the mortals. A fruit tree growing wild does Demeter no good. It is the act of cultivating it that makes it agriculture and fuels her gift."

"Why are you telling me this?" Persephone whispered.

"It was interesting enough when your gift appeared to be tied directly to the flowers themselves. Now it is apparent that it is tied to the Lethe, where the shades go to return to the mortal world, and the life there," Aidon coaxed her down the path.

"My mother would never have been able to help me, even if she wanted to," Persephone sighed.

"It would have been hard for her to understand. Apollo or Artemis would have had to recognize something similar within you," he agreed gently before standing up. "Come, there is something you should see."

They flew together on Ammie, soaring away from the comforting rush of the Lethe. They were almost on top of the river of fire before Persephone realized where they were going. She had gotten so used to the Phlegethon glowing in the distance that she never noticed it anymore. For the first time, she flew over its flames, the heat reaching up into the sky to ripple the air around them. Aidon guided Ammie down into the cranny above the river that led down to Tartarus, to the pit. The heat intensified.

Persephone was caught between the urge to bury her face in Ammie's mane to escape the heat and crane her neck to get a better look. It was a place of horrible stories from when she was young, a place she had only heard more about in Hades. Despite the flickering firelight, there was not much to see, simply sooty black walls. They seemed to go down for a long time before the passage widened out. Not into a huge cavern like Hades, but a smaller bubble of space. Away from the river of fire, the cavern stretching back into the darkness was only slightly cooler. She could see shades caught in various punishments. Leathery wings flapped in the darkness, and she flattened herself to Ammie's back. She caught a glimpse of a thief she had seen only the season before, buried to the neck in hot golden coins. She looked hopeless.

The cave narrowed once again, barely wider than the river below. But the journey was not nearly as long before the cave widened once again. This one was smaller. Persephone recognized more of the shades. Tantalus stood in his pool of water, food just beyond his reach. She thought of the dead child. She could not find it in herself to be sorry that he was here. Other mortals from her father's stories called the cavern home too. It was a place for the foulest of mortals.

But they didn't stop there either. The cave sloped down, following the river as it flowed more steeply than ever before. Far away from the cave holding the mortals, the river widened into a fiery lake that lapped at the shores of several tiny islands. On each island, a shadowy form knelt, limbs twisted together in awkward angles.

For the first time, Ammie drifted lower, and Aidon spoke. "Welcome to Tartarus. Where we imprison Theoi."

The Theoi on the first few islands looked normal to Persephone, although their bodies were twisted by the ropes that held them and exhaustion showed on their faces. Only one made any kind of movement that acknowledged their presence. As they flew deeper into the cave the Theoi became stranger. Their features were still symmetrical, and their hair and eyes were bright even in that awful place. But their brows were heavy and their bodies blocky.

"The firstborn Titans," Aidon explained. "Apollo, Artemis, and Poseidon were once something like this. But their new incarnations were influenced by the humans of later ages. Poseidon is not even quite Titan any longer. Ocean is a very human concept, drawing arbritrary lines on the water."

But if Persephone thought the Titans were strange, she was completely unprepared for the monsters at the back of the cave. Apollo had brought a monkey to Olympus once. She thought they looked something like it had, even their faces had some hair on them.

"The Primordials," Aidon said in her ear. "Tied to the fundamental forces of the world. As we are. They lived to wreak havoc. As queen of the underworld, you would have them in your charge soon enough. We visit them today to remind ourselves of what never to become. And why Apollo, Artemis, and Poseidon do not advertise their difference. We must not either."

Persephone tried to focus on things other than what she had seen in the pit. There was plenty to keep her attention. In the distant haze of her memory, Persephone could remember when Aphrodite and Hephaestus had gotten married. A big production had been made on Olympus. Even the Chthonics had been invited, and most of the Neptans had come. It had been a wonderful celebration, food, music, entertainment, a special sunset with green in it from Apollo. If only you hadn't looked at the bride and groom. It was Hera's idea and neither of the Theoi actually in the wedding were happy about it. But Olympus didn't have weddings very often, and Hera was bored. As soon as the ceremony was over, both Aphrodite and Hephaestus studiously pretended that nothing had happened.

It was with that memory that Persephone had recoiled when Aidon had asked her what kind of party she wanted to have to announce their union.

"I don't need a party. None of the Olympians or Neptans would come, except maybe Eros or Iris," Persephone said, shrugging. "We can just have the court here and call it a day." She looked at him sideways and smiled slyly. "It's not like we need to get permission from our Lord, My Lord."

Aidon didn't rise to her bait, still frowning. "I know what happened to you when you went back to Demeter. Forcing Zeus to acknowledge this will give you more protection."

"I'm fine."

"No, you were not. Thanatos bribed some of the mortals in that town."

Persephone whipped around to face him. "You didn't!"

"Mortals are very polite when the Theoi of dying asks them questions. Helpful as well," he smiled. "The shiny rocks were unnecessary."

Persephone groaned and rested her head in her hands. "Fine. We can go ahead and get it over with then." The triumphant look on Aidons's face was a bit too much, Persephone decided. *He could have found another excuse to force the other Theoi to come to the underworld.*

Thankfully, Orphne and her small army of shades took care of most of it. How Aidon found the time to plot with them, she didn't know. Persephone was chained to the table, adding her own energy to each crystal. Every Theoi needed their own invitation(why) and each one needed to come from them both(groan). Aidon had been able to simply wave his hand and create them with his own signature(showoff), but Persephone's control still wasn't good enough.

She did take a grim sort of satisfaction in the fact that she was getting better, faster and less sloppy. She poked at the finished stone, her own red swirling through the smoky gray that Aidon had left it. The imprint was strong, reaching immediately for her mind as soon as her skin brushed its surface. The image and sound were sharp and clear, as a new crystal should be. She sat next to Aidon in the throne room, a perfect matching pair. Lord Aidoneus of Hades, Theoi of Death and Lady Persephone of Hades, Theoi of Life invite the courts to attend their wedding on the Winter Solstice.

The thought of the consternation that message would cause on Olympus and among the Neptans was almost worth Aidon's plotting.

The nights grew longer in the mortal world above, as the underworld remained unchanged. Beneath the steady cycle of the Lampad's light, things were beginning to be transformed. One of the best entrances to the underworld was selected by Thanatos and carefully coaxed and tamed wider. The Lampads enlarged the glowing balls of light they had created and hung them in the air along the route to the palace. The shades made countless lanterns that Charon would supervise releasing on the Archeron, lighting its broad bends. The underworld didn't often see snow or frost, but Asca was planning to decorate his forests with a light sprinkling of white to mirror the deep drifts in the world above. Even the shades of Asphodel collected wood and flowers for bonfires and leis in honor of their new mistress.

Persephone heard of most of these preparations through Orphne and Gyra; Akhea was annoyingly tight-lipped. Persephone wasn't even allowed to see whatever creation had been created for her to wear. Aidon's was magnificent—-black and purple, highlighted in silver. Persephone speculated that hers would probably be a match in some way.

The only thing she was given free rein over was the food. Thanatos brought down ingredients from the mortal world, and the kitchens prepared them to complement the underworld tastes. The subtle differences would be interesting to Theoi who had never visited before, she was sure. But it was her garden that had given her ideas for her masterwork. The fruits on the mature trees were sweet and crisp as they grew, and heavy with juice when fully ripe. The exotic taste would be new to all the Theoi, no matter what court they belonged to. She wasn't sure what to call the strange fruit she could only coax to life in the underworld. The shades who worked the kitchens helped her squeeze the ripest ones. They made a thick juice, almost clear with golden overtones. There were only so many trees, and she was loath to push the young saplings too much. The firmer fruit dried beautifully in front of the fire, crystalizing into tiny, sweet, candy-like bites.

Every day messengers brought gifts and replies from the other courts. Persephone watched anxiously for her mother's reply. She wasn't sure what would happen if Demeter deigned to visit the land of the dead. Perhaps it would finally make her mother recognize that things would never go back to quite the way they were before. She shouldn't have bothered. The goddess never sent anything at all. The earth simply grew colder and remained dormant.

The light shining through the mist of the underworld began to dim, and the sounds from the stables rang with being readied for many guests. The glowing orbs of light ran down over the hill and swooped low over the palaces of the other Theoi on the slopes before soaring up and disappearing into the mist above. Persephone thought they looked like a string of glowing pearls, like the ones that Iris had once brought to Olympus.

"My Lady," Orphne insisted, anxiety seeping into her voice. She held the red and gold veil, in her lap ready to begin to pin up Persephone's hair.

"None of the other Theoi have even arrived yet," she complained. "And I'm not even supposed to go down until everyone is here!"

Persephone turned away from the glittering window and allowed Orphne and Gyra to run the brush through her hair. She could feel the nymph's small powers stirring and doing something she never quite understood. Despite what she had guessed from Aidon's costume, the tailors had other ideas. Beneath the red veil embroidered with flowers, fruit trees, and waves of grain a white chiton, in the same style she wore to meet Aidon shone through the veil. It was plain to her waist, where it rapidly darkened through purple to deep black at the hem which trailed behind her. Persephone could see where it was inspired by Peisinoë's effort. Small glowing gems scattered through the darkest parts, mirroring the Lampads above. It was beautiful, but Persephone wished that the tailors would one day make something formal that was not dreadfully heavy. And the veil wasn't even on yet!

"Look," Akhea shrieked, pointing to the window. The first chariot came barreling down out of the mist, flying low over the roofs below. It shimmered golden and glowed in the soft light. "I wonder who it is!"

Persephone leaned on the windowsill and watched Apollo's golden horses galavant as they always did. It occurred to her that the lampads had probably never left the underworld. Even the most recognizable Theoi would be new to them. "Apollo's sun chariot," she commented. "I've heard that it can glow so bright it's painful to look at and the hooves and wheels can scorch new grass."

The nymphs gasped, momentarily and wonderfully distracted from the heavy veil. A handful of other chariots followed Apollo's before the sky was once again clear. "That was exciting," commented Orphne, turning back to her work.

The tide of chariots picked up after that, and they often watched the view out of the window as the hour grew closer. Orphne carefully pinned the veil to Persephone's hair, while Akhea draped it across her back and pulled it over her head. It was very sheer despite the embroidery. It just looked like the world had blushed a bit.

The crowd in the hall below had grown large enough that they could hear it below them, sounding like the distant roar of the sea. The nymphs helped Persephone down the stairs to the doors of the great hall below. The great ebony doors were swung wide open, and the path to the dais that held the thrones was lit by lampads holding balls of light that glowed like the moon.

Other Theoi, more than Persephone had ever seen in one place, filled the sides of the room, milling by the feasting tables and divans. They all turned to watch her.

Persephone tried to keep her eyes straight ahead where Aidoneus and the members of the high court waited on the steps, but the riot of colors was too much. Near the front she saw Zeus, as well as Eros and Iris. Scattered among the crowd were other familiar faces, but she realized with a jolt that she knew less than one in ten of the hundreds of Theoi gathered together. *I thought they were scared and disgusted by Hades,* she thought dazedly.

As she passed each pair of lampads, they joined the procession behind her, seemingly extending her train tenfold. Just behind her she could feel her maids, their glows the brightest of them all. Asca helped her up the four stairs to stand before her throne across from Aidoneus. They turned to face the mass of Theoi. She scanned the crowd for her mother's distinctive shade of deep golden hair. Zeus stepped up out of the crowd to drone on about something. Persephone finished searching the far corners of the room as Zeus stepped down.

Aidoneus's gentle fingers untangled the veil from her hair, and the world suddenly exploded back into full color. His gray eyes smiled down as her as the veil fluttered to their feet. The kiss was soft and sweet-tasting and gentle in front of the crowd, but there was an edge to it. All thoughts of missing guests fled from her mind.

There was music and dancing—a mix of the parties she had sat in the shadows of and the one now dedicated to her. There were musician shades and Apollo's lyre. She danced in a circle with Eros and Iris, spinning in circles across the floor. Iris teased Eros as they spun, "You disappear for moons, but show your face for Persephone's wedding? I know who the favorite friend is!"

Eros only laughed and shook his head. "My feathers do not like to get wet. The salt makes them itch."

Several of the Theoi complimented her on the juice and dried fruit. Just the taste was invigorating, and most of the guests managed to swipe a bite or two. The other Theoi only left her alone when she danced with Aidoneus. They cut a wide swath across the floor, a bubble of calm in the storm. She was grateful when they managed to sneak away, laughing as they climbed up one of the back staircases to the roof.

XXVI

Prometheus made his way back to the other Titans. Hyperion, Atlas, and Epimetheus stood apart from their parents. None of them looked happy.

"Where have you been?" asked Epimetheus.

"We have been hiding," answered Prometheus.

Hyperion, the eldest, spoke harshly. "Hopefully not with those creatures. Themis says they are fated to destroy us all and Themis has always known these kinds of things."

"The Olympians are not so very different from us," answered Prometheus weakly.

"I will not be bound and thrown into a pit in the earth," insisted Atlas, grabbing Prometheus' arm. "Show us where they hide."

"At least let me try to convince Metis and the others to come away!" Prometheus begged.

"One day," Hyperion growled.

Being crowned queen of the underworld made surprisingly little difference to Persephone's life. She sat with Aidoneus during court, tended to her growing garden, and explored with Aura. It was Orphne and her sisters who moved her things into a new suite adjoining Aidon's. And she still had to dread leaving her new home when the seasons turned. But she still had time until the equinox. Iris visited three times, and Eros twice, their nervousness melting a bit every time.

"They are beautiful!" exclaimed Iris when she saw the fruit trees by the river for the first time. "I've never seen anything like them before." She tried to pluck one of the ripest fruits from the branches after Persephone had shown her how to choose a good one.

Persephone spent a minute laughing as her friend fluttered her rainbow wings, pulling back against the recalcitrant fruit tree.

"You get it!" Iris finally said in frustration.

The fruit hung low, heavy with juice, the reddish overtone almost faded from its skin, leaving only the rich gold. It came away easily in Persephone's hand. It was almost overripe, although she hadn't seen any on the ground as most trees would with their best fruit. She had thought that animals must have carried them away, or perhaps Asca, in his wanderings. But the look of surprise on Iris's face as she held out the fruit mutely made her wonder.

Eros couldn't pick the fruit either and one of his arrowheads couldn't cut the stem. He stood back from it with a laugh, bowing deeply to the tree. "Lord Tree, I admit defeat! What should I call my conqueror?"

Persephone picked a fruit for him too, this one crisper. She was embarrassed to say she hadn't thought about that too much. They were just her trees. She bit into her own fruit, the juice running down her chin. "Malon?"

"I might not be a mighty Theoi of the earth," Iris commented. "But these aren't apples."

"They aren't anything else either," Persephone huffed. "Golden apples?"

"*Golden* apples," Eros laughed. "I'll have to take some to my mother. She'd love to have golden apples."

"They make me feel as if I could fly off with a boulder," Iris sighed as she licked the last of the sticky juice from her fingers.

"Golden apples really are something," Eros agreed.

Persephone hummed noncommittally. They tasted good, but she hadn't noticed anything overly special about them.

Persephone rode Aura back to the entrance of the underworld as Iris and Eros flew beside them, teasing her mare and each other. Aura led the way through the tunnel, her sure feet finding the smoothest path. Persephone held the orb that Orphne had given her in her lap, its light pooling on the walls. She was getting better at making the journey and soon they emerged into the world above. That entrance opened out from a small hillside in a rocky clearing.

Aura picked her way gingerly to a patch of grass that was stubbornly clinging on through the snow, as Persephone joined Eros and Iris. They were arguing about the best way to explain Traveling. Finally, Eros turned to her. "It's easiest to go somewhere you can see, or at least have been to before. Some of the older Theoi claim to be able to Travel to new places, but I've never seen them do it."

Iris pointed to a clear spot a good distance away. "Just imagine yourself there and kind of fling out your power towards it. Since it's just you, you don't need to make a doorway like your mother does. Just kind of step forward."

Persephone did so and promptly fell over. Iris tried valiantly not to laugh. Eros didn't. It took most of the afternoon for Persephone to get the hang of it. You had to want it really hard and then find the place with your power. Even the sensation of Traveling with other Theoi hadn't prepared her for it. She was happy that the Chthonics preferred horses.

She pulled a picnic out of Aura's saddlebags and Iris reached out for one of the less squashed rolls, but Eros backed away. "I have to go soon."

"Eros is in love," Iris whispered loudly.

"Hey come back," Persephone insisted. "You have to tell us. Boy or girl? Nymph or Theoi!"

Eros laughed nervously and disappeared. Persephone turned to Iris in confusion. "At least I didn't keep 'Pluton' hidden."

"I think it's a girl from some of the things he's let slip," Iris mused, munching. "But he won't tell me much, and won't bring her to meet us. Probably a nymph, they're shy around Theoi."

Three moons seemed to slip through Persephone's fingers, each day faster than the last. Even with her newfound and fledgling ability to Travel, she didn't want to get stuck at her mother's temple again. It hadn't been what she had thought when she made the deal. Persephone wanted her freedom to wander through the mortal world. Surely her mother could be happy with seeing her every few days. Traveling would make that much easier.

With her revelation of the truth of her gift—that it was life that pulsed within her—Persephone grew ever more confidant with her powers. Asca, Hypnus, and occasionally Gorgyra helped her master herself. She called Asca's animals and grew tall pine trees to replace those that fell. "It's almost not so much fun to hunt with you when you cheat," he said dryly one day.

Persephone had the feeling he could do much the same with the animals in his domain, but it did take some of the fun out of it. Hypnus was skilled at reaching out with his power and shaping things outside of his direct domain. Persephone laughed with joy when she conjured her first piece of ribbon. It wasn't very pretty, but she made it appear where no ribbon had been before.

It made reaching out to push others' power back easier when you knew where your own power began and ended.

When the shades began to gather thickly on the banks of the Acheron, Persephone knew that it was time to return to the mortal realm and the temple of her mother. She was determined that this season would not be like the one before. Persephone packed saddlebags for Aura full of furs, soft clothes that the tailors had woven, and chitons with subtle patterning that included gemstones as well as sheaves of grain. She even packed a few of the dried golden apples. Persephone didn't think that her control was good enough to protect the whole fruit.

Persephone was proud to arrive at the Eleusis temple under her own power, not dragged. She turned Aura loose in the icy fields and brought in her own bundles. A small swirl of her power protected them in her room. Her clothes would not be burned this year, nor her furs stolen from off her bed. She stood straight in front of her mother, and although the grip of Demeter's power clung like roots, Persephone slipped through it like water. The expression on her mother's face was priceless, although she said nothing. Persephone still did not fancy her chances of direct defiance, but she would no longer be chained. Even the nymphs sensed something shifting, and she could see Calli smiling at her from where she stood behind her mother's shoulder.

Peisinoë attended her as she sat at the table, and Persephone offered her a basket of dried fruit and finest rolls from the kitchens of Hades. The nymphs exclaimed at their exotic flavor.

"My Lady Kore, are these the fruits that we have heard about the last few moons? The ones from your feast?" Peisinoë asked as she nibbled on the amber crescent.

"They are," Persephone answered. She noticed the nymph's careful avoidance of the proper word. "I thought you should all get a chance to try them as you could not come to my *wedding*."

Her mother refused her slice. "What good can come of the earth of the underworld? It is a wonder they are not actively poisonous," Demeter sneered derisively.

But no matter what her mother wished, things had changed in the season that Persephone had spent in Hades. Nearly all of the nymphs were at the table, even the nymphs of the fields. They might not have looked hale and healthy, but they were a far cry from what they had been before. An entire growing season to prepare did wonders. In the two days before they set off for the sowing, Persephone saw many of the same things in Eleusis. Mortals were thin, but bright-eyed as they watched her from the doorways and windows. She was not mobbed as before. *Some Theoi must have taken a mortal or cursed a nearby town,* she thought. *Mortals are always timid after that happens.*

The procession moved from town to town, the mortals were livelier as they left the surrounding area. Persephone once again walked behind her mother, making the hedgerows bloom. But now she made sure to energize the forests as they went. They had sustained the mortals better than she during the cold season. Persephone no longer was ashamed to make the wildflowers blossom along the road, and small children picked them as they ran behind her. Some of the story must have spread because she was showered with more flower crowns and petals than ever before. It was a much more comfortable season. Aura followed them, and in the afternoons Persephone would ride through the trees and jump the mare over streams. Her furs were warm at night, and she managed to intercept two baskets from Thanatos before her mother ordered them destroyed. Persephone devoured the messages from her friends. Most precious was one from Aidon. He whispered his love in her ear every night as she fell asleep for weeks, the smokey crystal clutched safely in her hand.

They did not return to Eleusis at the end of the sowing season, but to another one of the temples. Persephone took that as one last sign that things were settling into a new pattern…one that was not quite the old one, but was, perhaps, sustainable. She only went back to Eleusis once, pushing herself to Travel further than she ever had before, to retrieve the last of her things. It was only two days later that Arce appeared on the steps of the temple.

She approached Demeter and nodded a greeting, but the crystal in her pouch was for Persephone's hands. The messenger darted off quickly.

"My presence has been requested by Lord Zeus," she said in wonder. "He heard that I brought more of that 'wonderful fruit' with me from Hades."

XXVII

Prometheus ran back to the cave and tried to convince Lelantus to help spirit the other Titans away. "I will not go," he cried. "This is wrong!"

The others awoke and surrounded Prometheus, who cringed away from the Olympians. "We must leave," he begged. "They will destroy us with them if we do not. Themis says they are destined to destroy the Titans!"

"I do not believe in destiny," announced Leto. "And is it so wrong if they are destroyed? If we had been born as they were, would we not have been eaten as well? No, I stand here."

Metis stood strong beside Zeus and Hypnos stood beside Aidoneus, whom he had befriended during their time in the cave. Zeus brandished his spear, and Prometheus ran with a cry.

"We must leave here," said Metis. "He will surely betray us."

Persephone had never received a personal invitation to Olympus and even her mother didn't say anything about her not going. Apparently, Demeter did not want to anger Zeus again so soon. There wasn't much of the golden apple left, but Persephone scraped together two bowls full. She hadn't brought any of the juice. Eleusis was far away, but Olympus had to be over twice the distance. Persephone thought about trying to Travel that far, but even with Aura helping her, she didn't think she would make it. And it still tired her enough that she didn't fancy trying to take multiple hops either. But Aura was a wonderful horse, fast even in the new world she found herself in. They soared over the fields and trees. Demeter had refused to allow her to take any of the nymphs with her, in an odd reversal of her methods last season. Persephone didn't mind. The air whipped through her hair and she loved the feeling of freedom, leaving the temple too small to see over the horizon.

It was only when Olympus loomed on the horizon and Persephone felt herself move from the mortal world to the realm of the gods that she became nervous. She had never been to the mountain alone. She wished suddenly that Eros or Iris would be there, hopefully waiting for her. They weren't. Instead, several of Zeus's nymphs whisked her down the many hallways and to the massive throne room. It was so much bigger than the one she had become used to. Persephone straightened her spine. *I am Queen of Hades,* she told herself. *Not little Kore, not even a member of Zeus' court. Equal to him or Hera.* It didn't help.

Despite how they had behaved at her wedding, she still expected to be ignored, or perhaps treated with the overtones of hostility that she had begun to see directed at the Chthonics. But instead, they all looked at her expectantly—everyone that she could name, and many she couldn't. All except for Aphrodite. She looked at Persephone like she was something that crawled out of the mud. That was new. Aphrodite had always been friendly, when she managed to remember Persephone existed.

"Lady Kore," Zeus thundered happily. "We heard that you brought some of that delicious fruit on your…ah…vacation. Perhaps you still have some of it left?"

Persephone blinked in confusion, as she summoned it from the saddlebags. That was what the message had said, but was this really about the fruit? *No matter how delicious Iris and Eros think it is, this is strange. And where is Eros?*

The two meager bowls of fruit slivers disappeared quickly. Persephone had never felt so popular, not even the day she returned to Hades or at her wedding. Everyone had something nice to say as they accepted their piece. Even when the bowls were empty, some of the minor Theoi who hadn't gotten a taste stayed to talk. "They kind of looked like pieces of amber in the bowl," one said sadly. "Does it taste as good as everyone says it does? Does it really make you feel strong?"

Persephone looked down at the picked clean bowl. "It tastes good, but I wouldn't really say it's anything special…" she trailed off. It was only then that Persephone began to accept that there might be something more to the 'golden apples' after all. There were even a few of the braver Theoi who asked if she was accepting visitors at her palace.

"Lady Kore," Hera called out from the far end of the room. "Does your garden produce many fruits, or did Demeter and her nymphs keep it all to themselves?"

"My Lady Hera," Persephone squeaked out. The queen of Olympus had never spoken to her before. "There should be more on the trees now, I didn't bring much up with me."

Hera waved her hand. "Lord Aidoneus has given you a horse. Why don't you go back down for a visit and bring back up some more? Perhaps even some seeds for our own gardens. I'm sure the dryads can cultivate it."

Persephone felt her heart start to beat faster and thoughts swirled in her head. "I would be happy to bring up some more dried fruit, or even juice. It's easy to make, even if the fruit doesn't travel well. It would be wonderful to see Lord Aidoneus again." She licked her lips. "The seeds don't grow outside the underworld, I've already tried, and I'm afraid Lord Zeus's decree forbids me from going home at the moment."

Hera shot a sharp look across the hall to her husband. "Send the girl down. Demeter can part with her for a night."

"Perhaps Lady Arce can take a message down for Lady Kore," Zeus hedged. "If it is as easy to make as she says surely one of their nymphs can handle it."

Persephone felt trapped between them as surely as she had once been trapped between her mother and Aidon. But the prospect of having one night of freedom was enticing. "I'm afraid no one else can pick the golden apples. Lord Eros and Lady Iris already tried." *Not to mention Aidon will probably refuse to send any out of spite. He was not happy to send me away.*

"The girl must go. I have become tired of this squabble. You should not have allowed Demeter to defy you so," Hera said haughtily.

Zeus looked unhappily across at Hera. "The mortal world was dying, something had to be done!"

"The mortals have always been fine before. They would have adapted. You were worried about your mortal women and demigod brats!" Hera hissed.

Zeus stood up forcefully, "Quiet woman!" He pointed down at Persephone. "Go pick your apples. Lady Demeter will not sense you have gone. Be back by sunset tomorrow."

Persephone practically ran out of the room and back towards Aura. This was more than anything she could have hoped for. She glanced at the sun, already low on the horizon. If she hurried she could have a whole day with Aidon!

It did not turn out to be quite a full day. Persephone and Aura rode faster than they ever had before, thundering down the tunnel almost as loudly as a full chariot. She shot out over the Acheron just as Charon was passing in his boat. Persephone shouted a greeting as she barreled towards the palace. Aidon was somehow there to catch her as she jumped off Aura.

He stood there, solemn, not smiling even with her in his arms. His armor and helmet were missing, but he clutched his trident so tightly his knuckles were white. "What did she do?" he growled.

Persephone couldn't put the pieces together for a moment, then she laughed and threw her arms around his neck. "Zeus wanted more of the golden apples, so he gave me permission to come down for a full day just to get some!"

Aidoneus blinked down at her. "What?" He asked again dazedly, arms loosening their grip around her. "He sent you here for fruit?"

"Yes, everyone seems to think it's delicious and that it also makes them feel...strong. Makes it easier for them to use their gifts," Persephone looked up at his face. He still looked confused and a little disbelieving. "You didn't try any!" She accused, shoving his chest.

He looked a bit sheepish. "I am sure that anything you grow in your garden is delicious," Aidon assured her.

"You really didn't!"

"There was not an abundance of your golden apples. I allowed the guests to sample them," he admitted.

Persephone dragged him off towards where Ammie was waiting. "Get on your horse! We must repay Zeus for letting me come today."

"It is Zeus who is part to blame for your leaving at all," Aidon grumbled as he coaxed Ametheus into the air.

The flight was short, but Aidon quickly relaxed and laughed at her stories of the Olympians. "I wish I had been able to see Zeus's face when Hera said that. Perhaps you will one day share the memory with me."

When they landed in her grove, Asca and Gorgyra were already there, conjuring wide baskets. "Your trees do not like us," Asca called to her.

Persephone laughed and walked through the grove in delight. They had grown several feet in only the last few moons and were now solidly trees, although their branches still spread low. A cluster hanging just over her head looked particularly ripe and she picked them first. She passed one to each of the Theoi. "Try it, Aidon. Pay attention and see if they do anything other than taste good."

Gorgyra finished her fruit first. "Perhaps the Olympians are not completely insane."

Aidon nodded in agreement. "They affect gifts. I feel stronger."

She began to pull the fruit off the trees, handing them to her helpers to put carefully in the baskets. Where before, there had been perhaps fifty apples, hundreds now adorned the branches. The mist quickly darkened and they headed back to the palace, leaving the full baskets for the kitchens.

The morning was also consumed by the grove, picking the remaining fruit. Persephone stared at the trees, their empty green branches rustling in the breeze. She gave each of them a boost with her gift, mentally apologizing for taking so many at once. They didn't look right stripped bare. Hopefully, with her help, they would not be so for long.

Persephone had only the afternoon to spend freely in the underworld. She could feel the deadline looming over them as they walked the wild garden and swam in the river below the palace. Persephone could feel Aidon's sadness even as he splashed in the water with her. She curled up on the large flat rock, warming the air to dry her clothes a little faster. They were silent as the rush of the river sounded below them. Her visit was over too fast, and her invitation to Olympus as well.

It was strange but the rest of the warm season passed quickly. Persephone visited Olympus regularly and even went to see Iris and the Neptans twice. Theirs was a beautiful underwater city of bronze, blue, and green. Everyone wanted to have more of the golden apples. She was forced to name them. The dried fruit that the kitchens had turned into little squares became ambrosia, for their amber color. The juice she called nectar. And although she found it delicious, Persephone could feel no difference in her gift. It was slightly unfair, but the feeling wasn't new to her. Even Demeter was forced to stop complaining about her wanderings in the face of such overwhelming support. But she still refused to try anything that Persephone brought back from Hades.

XXVIII

The Olympians and their Titan allies ran from village to village for a double handful of seasons, staying just ahead of the firstborn Titans as they honed their gifts. The Olympians, fueled by the worship of the newest breed of humans, discovered that they were as powerful as the Titans. Aidoneus's power over death was particularly strong, fueled by fear inspired by new stories about what happened to dead souls. When the firstborn Titans at last tracked them down, they were ready to make their stand. Although Metis first called out for peace, only ashamed Prometheus stepped aside. Not even Rhea was willing to spare her children.

Even to Persephone, the season passed quickly. She was almost surprised when the Harvest festival and her return to the underworld came again. It did not seem like an entire season had passed. Some of the mortals brought offerings for her as well as her mother. Little charms of flowers and vine. Wishes for a short cold season. A child to be blessed. Peaceful journeys. Persephone wasn't sure if she could do any of that, or even what they had heard to make them think that she could.

The sun was setting, the sky in the west was already glowing orange. Persephone bolted towards the doors and Aura, not waiting for an escort, her mother's shouts ringing in her ears. *Zeus didn't specify exactly when my time ends.* The heavy oak doors slammed closed in front of her, Demeter's attempt to seal her inside the temple. Persephone drew upon her power, pulling it up through her chest. She hadn't decided if she would try to Travel, or just blow the doors into splinters, when they blew abruptly back open.

The nymphs were thrown off their feet, and even Demeter skidded back a bit from where she stood on the stone floor before the dias that held her throne.

"You will *not* hold my wife against her will," thundered Aidoneus from where he stood on the road, still well back from the temple entrance.

Persephone snatched up the basket holding her things in delight and made to run down the steps towards where Aura was standing beside Ammie. She only made it a few paces before another burst of power buffeted her. This one was not gentle as it flowed around her.

"This is my daughter Kore's home. I will defend her here!" The power that flowed from Demeter tinted the air in swirls of gold and green.

Persephone pulled in a gasp as it rushed towards Aidoneus and a strangled noise escaped her throat. He did not need her warning. The burst of power dissipated just before it reached him, swirling futilely around him and the horses.

"I suggest you show the Queen of Hades some respect," Aidoneus said in a low voice. It echoed around the temple. "She has made her choice of address and desired home quite clear, if you would only speak to your daughter. Listen to her, Demeter."

Her mother stalked towards the temple doors, trying to cut Persephone off from the exit. Persephone darted ahead of her and danced down the steps out of her mother's reach. The nymphs who had flattened themselves onto the floor to escape the display of power were only beginning to pick themselves up. Persephone looked from her love to her mother. She stood stock still in the hopes that the display would not start again. "Stop!" Persephone cried. "I wa..."

Demeter cut her off sharply. "I did not give my permission for such a match. You are in my place now, Hades!" Her power crackled through the air.

"I said listen when Persephone speaks!" Aidoneus roared. "No Theoi should be treated this way, let alone your own daughter."

This time it was his power that swirled gray around Demeter, dampening the air around her as if she was enclosed by a case of solid rock. Aidoneus tipped his head towards where Persephone stood frozen on the steps.

"Mother, I love him," she said desperately. "I went with him willingly, I married him willingly, *happily*," her voice was getting stronger. "And for the last time, my name is not Kore. I should never have been called such a thing!"

The shield around her mother was growing thinner, and her voice could escape, quiet in the evening air as Persephone walked down the last of the steps, her head held high.

"My sweet daughter, come back! I love you, I have always loved you, we can get past this. You just have to stay here where things are green and living. Don't let him trick you."

Persephone didn't look back, her pace quickening until she almost crashed into Aidon, "You still refuse to listen, Demeter. Change course before it is too late," he said coldly as he helped her tie her basket onto Aura's saddle.

They picnicked on the ground outside the cave entrance. If it was not as romantic as the meadow had been, Persephone thought she could smell the scent of her home on the breeze slowly sighing through the cave. She sat beside Aidon on the ledge and watched the sunset. It was romantic, she supposed, something that the mortal poets sang songs about. They had never gotten to do it before. He had always had to return to his duties, or they had been in the underworld. The sky of Hades might be beautiful, but there was no sun.

Persephone sometimes missed Apollo's light during her stays beneath the ground, and she luxuriated in the feeling of the last warm rays on her skin. Aidon pulled her close and put his arms around her, closing his eyes and tilting his face to the sun. Persephone smiled softly. He looked almost as he had that first time she had caught him napping in the sun. What a stupid girl she had been to think he was a mortal.

"I wonder if this is what Thanatos does when he lingers returning home," Persephone mused.

Aidon muffled a soft laugh. "He bathes in the beauty of something, I am sure. But I do not believe it is Apollo's light."

Persephone turned in his arms, trying to see if he was making a joke. "Really? When there are so many willing shades and nymphs..." She started to laugh too. "I would never have guessed. The mortals must be in for a bit of a shock when they wake up and realize what Theoi they bedded."

"I do not think he usually tells them. Thanatos gets tired of their fear, though I do not know how he hides his aura so successfully."

The sun was almost gone, only a sliver on the far horizon. Aura was nosing at her hair, the rocky hillside did not offer much for a horse. Unlike the extravagant ball from last season, Persephone found her welcome to the underworld like a warm hearth instead of a bonfire. Aidoneus's court, her friends, were waiting for them. There was wine, and sweets, and even a few glasses of nectar someone had saved. Persephone sat with Makaria and Asca. They kept shooting glances across the hall at Thanatos and giggling. He didn't get the joke. There was less strain in the air than there had been before. It was amazing the difference that being able to see everyone even for only a handful of days across her season of exile had made.

Back in the underworld, she was inundated even more than she had been before with requests from other Theoi for the fruits of her garden. The underworld had not been so popular since Aidon and Hypnus had first disappeared into a crack in the earth. The other courts feared them because of Aidoneus's contributions to the war, the red glow of Tartarus, and the pall of death. Occasionally one of the Theoi would ask for special treatment for a mortal they had grown attached to. But now Theoi actually came to visit, Theoi who were not messengers under duress. Persephone formed tentative friendships. Aidon counseled her to make the most of them. "It is always best to have connections in the other courts. They may be able to help you when you are with your mother. And if they like ambrosia and nectar, you have bargaining chips now. Use it if you can."

Persephone loved spending time in her garden, puzzling over the other plants and tending to her grove. It was steadily growing, two more trees had sprouted and the adult trees happily produced fruit when fed with her power. She was running a sweet-smelling herb through her fingers, sniffing at the oil it left behind when the sound of frantic wings filled the air. She looked up, but she couldn't see anything but a few scraps of mist through the green leaves. There weren't many—any—birds that big in Hades. She had never seen anything like a roc here. Thanatos had wings, but he rarely flew in the underworld. His duties gave him enough of that in the mortal world. Persephone began to run to the bank of the river. *Eros?* Iris's wings were silent, and he was one of the only other winged Theoi who could find her there.

Eros landed half in the river with a splash, and yelped, holding the bundle in his arms high above the water. He climbed quickly out of the river and Persephone met him at the edge of her grove.

"Eros, what's going on? Are you all right?" Persephone asked, watching her friend's wild eyes.

Eros carefully knelt down and set his bundle on the ground, unwrapping the heavy cloak. A girl lay on it, a mortal girl. She was beautiful but barely breathing. Persephone had never seen a living mortal in the underworld. She hadn't even been sure if it was possible to bring one. "You have to help her," Eros begged, brushing the girl's blonde hair off her face.

Persephone stood there stupefied for a moment, before joining her friend on the ground. Mortals, especially sick ones, were not her specialty. But Eros was the one asking. She would help if she could. Persephone belatedly realized that this was probably the girl that Iris had told her about. *Oh Eros,* Persephone groaned. *Nothing good ever comes from falling in love with the mortals.* She reached out tentatively with her powers, trying to ignore Eros's panic. Persephone couldn't find any cuts, bruises, or broken bits beneath her skin.

"Psyche didn't know," Eros sobbed. "I didn't tell her, and she opened it, and now it's all my fault." He held her hand tightly to his chest.

Persephone pushed deeper into *Psyche*, past her skin and bones, searching for something broken. Her gift told her something was wrong at her core. Persephone couldn't describe it, let alone fix it. But the life in the girl was flowing out. "What happened, Eros? Why didn't you take her to Apollo?"

Eros took a deep breath, his voice hitching. "I found her two seasons ago. She was a princess, and some of the mortals started worshipping her as Aphrodite incarnated."

Persephone winced. Aphrodite was a jealous goddess, and no story that started that way could end well.

"Mother told me to do something about it. I'm sure she meant kill her or make her fall in love with a bear, but she was so kind. I took her away to my palace. I couldn't let her go. She seemed happy even if I didn't show her my face or let her leave the garden." Eros buried his face in his hands. "But I got careless. I was making my arrows and left the box of venom out. I wasn't thinking, it doesn't harm Theoi or nymphs, but she's human. Psyche spilled it on herself and she collapsed!"

Persephone looked sadly at the mortal girl. She looked so young curled up like that. Theoi powers could be overwhelming to them. The poor thing would not be the first accidentally killed. Olympus was dangerous even for demigods. "I'll make sure she finds a nice place here," Persephone soothed. "You can visit her on the Isles of the Blessed."

Eros pulled the girl back into his arms. "No!" he snarled. "That's what would have happened if I took her to Apollo. He can't fix something like this, but maybe the golden apples can. They make gifts stronger, maybe they can help her fight it."

Persephone watched her friend clutching the tiny body of the girl in his arms. She was going to die and he was going to *shatter*. The same thing happened every time. "Your Psyche can try the apples. I don't have any nectar or ambrosia here." Persephone bounded up, eager to get away from the doomed scene. The goddess looked quickly for the softest apple she could find. If Eros was going to try to feed it to her, she might as well make it as easy as possible.

Eros didn't even bother to use his power to slice the fruit, he tore it apart with his fingers. He had the girl propped up against his shoulder as Persephone helped to hold her head. The ragged slivers of apple he slipped past her lips did not seem to be doing much. But they were small and enough for her to swallow easily. Persephone was grudgingly impressed with his dedication. He managed to get almost half the fruit down her surprisingly quickly. Psyche suddenly jerked to life in his arms, and Persephone scooted back. She had the wild thought that Eros's plan had worked and the girl would not appreciate a strange Theoi looming over her.

But the girl didn't open her eyes. Instead, she began to violently shake, limbs flailing. Eros had to hold her down for several minutes, murmuring sweet apologies. His face showed nothing but fear. Persephone wasn't sure what to do. She had never seen a mortal sick like that. If not for the fact that Psyche was dying anyway she might have thought the apple had killed her. When at last she stilled in Eros's arms, her face was flushed deep pink. Her hands still trembled.

Persephone knelt again next to her friend. The mortal was burning, far warmer than she should have been. She no longer looked like a corpse, but Persephone was not sure if this was an improvement. Eros ran his hand through her hair again. It was already darkening with sweat and sticking to her forehead.

"We should take her back to the palace. She can lie down, and maybe one of the others will know what to do for her," Persephone suggested. She began to wrap the mortal back into the blanket.

Eros numbly followed her instructions, carrying Psyche gently to the edge of the water where he could spread his wings. He was flying slower and Aura was able to keep up easily. Persephone left the mare at the stables and led Eros through the palace to the guest suite where she had once stayed. Gyra spotted them in the hall and stared at the mortal with wide eyes before disappearing.

Eros laid Psyche down on the bed and Persephone brought her some water. Not much went down the girl's throat, but it might help cool her off. Persephone threw open the windows and the door to the balcony. Hopefully, the coolness of the underworld would keep her from overheating.

Aidoneus strode into the room followed by Hypnus. They looked down at the girl in pity. Persephone joined them in the corner. "Eros has been hiding her on Olympus for quite a while. Psyche got into something she shouldn't."

"I would say that Hades is no place for a living mortal..." Aidon trailed off.

"He wanted to feed her the golden apples. I think they made her worse. She seemed to be slowly fading before. Now she is sick as well," Persephone gestured helplessly to the bed.

"No Theoi can cure death," Hypnos said. "Not the Primordials, not Titans, and not now. It is sad each time a Theoi loses their heart to one. Before, your friend Eros might have tried to bind her life to something and make her a nymph, but not now. Most do not survive that either."

Persephone sat with Eros as he watched Psyche, while the sky outside the open windows darkened and the mist receded. She had held out hope that Thanatos, with his experience with dying mortals, might be able to do something. But he took one look at the girl on the bed and shook his head, slowly backing out of the room. Aidon came to sit beside Persephone as night stretched before them. He did not bring dinner as he usually would when she became too distracted by a project to join him for a meal. Aidon just sat with her in the large chair, arms pulling her against him, slowly stroking her hair as the hours of darkness passed.

Psyche burned with fever on the bed. It never broke, and sometimes she shook as she had in the garden. Eros had to hold her to keep her from thrashing off the bed. It was the only time she seemed to have any strength in her at all. Persephone watched her and waited for her to die. Aidon hummed something soothing in her ear. It was nice to feel his warmth against her skin in the night chilled air. Eros didn't even have any idea that she was here, and Aidon made her feel less alone. The little mortal was very stubborn and to Persephone's surprise, she was still alive when the mist began to cover the cavern. Aidon ran his thumb over her knuckles and kissed her gently before he left.

The girl began to shake again, this time more violently than ever before and Persephone reached out with her gift. Something was changing inside Psyche, an energy that wasn't there before. For the first time the girl opened her eyes, although she did not seem to have any concept of where she was. Suddenly something snapped inside her and she collapsed back down onto the bed. Persephone thought for a moment that she was finally dead, but her chest was still rising and falling. For the first time since Eros had brought her to the underworld, Psyche only looked asleep. But there was something about her that did not feel the same anymore.

Orphne brought Aidon back on Persephone's orders. He opened his mouth in the doorway, clearly having prepared a comforting speech for Persephone's oldest friend. He stopped short and closed his mouth. Psyche was sitting up in bed, eating a bunch of grapes that Gyra had brought. When she caught sight of the Lord of the Dead she immediately tried to hide behind Eros. He caught her and held her gently, relief and shock still mingled on his face.

"That was a mortal when I last saw it," Aidoneus said slowly. "I may not interact with them often, but I can tell mortal from Theoi."

Other members of the court pushed in behind him. They all gawked at the girl on the bed. Thanatos especially seemed to be completely at a loss. "What did Lord Eros say she was poisoned with?"

"The venom he uses on his arrows. It is simply meant to stun mortals so it is easier for him to use his gift on them. But it is reasonable to think a whole box would be deadly. And Psyche was dying. I felt it!" Persephone insisted, half-hysterical.

"And then you fed her your magical golden apples," Charon mused, looking thoughtful.

"I feel as if the ground has tilted a little under us," Hypnos sighed. "This will change things. I fear it will not be entirely for the better."

"Several Theoi have already eaten the golden apples whole?" Aidoneus asked, his voice hard.

Persephone nodded helplessly. "Nymphs have tried both ambrosia and nectar and not been too affected."

Aidoneus turned to Makaria. "I want a mortal shade and a demigod shade. Volunteers, but choose *carefully*."

The demigod, a daughter of Ares went first. She seemed both awed and scared to be in the presence of so many Theoi. She chewed the small slice of ambrosia slowly and took a tiny sip from a bottle of nectar. The red-haired girl swayed slowly and sat down heavily in a chair. "I do not think I should eat any more, My Lord."

"Nothing much seems to have happened to her," Asca pointed out.

"I feel too big inside," the demigod said. "As if my heart could explode."

The shade who had once been a mortal touched his tongue to the piece of ambrosia gingerly, before throwing it away and shaking. "My Lady no more," he gasped to Makaria. "I think that would have been the end of me if I were still alive."

"Do we feed an apple to a nymph or the demigod?" Charon mused.

Persephone noticed that Orphne and her sister had somehow disappeared.

XXIX

The battle was horrendous. Humans fled from the Theoi, and the land around the battle turned to hot sand as it raged across the earth. Hypnos played distracting lullabies on his lute, Metis directed the battle, and Hestia caused Anchiale's fire to go awry. Demeter tangled the firstborn Titans in her plants, tripping them so Lelantus, Leto, and Hera could bind them. But it was Poseidon's waves, Zeus's lightning bolts, and Aidoneus's two-pronged spear and knack for slipping through the shadows that carried the day. Themis and Hyperion had been killed, and Metis had been badly wounded.

Persephone never knew who told. Eros was still in the underworld and seemed to be planning to hide Psyche somewhere in the mortal realm forever. But Zeus and Poseidon sent a joint message only the next day demanding a demonstration. Aidon tried to hide it, but Persephone knew that he had been hoping to prevent that from happening. Indefinitely if possible. Too many Theoi knew about Psyche for him to ever make it go away, but a large disturbance on the board causes trouble for everyone.

She carefully picked one of her apples. It was not quite as soft as the one they had fed Psyche. Persephone was planning to carry it in her lap during the journey to Olympus. Hopefully, the chariot would not bounce it around too much. Presenting Zeus with a smushed apple that probably wouldn't even work would have been embarrassing. Persephone wasn't sure if *she* wanted it to work or not. She might have been forced to admit that the golden apples were special but what happened to Psyche could still have been a freak combination of circumstances. Her life was just beginning to be ordered in a tolerable fashion.

The hall on Olympus was nearly deserted. Persephone's eyes were drawn to a boy who was trying valiantly not to cower at the foot of Zeus's throne. He bore the distinctive bright gold hair that all of her father's demigods seemed to share. A handful of other important Theoi from both of the other courts were already scattered around the room. Even her mother was there, standing near Poseidon. Interestingly, normally mild Apollo was glaring at the mortal boy.

All eyes were immediately fixed on the apple Persephone cradled in her hands.

"We have found you a volunteer to test the powers of your apples, Lady Persephone," Zeus said magnanimously, but his eyes betrayed more than a little greed.

"I brought your brat here to be punished!" Apollo spluttered looking from the apple to the boy. "This isn't what I had in mind."

"You should have burned him where he stood if you wanted to punish him," Zeus chuckled. "And really, Lord Apollo, you let a half-mortal child steal one of your cattle?"

Apollo growled and took a few steps toward the boy, who had perked up. Seemingly picking up on the fact that he wasn't immediately slated for death.

"His punishment is to try the apple. Take heart, Lord Apollo. You may still get your wish, the other nearly died. And what Hermes did was clever. Perhaps he will be entertaining to have among us." Zeus's power whipped out and shoved Hermes into the center of the hall, in full view of the assembled Theoi. He skidded to a stop at Persephone's feet.

"It may not work at all," Persephone hedged. "And it took a day and a night for Psyche to...change."

"Yes, the girl," Zeus said animatedly. "Bring her out. We shall see the specimen before the experiment!"

Eros had lingered at the back of the column of Chthonic Theoi, trying to shield Psyche from sight. Her eyes were as wide as saucers as she stood in the Hall of Olympus. Eros took her hand and led her out to face Zeus. Psyche stayed on her feet but swayed as Theoi all around her stretched out their powers to prod at her.

"Not very powerful," sneered Hera at length.

"But Theoi, and only hours old," Zeus mused. "We should not make any judgments until she has had time to find her gift, if she has one. You may keep her, Lord Eros."

Eros grabbed Psyche and Traveled away, taking Zeus's statement as a dismissal. All the eyes in the room turned back to Hermes, who was still sprawled on the floor. Persephone did not know what else to do except offer him the golden apple. For a second she thought the boy would try to flee. Bolt out the door and steal a horse as he had the cow. But Hermes took the apple and turned it over in his hands before unceremoniously taking a large bite. He managed three before his hands began to shake too badly.

The assembled Theoi watched both boy and apple fall to the floor. Most of them seemed to expect some sort of flash of light or dramatic death throes. Persephone was just curious as to if the boy would throw off the fever more quickly than Psyche had done, or simply die. She was quite surprised when almost all of the assembled Theoi were still watching over an hour later. Aidon had created more divans for their party, but not much else had changed. Few in the hall even spoke a word.

"What will happen if the boy dies?" Aidon mused into her hair. He kept half an eye on the others in the room, but most of his attention was fixed on the demigod.

But Persephone watched the faces of the Theoi most of all. She had already seen the drama once with Psyche. The only real difference among them that she could see was Poseidon. He watched the lump on the floor particularly avidly. Zeus was beginning to become bored. Her mother was disgusted. Apollo looked vaguely and grudgingly impressed that the boy wasn't crying out.

Zeus cracked as the sun was going down. The room which had been sealed was opened to nymphs bearing platters of food and drink. Persephone was amused to see ambrosia and nectar among the offerings. A few other Theoi slipped in with them and settled down to watch, but Zeus kept most of the others out.

Stars came out, shone, and then winked out as the sun rose. Persephone thought Hermes's fever might be lessening. He did not twitch as much. It was Poseidon who spotted it first, sitting up straight on his divan. Hermes's face was no longer flushed a deep red. The scar on his left cheek was gone, and if it was possible his hair shone even brighter. The boy pushed himself off the floor, seemingly surprised at how easy it was after the dark night. He turned to smile at Apollo. "I'm still hungry."

Pandemonium reigned. Theoi who had been half asleep sat up and pressed in a knot close to the boy. Persephone noticed that the other half of the apple was no longer on the floor by the boy's feet. The Olympians and Neptans were talking at once, shouting over each other. Persephone was going to edge closer, to try to get a better look at the boy. Was he truly a Theoi now, or simply still alive? Then she felt a tug on her shoulder. Aidoneus and Hypnus were urging the Chthonics out the door.

XXX

The Olympians stood over the bound Titans and tossed them onto the scorching sand of the desolate battlefield. Even defeated, none were willing to bow to the three Olympian brothers. Fearing that Metis was going to die, Zeus pulled her essence into himself so she did not disintegrate like Themis and Hyperion. Zeus used Atlas's great strength to hold apart the mortal world from the new plane where the Theoi could live. For his treachery, Prometheus was given to one of Uranus's great rocs to feed upon. Poseidon took Coeus to form a domain under the waves. Aidoneus warped Anchiale's fires from the first prison to expand the cavern and volunteered to house the rest of the prisoners among the dead. Each brother had a realm and they drew lots to choose their supreme king. Zeus won, perhaps with a bit of help from Metis.

The underworld showed its unrest in a different manner than Olympus. The Theoi of the mountain gathered in large groups, many trying to push into the hall to see the newly minted god. They shouted over each other, including Hera and Zeus. Each seemed to be somehow trying to blame the other. The news of Psyche had time to spread to every corner of the underworld by the time Hermes awoke. While many of the Chthonic court gathered in Aidoneus's hall, they stood together in small knots and spoke in low voices. Others visited friends in their homes to gossip. In fairness, Hades had far fewer Theoi and longer to digest the news by the time Persephone returned with the council.

Orphne began questioning her immediately as she helped Persephone strip off the fancy clothes she had been in for far too long. "Did Lord Zeus really give the golden apple to three of his mortal mistresses?"

Persephone laughed dryly. "I don't think Hera would have stood for *that* one. It was only one of his demigods. But it did work. The boy looked almost as sick as Psyche did. Some of them are not going to survive it."

Gyra shuddered. "It looked awful, my lady. And someone will try it on one of us soon. Poor thing."

"You wouldn't want to be a Theoi?" Persephone asked.

"Some will," Akhea commented darkly. "But we already have long life and power enough. Many die trying to become nymphs. It will be the same with the apple."

They brushed out Persephone's hair while she thought. Despite what her handmaids thought, she had the sinking sensation that many people would want the apple. A part of her thought wildly of burning her grove, sucking the life out of it and refusing to ever grow any more. But there was no going back, whatever chaos would come was already knocking at the door.

The day was not even over when the first casualty was escorted by Charon into the audience hall. The shade had been a living mortal only a few hours previously. Even as a shade she looked small and fragile. "She caught me as I was walking home from the stream," the shade whispered to the floor. "The Lady rode on a white horse, but I did not know her. She asked me if I would like to try the food of the gods."

The tears began to leak from her eyes. "It smelled wonderful and looked delicious, but my mother always told me that Theoi do not bring good gifts. I tried to run but she caught me. It tasted like heaven for a moment but then it began to burn and I couldn't feel anything anymore. The Lady forced me to eat and drink and then I woke up beside the river." The shade hung her head lower.

Persephone sat in shock next to Aidoneus as he waved his hand. Makaria came and led the shade away. She went quietly with the creature so like the one that had killed her.

"There have not been any others, Aidoneus, but she will not be the last. Several Theoi will try it before it is accepted to be impossible," Thanatos said.

"Will Zeus and Poseidon control their courts?" Hypnus mused.

"It is not so different from their normal activities," Charon pointed out. "As long as no one kills mortals belonging to another Theoi it will be ignored."

"We can stop sending them ambrosia and nectar," Persephone suggested. "They are quite enamored of its gift enhancing properties. If they only have a limited supply they might keep it for themselves."

Aidoneus shook his head, "The Theoi planning to try that method have already made their decision. And much as we dislike the other courts they are not complete imbeciles. This will stop soon. We must decide what to do when that time comes."

He was proved to be right. Four more shades killed by nectar and ambrosia were found by Chiron or Thanatos in the following two days. The last was even a demigod. Encouraged by his immediate survival, Dike had fed her son until even his demigod constitution had been overwhelmed. Persephone was grateful when that seemed to be the end of it. She sat staring at the golden globes, green leaves, and patches of grey sky. They blurred together through her tears. *My fault.*

To her surprise things calmed down for most of a week. There was no news from Olympus or the Neptans. Persephone was on edge, waiting for the axe to come down on their heads. It was poor Arce who was tasked with the journey again. She looked just as uncomfortable as she had on her first visit. As if the last few seasons had not passed. She was not one of the minor Theoi who had begun to visit Persephone.

"My Lord Zeus has commanded that Lady Kore share the secret of her golden apples. The trees are to be grown on Olympus as well as in Hades," Arce announced.

A few nymphs hustled her into the corridor while Aidoneus turned to Persephone. "It would mean the loss of a bargaining chip, but also less scrutiny. They are your creation. Will you send some for Zeus? I would not, but my brother has annoyed me of late."

"I already brought those seeds to the mortal world," Persephone began.

"When?" Aidoneus asked in surprise.

"The first time I went to visit my mother, I had leftover seeds from when I planted the grove. They never grew," Persephone mused. "I do not think they will grow on Olympus either."

A slow grin stretched across Aidoneus's face. "You are wonderfully clever, my dear. Core one of your golden apples and send him the seeds so they cannot doubt what they are. It will buy us time before they realize the joke."

Persephone ended up coring two apples, one for Olympus and one for the Neptans. There was barely any flesh left on them, but the golden skin on the top and bottom of the core left no doubt to what they were. Arce was allowed to watch the procedure and sent home, for once happy that her duty was complete. Eros, more knowledgeable about the apples, passed her word on the Olympians comical attempts to make them sprout. Even her mother had been enlisted as a reluctant participant. First the strongest of her mother's orchard nymphs had failed and then Demeter herself. Eros had almost lost himself in his laughter at that point. Flying high above with Psyche and her new wings, they had seen the whole spectacle. Demeter may have been dismissive at first, but soon her pride was on the line. However, nothing could so much as crack the casing on the seeds.

She hadn't heard from Iris about what the Neptans were doing with their share. Persephone hoped that her friend was keeping her head down. She didn't have any secrets to share, but Theoi were not always known for listening to reason.

Almost a moon had passed when the sounds of a chariot landing on the terrace woke Persephone one morning. She was not sure of how she was able to tell, but it wasn't one that was familiar to her. The glow beyond the corner of the building betrayed Apollo.

He was in a good mood when he reached the throne room. Aidoneus was absent and Persephone had rushed to meet him. She remembered vaguely that Apollo had been kind to her when she was small. And even later he was generally of good temper. He had a mortal with him, young and handsome. Persephone's heart sank. Apollo was one of the few gods who was able to fancy himself in love with a different mortal each season. Who knows, maybe he was. Unlike Zeus he actually spent time with them before leaving for a new distraction.

"This is Hyacinthus," Apollo said happily, catching the youth's hand. "He would like to try his luck with your apple, Lady Persephone."

She gestured for one of the nymph attendants to distract the handsome mortal. The Lampad blushed and seemed quite happy to comply. "Lord Apollo, your lover may die," Persephone said when the youth was gone. "We have been lucky so far, but the mortals were near death both times."

"Hyacinthus is young and strong," Apollo insisted. "I told him of the suffering. He is willing to bear it for his chance for glory."

Persephone winced inwardly. "Apollo, I might not have been important, but I lived on Olympus for many seasons. I have seen and heard of your other mortal loves. If this one survives, you will be stuck with him forever. Are you sure this is the one you want to keep?"

Apollo puffed up in offense. "I love Hyacinthus! It is a wonderful thing to be able to keep one of them, not a tragedy."

Persephone stood with a sigh. "I will take him to the grove, if that is what your Hyacinthus wants." The nymph let the youth back into the hall.

Apollo caught his hands and spun him around the hall. "You are to become Theoi," he enthused.

Persephone pursed her lips, but led them to Apollo's chariot. She directed him to land down the river from her garden, and led the mortal alone to the grove of trees. His eyes lit up at the sight of the ripe fruit.

"Wait!" Persephone cried. "This may kill you, do you understand? We can go back to Apollo now and tell him you were unable to pick an apple," she said, thinking fast.

"Thank you for your concern, My Lady," the youth said politely. "I would risk far more to stay with Apollo. I love him. What should I do?"

Persephone gestured to the trees. "It is your life. You should pick the apple you will risk it for." The mortal shot off among the trees, stopping to examine some of them minutely. She watched with interest, unsure what he would do when he realized that he could pluck none of them.

Hyacinthus studied many golden apples before he decided to pick one from the tree. He did not seem fazed by its reluctance to let go. It was not until he had repeated the process with four others that he seemed to become concerned. Persephone watched as he tried to pull first one and then another from the tree, waiting curiously to see how he would solve the problem. At long last, he returned to her, head bowed.

"I am ready to return, my Lady. I am unable to pick the golden apple," he said quietly.

Persephone got up, and walked over to the first apple he had selected. It hung innocently on the branch, but it released easily into her hands. "Even Theoi cannot do everything. Remember that." She handed him the apple, and led him back to Apollo and his chariot.

They returned to the palace, and Hyacinthus never let the golden apple leave his hands. Persephone led them to one of the guest suites, and instructed a passing nymph to bring them food and water when they needed it. Apollo was almost incandescent with excitement.

Hyacinthus did not survive. The next mortal threw a temper tantrum below the trees and was not given an apple. A demigod brought by Eunomia survived, and then two more deaths. Persephone sat alone among the trees and did not hear any more petitions.

XXXI

Aidoneus with the help of Hypnos led the captured Titans to his new realm he named Hades. Lelantus and Leto chose to accompany Poseidon to his new home. Zeus and the rest of the Theoi built a palace in the realm apart above their mountain, where they were often joined by Poseidon and his court. Zeus took Hera for his queen, but she soon found him to be unfaithful. First Leto fell pregnant, and though Hera chased her across the world, she bore a set of curious twins. Apollo, of the sun, and Artemis of the moon, who disturbed the Olympians by bearing memories of times before, memories they had no right to. When their sister Athena freed herself from Zeus's temple, the last rule of Theoi existence was alarmingly clear. Theoi cannot be killed, simply banished back into the unformed thoughts of nature and humanity. When they return—and Theoi always do—they might be the same entity reborn, bring with them foreign memories as Artemis and Apollo, or simply similar traits like Athena. Zeus sent a messenger to Hades to warn Aidoneus that none of the prisoners could ever be allowed to be reborn.

The minor Theoi were the first to recognize the new power held by the Chthonic court, followed by a handful of the bigger players. Hera and Zeus were reportedly fuming and each trying to blame the other, while Poseidon and his court, even Iris, had been quiet. Suspiciously quiet, Persephone came to realize when Iris, acting in her official capacity as messenger instead of friend, had arrived. Iris carried a message buried in a deep blue crystal from the Lord of the Sea. Persephone looked up at her in surprise when she realized what he was asking.

"What mortal does Poseidon want to bring to meet me?" Persephone asked in disbelief. "I have never heard of him associating much with mortals. Or fathering any demigods at all recently."

Iris shrugged before sitting down next to her on the bench and grinning conspiratorially. "No one knows. He didn't let anyone so much as touch the seeds you sent. Disappeared into the private wing of his palace with them. Only came out yesterday."

"How strange," Persephone mused.

"You have to say yes just to find out," Iris insisted. "Maybe he's taken up with one of his nymphs. It would be interesting to see what would happen if one of them took a bite of the golden apple."

Persephone sighed deeply. "Several mortals have already died eating ambrosia, nectar, or the apples themselves. I don't want nymph deaths too. Still, I can't offend Poseidon either. Tell him that he can come, but no promises."

To her surprise, only hours passed before Iris returned flying ahead of Poseidon's chariot. She shot a strange expression at Persephone as they landed, but scurried away when Persephone tried to find out more. The chariot was the largest one she had ever seen. It was carved with leaping waves and coral. The stallions at its head had been bred to be the blue white of sea-foam.

The god stepped out of the chariot, largest of his brothers. The monstrous contraption almost seemed appropriately sized with him standing near it...until you took in the stable hands hovering nervously. He held out a gentle hand to help a woman down its steps. She was bundled up heavily, excessively so, Persephone observed. *It may be chilly here, but not by that much, even compared to the heat of the undersea palace.*

Persephone tried not to be too obvious about straining to get a glimpse of her guest. Her eyes narrowed as she caught a glimpse of what appeared to be a withered hand as the sleeve fell back a little. It was a fine cloak, whatever was beneath it.

Poseidon looked up darkly at the low hanging mist. "Lady Persephone, may we retreat to your hall, I do not like how cold it is here." He pulled the bundle to his chest, shielding it from a nonexistent wind.

She nodded, perplexed and led the way through the doors and into a smaller chamber near the main hall. It was one of the few rooms in the palace that always had a fire burning. Persephone had gotten much better at using her powers to sense what was going on around her, especially in the underworld. She didn't think Poseidon was aware, but Aidoneus was somewhere nearby, watching. After Zeus and Demeter, perhaps he no longer trusted any of his siblings. Poseidon gave her a grateful smile and began unwrapping the figure. Two layers later, and it was much smaller than Persephone had expected. A very old woman, frail, but with thickly curling white hair on her head. The Theoi looked at the shriveled woman, the depths in her eyes and her lined face. For a moment she thought Iris had been right, and it was a nymph at the very end of its life that had been brought before her. But the eyes lied, there was no trace of power in her bones. It was a mortal. Persephone supposed she had been beautiful once. The old woman sat down on a divan and managed a smile at Poseidon who hovered over her.

Persephone shifted from one foot to another, unsure of what to do. This was unlike anything that had been brought before her yet. "Would you like something to drink?" She asked the woman.

The woman glanced up at Poseidon who responded for her. "Something warm would be nice. The cave entrance was even colder than it is here." He turned smile softly at the woman. "Amphitre, this is Lady Persephone. She may be able to help us." He turned to Persephone. "Lady Persephone, may I present my wife, Amphitre."

A nymph arrived with a steaming cup of something. The lampad seemed to be just as surprised as Persephone had been to see such a mortal. It was unlikely she had ever seen anyone so old before. Even shades in Tartarus could appear the age they wished, and almost no one would choose that.

The woman—Amphitre—took a sip of her drink. "Hello, Lady Persephone. Please forgive me for not greeting you earlier. But I have spent a long time around Theoi, and learning to hold your tongue is an important survival skill."

Persephone had never met a mortal who was so unsettling. Even old mortals did not have fathomless eyes. At her gesture another few nymphs brought a platter of food into the room. It was Poseidon who spoke as Amphitre ate.

"When I first met Amphitre she was the daughter of a merchant who walked the coast every morning. She swam further out to sea than any other mortal I have ever met and would search for clams on the sandbars." He took a deep breath. "I fell in love with a mortal, ill-advised as that is. I would have bound her soul to her precious sandbars, but I have never had much skill at creating nymphs. Amphitre would have died. Instead I tried to extend her life. It has worked for nearly three hundred seasons, but it left her barren. And it will not work much longer." His voice broke at the end.

Persephone was taken aback. She had never seen the Lord of the Sea so moved. He had always seemed to her to be far more in control than Zeus, though he rarely left his domain.

"That has never been your fault," Amphitre said gently. "I have lived a longer and far richer life than I ever had any right to expect as the daughter of a poor merchant."

The helpless anger boiled in Poseidon's voice. "A wonderful life I have given you, trapped in one wing of a palace. Afraid to introduce you to my subjects."

"It was not always that way," Amphitre said wistfully. She turned to Persephone. "No matter what he tries to tell you I have had a good life. Before I aged so visibly, we visited what seemed to be every beach and sea-town in the world."

Persephone nodded, unsure of what to say.

"Zeus demanded you return to Demeter, ambrosia and nectar, a golden apple for Hermes, and seeds for your garden. I and my court have demanded nothing. Lady Persephone, I ask you as Queen of Hades to give Amphitre one of your golden apples. I believe an alliance would be beneficial to both of our courts."

Persephone had thought to earn the goodwill of the other Theoi with the power she had stumbled into. It was hard to believe that in only a handful of seasons she had gone from nothing to a Theoi that Poseidon of the Neptans would want an alliance with. "What if your wife dies?" Persephone asked bluntly. "I will not lie to you, we have already had deaths."

Poseidon nodded sharply, acknowledging her point. "I once thought I could order anything within my domain. But I have been forced to confront my limits. My love will die soon regardless of what happens today."

"Then I will give her an apple," Persephone decided. Aidon would be pleased that she had managed to snare the good favor of one of his brothers after what had happened with Zeus. Perhaps she could finally force her mother to be reasonable.

Poseidon fussed over his wife as they made their way back to his chariot. Persephone felt a strong sense of deja vu. The last love of a god she had brought to the grove had died horribly. She hoped that would not happen to the mortal so captivating she had managed to keep the sea god's heart for an age.

It took some doing to leave Poseidon at the edge of the grove, but Persephone was the one who took Amphitre's arm and led her deeper through the trees. Persephone was tempted to call out to Aidon, ask him to wait with the Lord of the Sea. But she decided to let him keep his own counsel, just as he was allowing her to choose what to do with the apples. They sat down on a tree root that had grown rather large.

"It is true that the golden apples have killed half of the mortals who have tried it. More if you count the ambrosia and nectar. They were all young and strong, and some of them demigods," Persephone watched Amphitre's face. She showed no fear or concern.

"And I am neither young, strong, nor a demigod," Amphitre finished.

"They died horribly. Even those that survived suffered for hours. I can tell Poseidon that you failed to get an apple. Perhaps he knows too much to believe me, but there isn't much he can do about it."

Amphitre smiled at her. "Lady Persephone, I have not feared death for many seasons. Less when Poseidon returned from your wedding to tell stories of the underworld, and not at all now that I have been here. I will suffer and die no matter what happens. I am a mortal. Poseidon wants this hope badly, and it hurts him to see me wither away before him. At least this death will be quick."

Persephone took a deep breath and gestured to the fruit hanging around them. No matter what the sea god wanted she would not give an apple to another mortal too weak even to try to get one for themselves. After watching the horrible business so many times she deeply believed that Psyche had gotten lucky. She had been half a breath away from death several times. Persephone would refuse to be party to any more force feedings.

Amphitre showed a surprising reserve of strength as she circled the tree. Her hands reached out to brush first one fruit and then another, before returning to sit next to Persephone on the tree root. She reached out to the closest apple and gave it a weak tug.

"They seem to be all the same, Lady Persephone, but I do not have the strength to pluck it." The old woman seemed quite untroubled by her predicament.

Persephone reached out and pulled it from the tree for her. Amphitre carried it with Persephone's help back to where Poseidon paced nervously. His face glowed with relief as he helped Amphitre back into the chariot. She disappeared behind its high sides.

"You are welcome to a guest room, or to take her back to your home, but the apple has to be eaten here."

Poseidon, obviously remembering Hermes shot her a sharp look before laughing. "Zeus will be displeased that you have a spine. But not quite as much as Hera. We will be happy to accept your hospitality."

A nymph directed them to their rooms, but Persephone refused to watch. She had done that too many times already. And although Persephone thought this particular case hopeless, Amphitre surprised her. She was, indeed, beautiful.

XXXII

The Olympians were far more fruitful than their Titan or Primordial predecessors (especially Zeus) and soon the halls of Olympus were filled with Theoi. Sometimes they left to join another court or to wander the earth below. To serve them, the Olympians created many classes of creatures inspired by Teyths's Naiads. Pan created Dryads, bound to the great trees of the forest, and Demeter created Meliades for her fruit trees. Poseidon's court had the Nereids and their beaches. And of course, many, many mortal demigods.

For the first time, Persephone was invited to visit Olympus during the cold season when she reigned as Queen in the Underworld. The invitation had come for her, not Aidon. He had laughed sardonically after the messenger had left. "You have done it, my dear. Something none of us have for seasons upon seasons. Persephone, we now have something that Zeus wants badly enough to sit at the table and ask nicely."

Persephone was not sure where her time had gone, and she could feel the deadline of the warm season bearing down on her. Less than two moons were left of the cold when they flew for Olympus. Aidon smiled the whole ride and occasionally chuckled to himself. There was a different air to the column than the other two times they had traversed this route. Persephone was not to be stolen away, neither were they called before the entirety of the Theoi to show proof of the end of an era.

She immediately spotted Poseidon's chariot as they encircled the mountain before curving down to a graceful landing. The Neptans were out in force, more than she was used to. Persephone wondered what kind of chaos the introduction of Amphitre was causing under the waves. Several of the nymphs they had brought from the underworld jumped down from the chariots with wide eyes, taking in the bright white marble and gold of Olympus. They began unloading the generous amount of nectar and ambrosia Persephone had brought with her. None had been sent from Hades to Olympus or the Neptans in over a moon. She had a feeling the other Theoi would enjoy it.

Aidoneus and Persephone strode into the grand hall arm in arm followed by their court and the nymphs bearing the platters and flagons. Orphne and Gyra had directed their carving. Each of the dark stones were native to the underworld, and they were decorated with gems of all kinds. The contrast with the golden liquid and deeper color of the ambrosia was striking. As they settled into the divans at their end of the room, Aidoneus waved his hand and created a three-sided feasting table on which the nymphs could place their burdens. It was a masterful display of power, each side carved and colored in honor of a Theoi court. Persephone could feel him relax next to her when the demonstration went off perfectly.

Their nymphs were relieved as well. Setting down their burdens they hurried off to the edges of the hall. It was good that they were light on their feet. Eager Theoi soon swarmed the table. Even Zeus came for his portion himself. Persephone watched in satisfaction. Poseidon and Amphitre, surrounded by the high-ranking Neptans, didn't move. Whatever was going on under the sea, they did not show any signs of unrest in public. Poseidon shot them a pleased look. Aidoneus nodded formally, and Persephone waved happily at Amphitre. She wondered if it was the first time the new Theoi had been to Olympus. Most Theoi seemed to have missed the new addition so far.

Finally, Zeus turned to them, lounging on his throne. "Persephone! I see you have brought Hades and some of the other Chthonics to my party! It seems no one can stay away from Olympus today."

He had the audacity to wink at her. As if bringing Aidon had been his idea. Zeus hadn't even remembered to invite her husband. And had regressed to the wrong name again. Persephone could feel Aidoneus tense next to her. She laid her hand on his arm as they regarded his younger brother.

"It is an interesting party," Persephone acknowledged as some of the Olympian nymphs took their place to sing with Apollo and his lyre.

"Zeus is an imbecile," Aidoneus muttered with annoyance into her hair. "It is clear why his court is always causing trouble. He cannot even see that there is more here than a party."

Persephone leaned her head against his arm. "It *is* a nice party. And the other Theoi don't stare so anymore."

"I do not know if more invitations to Olympus are a good thing," he countered. "We were left nicely alone until you came and let all this noise and nonsense in," Aidoneus teased.

"Just this once, and we won't have to come to his call again. And Poseidon really seems genuinely friendly. Perhaps he has better parties."

"We would not have to come at all if you would let me put Zeus in his place," Aidoneus pointed out. "If we refused to let shades in or out of Hades he would lose his nerve in days. Or I could simply take away that spear and crack it over his head." He smiled happily at the prospect.

"The spear shoots lightning," Persephone reminded him. It was something she had only seen twice.

"Ha! Sometimes I forget you did not see the war with the Titans or the giants. Zeus is a poor commander. It is a miracle Hera has not disposed of him yet."

"No one likes Hera," Persephone sighed.

"I doubt many like Zeus much either," Aidoneus's head suddenly whipped around to follow someone in the crowd.

Persephone followed his gaze to see her mother moving to sit near Aphrodite. She was more than a bit surprised. Her mother still insisted she was paralyzed with grief whenever she was gone. *Perhaps Zeus let slip I was going to be here,* Persephone thought in annoyance. *Maybe it's for the best. Get the resistance out of the way at the start.*

The ice nymphs were building another sculpture and Persephone watched it take shape into an apple tree. She smiled. The entertainment continued into the night. When the sky was finally dark, Aidoneus directed some of their own nymphs to create a dazzling display of dancing lights. The other Theoi were enraptured.

"What a wonderful night, and a delicious feast!" Zeus boomed when the display was concluded. "Perhaps Lady Persephone will honor us with her presence again on the next full moon."

"Unfortunately that will not be possible," Persephone said loudly. "I must soon return to my mother, and there will not be another harvest until I can attend the trees again." This was not strictly the truth. Her golden apple trees happily grew the fruit when she wasn't there, replacing anything she took quite quickly.

A murmur went up around the room. The Theoi had become used to a regular supply of ambrosia and nectar. Going without it was an unpleasant thought. Zeus shifted uneasily on his seat. "Surely you can return occasionally as you did last season. Lady Demeter cannot possibly need you every day!"

"Return? Return to the Underworld!" Demeter suddenly yelled from a divan, quickly standing. "First you allow my daughter to be kidnapped by Hades half the year, then you require her presence during the time I have left! And you sent her back to *that place* for cursed produce?"

All eyes were on Demeter, her righteous fury ringing throughout the hall. But unlike before, the other Theoi were not apathetic, interested only that the mortals have the food they needed for worship. Demeter was threatening *them*. Their gazes were harsh, and Theoi murmured to their companions and shot glances around the room.

To Persephone's delight, her mother was not immune to the sentiment. She seemed to deflate before her eyes, the power which had been crackling ebbing away. Even Demeter was unwilling to face the united disapproval of the other gods and goddesses. The other surprise was Hermes. Persephone hadn't noticed him before, where he leaned against a column. He still looked very young, but much more confident than when he was shivering before Zeus's throne. The new god's eyes glittered with suppressed mirth as he watched the proceedings.

"Our daughter volunteered to return to the underworld," Zeus said firmly. "Surely there is a way to make sure everyone has what they need."

Persephone smiled. "You are right Zeus, my mother only really needs me for a few moons out of her time. The rest could be more flexible?"

Zeus looked uncomfortable again, unwilling even in the light of her new support to completely change his mind on the topic.

"If I visited my wife during her stay in the mortal world, perhaps Queen Persephone would be more willing to spend more of her time in the underworld tending the grove," Aidoneus suggested.

"I will not have a creature of the underworld at my temple," spat Demeter

"For most of the year, I once wandered the mortal world. Perhaps I could do so again if the thought of my husband is so distasteful to my mother." The look of betrayal her mother sent Persephone was almost comical.

Zeus nodded slowly. "Persephone will live one season in Hades, and the other on the living world. Other than attending her duties with Demeter during the planting and the harvest, her time will be her own, although Demeter is within her rights to ban any Theoi from her temple."

Persephone let out the breath she had been holding and relaxed into Aidon's arms. She felt him squeeze her arm in comfort. Persephone watched her mother splutter at Zeus, standing alone amongst all the other Theoi. *If she had not pushed so hard, she would have more of what she wants,* thought Persephone. *But my mother could not let go of the idea of having everything, and now she has next to nothing.*

The tension slowly bled out of the atmosphere as Theoi went back to the party. Some slowly drifted out of the hall, others grazed what was left of Persephone's feast. Her eyes were half-closed, content when Amphitre walked over to where they sat.

"Hello, Lady Persephone," Amphitre said with a sly smile.

"Somewhat different from how we last saw each other," Persephone observed. "Theoi and mortal. And now the bargaining chip of the gods and the Queen of the Sea."

"Surely it is not so bad as that," Amphitre replied, blushing a bit.

Persephone smiled to herself. There was still something a bit mortal about the new queen. Perhaps that would pass with time. "You seem happy."

"It is past time that all of the courts had a queen," Aidoneus noted. "I tarried longest, although few knew it until recently."

"I am glad the sea court seems to have come to terms with its new circumstances," Persephone observed. "Were they surprised you knew so much about them?"

"Some were," Amphitre allowed. "Although I never expected to put my knowledge to use. Even when Poseidon returned from Olympus with news of a magical golden apple, I did not credit it much. But I understand so much more about Theoi than I ever did before. I can feel the sea in my bones too."

"If you did not expect it to work, why did you take the apple?" Persephone asked curiously.

Amphitre sighed and sank down on the bench next to them. "I had plenty of time to make my peace with death. But Poseidon never did. If I did not try, I think he would have broken. And it would have been a quick death."

Persephone nodded slowly and wondered if the addition of the former mortals would have more of an effect than anyone had thought.

"We would be honored if you would visit us," Amphitre said. "I have seen your home, but you have not seen mine. I think it should still count as the living world." She gave Persephone a conspiratorial grin before dashing back to join Poseidon.

"If only someone could have told little Kore that she would have an invitation from the Queen of the Sea," Persephone sighed. "I do not think I would have believed the messenger."

Aidon leaned close to whisper in her ear. "I would have."

XXXIII

Hera was somewhat mollified by her three sons, Ares, Pan, and Hephaestus. Poor Hephaestus she loved least, for he was ugly in the eyes of gods, with great hands, hulking shoulders, and thickened skin for his work. By the time her sister Demeter fell pregnant by Zeus, even Hera was tired of chasing down the adulterers. After all, half of Olympus had been filled by Zeus. Demeter could not wait to meet her first child, and she stayed away from the other Theoi, walking her among her fields of golden grain.

The forests and rivers of the mortal world had not changed at all since Persephone had last been free to explore them. Even the towns and fields were almost unchanged, recovered from the brutal end of the Cold Growing season. It was only Kore who was gone, Persephone walking the trails in her place. She could feel the life thrumming around her, forming a lush weave around her. Her eyes and ears trained by Asca caught the signs of the passing animals. She smiled as a deer raced past. Perhaps it was one she had met before. There was something comforting about returning to her trails.

Persephone returned to the little mortal village where she had grown her flowers. The merchants' wares looked drab compared to what was made in Elysium. Still, she bought a red cloak for the girl she had been. It helped her blend in among the mortals. The legends of the golden apple did not seem to have found their way to the mortal world yet.

But things were not what they had been before. It was not unusual for her to have visitors seeking her out. Aidon always came in the mornings, just after dawn. He came often, but it was always a surprise for Persephone which day he would bring her breakfast from Hades. The first time he came she had been growing a patch of flowers to take into town. A merchant had been kind to her the day before, and she had wanted to thank him.

Persephone had been so engrossed in her flowers that she hadn't seen or felt him approach. When the flowers were done she looked up, blinking in the weak morning sunlight to find Aidoneus sitting before her, patiently waiting on a fur, breakfast spread around him.

"Aidon!" She had shrieked in delight, abandoning her project on their stalks. Persephone threw her arms around him, and they collapsed onto the blanket almost crushing the basket in the process. She buried her face in his neck breathing in the scent of him and the clean smell of the underworld. Persephone noticed distantly that she was shaking. She had only been released from her planting duties for two days. Deep down she had not been really sure if she would see him. After a long while they sat up and Aidon handed Persephone a bit of roll with nectar spread across it.

"This is actually quite good," she said, chewing thoughtfully. "I wouldn't have thought to do this, use it like honey."

"One of the nymphs in the kitchens figured out how to thicken the nectar in the ovens," Aidon explained. "Ambrosia also comes in squares now. It is easier to pack."

Persephone laughed dryly. "I think I have created a monster."

"It gives the kitchens something to occupy their time. And something for us to trade with the other courts," Aidoneus said.

"Hold over their heads, you mean."

"That as well."

Persephone wasn't happy when Aidon stood up and collected the blanket and the picnic, but something had calmed inside her heart. She would see him again, and soon. Perhaps not every moment of every day, but soon. He pulled her to his chest and ran his hands through her hair before kissing her gently. "It is a beautiful world you have here. Remember that too."

Persephone took the flowers to the merchant. He was thrilled to see them, marveling at their color, varieties he had never before seen in his life. She watched from her seat on the fountain as he showed them to his wife and various customers. She smiled to herself. *Aidon is right. This world is beautiful too.*

Interspersed with Aidon's visits were the unpredictable attentions of the other Theoi. She was not hard to find for any Theoi who took the time to look. Persephone wasn't bothering to hide, her mother was sulking in her temple. And the last season had increased her confidence in her abilities to defend herself. Or at least escape. Sometimes the Theoi brought her gifts, trying to earn her goodwill for their eventual choice of mortal. Others came to tell her stories of their wonderful children and beautiful loves. She had never known how many Theoi were attached to at least one mortal. And some brought their choices to meet her directly. None were nearly as old as Amphitre had been, but Persephone was introduced to a newborn baby and a toddler. Those were easy to dismiss. Children deserved to have a choice in how to shape their lives.

Greedy kings, arrogant demigods, and passing fancies of Theoi were easy to weed out. Apollo already had another mortal, this time a girl. It was incredible to Persephone, but he seemed just as besotted with this one as the last. But some were harder for Persephone, and could not be refused out of hand. She pointed out that nothing could be done until she returned to her home, but that just put off the awful choice. The most moving was Artemis's friend.

The girl was painfully young, but on the edge of adulthood by mortal standards, already at her full height. She fell to her knees before Persephone. "Please, my lady. I do not want to marry the man my father has chosen. He might provide well for me, but I do not want to marry at all." The mortal shot a pleading look at Artemis. "I would take the same vow as Lady Artemis."

Persephone looked down at the mortal girl at her feet and then back up at Artemis. Of all the Theoi she had not expected to ever see Artemis bring a mortal before her. Who could she possibly bring if not a child or a lover? This pitiful creature was much worse.

"She is quite skilled with the bow," Artemis said. "She can be my handmaid and join my nymphs on the hunts."

Persephone nodded slowly. "Bring her to me when the season turns. We will see if she can choose an apple."

It is good the mortals do not remember much, Persephone thought to herself. *I can continue to use my trick. But I think that one will pass.*

But that still left her with the problem that there would never be an end to the parade of mortals before her. It would be so simple if all were like Psyche or Amphitre. There was no guarantee that a new Theoi would be powerful. In fact, other than Hermes all the new Theoi had small gifts. Artemis would not abandon her girl. She was always taking in new nymphs for her hunt. But what of Theoi like Apollo?

The light under the sea reminded Persephone of Hades in a way. It seemed to come from everywhere, but in Poseidon's palace it flittered and concentrated in flashes instead of a uniform glow. The bronze and blue colors interwove with walls of coral and deep pools of water. The rooms and courtyards of the large complex were filled with humid air but most of the windows looked out into bright water and schools of fish. For all the stories of the underworld Persephone had heard, she found the home of the Neptans far stranger than Hades ever was.

She might not have needed air, but she was used to it. The Theoi and nymphs of the Neptan court seemed to view air as completely beside the point. Hours of their time were spent in the underwater gardens, even talking to each other through the water in their throat. The nymphs grew tails when their bodies hit the water, and even many of the Theoi used fins of some kind. Persephone's mouth dropped open when she saw Iris flying through the water towards her, before surfacing in a pool and shaking off her rainbow wings. The water seemed to slide off her like rain sluicing down a rock. By the time she was standing on her feet, Iris was completely dry. That was good, as she immediately launched herself into Persephone's arms.

"I can't believe after all this time you're here! I've always wanted to show you where I live," Iris gushed happily.

"It is very beautiful," Persephone said. She suddenly believed she knew what the other Theoi felt when visiting the underworld. The underwater palace was beautiful, but she felt very out of place.

Thankfully Iris didn't notice. She showed Persephone many rooms, some of which had pools of water leading outside or streams running over rocks in the floor. There were beds of underwater plants that Persephone almost recognized and wild kelp forests. She never did get used to speaking with her mouth full of water. It might have been frightening, but the palace was in shallow water. Persephone could see the waves breaking up the sunlight above her.

The fish had started to glow, something that Iris ignored, when they began to swim back to the palace. Persephone kept trying to catch the glowing creatures along the way. They reminded her of the lampads of the underworld. The fish kept wriggling out of her fingers, and she never figured out what was making the light. Iris swam to a large wing that was somewhat disconnected from the rest of the palace and led Persephone up through one of the pools in the floor. They surfaced in an entrance hall, richly decorated with patterns of waves and leaping fish. The whitecaps were made of pearls and the fish scales of coral in a rainbow of colors. Iris was instantly dry, but it took Persephone a few moments to copy the trick so she could follow her friend.

Unlike the other wings of the palace, this one was more richly furnished but sparsely populated, Persephone only saw three nymphs hurry past. There were no pools of water connecting it to the outside world, although there were many of the little streams running across a sandbar. The wing suddenly opened up into a massive pool of water, floating platforms trailed across it. Though it was incredibly deep and wide, Persephone did not see an exit to the wider ocean. Amphitre sat on one of the floating platforms, a pod of dolphins excitedly surrounding her and taking treats from her hand, completely ignoring the rich schools of fish their pool was stocked with.

Iris led Persephone across the water, hopping from walkway to platform to walkway. They swayed slightly beneath her feet like Charon's boats. When they were halfway across, Amphitre turned to smile at them, throwing the last of the food to the dolphins. They clicked unhappily and then disappeared back into their pool.

Amphitre's platform in the center was by far the largest, equipped with divans and food for Theoi in addition to dolphins. Persephone took the last jump carefully and settled herself onto the divan across from Amphitre. Iris dipped her head to her queen and made her way back across the platforms, the dolphins chasing her beneath the waves.

Persephone looked around the room. It was beautiful, peaceful in a way that the rest of the court was not. It seemed like its own little world. The ceiling was bright blue, almost reflecting the water below. The walls were a jungle sloping down to a beach Persephone hadn't noticed on the far side. She closed her eyes for a moment, breathing in the warm salt smell of the pool.

"I see you like my wing as well," Amphitre said, handing her a glass of nectar.

The pieces fell into place in Persephone's head. "This is where you stayed before. That's why none of the pools lead back out to the ocean."

Amphitre nodded. "The nymphs are adding exits now, but before they were all like the dolphin pool. Enclosed ecosystems." For a second her gaze became sad as she watched one of the smaller dolphins play. "I wonder what will happen when they open this pool. The dolphins here have not left for generations. When I was a girl on my father's docks I would play with the dolphins who came looking for treats. The first thing Poseidon gave me were my companions. They seem happy but I worry they will not know what to do with an ocean."

"You seem to have adjusted," Persephone pointed out. She did not know anything about the gray creatures, save that they were lucky in their mistress. Persephone could feel the tie connecting them to their Theoi. She wondered if that was the extent of Amphitre's gift. It was good to see at least one of the newborn Theoi thriving.

Persephone stayed in Amphitre's wing for several days, enjoying its peaceful rooms and the ocean like she had never seen it before. Poseidon's love was stamped across every surface. Even the nymphs still hovered over their mistress as if she was a fragile mortal. It was easy to understand why she had been so happy even with only a corner of the Neptan palace. Persephone hoped that in three hundred seasons she would be as happy with the life she herself had chosen.

XXXIV

A week after her daughter was born Demeter brought her to Olympus, where she was cheerfully acknowledged by Zeus and pointedly ignored by Hera. As had become custom, Zeus took his newborn daughter to the Moira Lachesis to learn her name. The child squirmed in his arms as they examined her with interest. Children born from two of the original Olympians were becoming somewhat rare. After a time the Moira announced, "This child will be known as Persephone."

Demeter snatched her baby back from Zeus, shielding her from Lachesis. "Bringer of death? What an awful name for a baby!" Demeter turned to leave but Lachesis only laughed. "Awful or not, it will be her name, Lady Demeter."

"Come now, Demeter," Zeus soothed. "It is not as bad as all that. It could also mean defender or to separate."

"No," Demeter said coldly as she turned to leave Olympus. "Never. She will be my beautiful daughter and follow me through fields full of sunlight and laughter."

It was not quite three hundred seasons later when Persephone had her answer. She loved Aidon, felt most at peace in the underworld, and would not trade Zagreus for the world. There was nothing like watching her son play by her river and run through the low underbrush of her garden. Zagreus had no idea that once upon a time nearly all Theoi refused to come to his home. He had plenty of playmates from all three courts. Even some young demigods would occasionally come to play with him while their parents talked. And if no one else, the shades in Elysium saw him as nothing but another child.

Watching her son play in the place Persephone had made gave her a feeling of contentment. Her son would never struggle to find his place in the world. He could find his gift in his own time, the blood of two courts flowed golden in his veins. Zagreus would have plenty of time to choose where he belonged. Maybe he would join Eros and Psyche's daughter in the skies or Iris under the sea.

But the days were growing longer again. It was the only unsatisfactory part of Persephone's life. She had long since made her peace with returning to the mortal world every year. The mortals needed her, and she rarely had to truly talk to her mother. Calli and Psione were fine company without her. Aidon would bring their son when he came to visit her on her wanderings, or on Olympus, or with the Neptans. Dionysus had grown slowly and this was the first year that he was walking well enough for Persephone to even consider taking him to planting season. She was unwilling to take a baby to a new town and new tent every night no matter how Demeter howled. Her mother had barely ever met her son, only deigning to come to her temple door when Aidon had brought him to a harvest festival.

But there were growing things in Zagreus's blood just as there was Hades. Persephone would not do to him what had been done to her. He would need to see the growing things of the world sooner or later. Even Zeus would agree on that, although she suspected that Aidon would ask for another season, and then another. Persephone smiled sharply to herself as her son ran unsteadily to hide behind another tree trunk. *If my mother tries anything, she will not get far. Not with the Chthonics refusing to provide nectar and ambrosia.*

"Mother look!" her child cried as he tried to climb one of the low-hanging branches of her apple trees.

The trees had grown over the seasons, gnarled branches sweeping low over the ground. Their leaves making a swaying curtain like a weeping willow. Their branches would easily hold the weight of a small boy.

Zagreus grabbed one of the glimmering apples, trying to pull himself higher into the tree. His hold suddenly gave way, and he fell a few feet to the ground.

Persephone hastily walked over. Her son was a Theoi, a fall would not hurt him. But landing on the hard ground wasn't fun. A golden apple had rolled a little away from him, resting innocently against a tree root. Zagreus got up and ran off, laughing, to try his luck on another tree. Persephone stared at the apple.

Hey reader!

(yes you.)

You spent hours to get here, spend one more minute to say thank you by rating or reviewing In the Shadow of Demeter where you bought it.

If you really liked it, say something on Goodreads!

Thanks,

Vic

If you would like to see more like this, including a preview of my next book,

Lorelei and the Airship, visit me at my website:
https://vicmalachai.wixsite.com/my-site
Or join me on Tumblr, Instagram, Twitter, or Facebook!
https://vicmalachai.tumblr.com
https://www.instagram.com/vicmalachai/
@MalachaiVic
https://www.facebook.com/profile.php?id=100072249970288

Don't miss out!

Visit the website below and you can sign up to receive emails whenever Vic Malachai publishes a new book. There's no charge and no obligation.

https://books2read.com/r/B-A-NVWP-QNGRB

BOOKS 2 READ

Connecting independent readers to independent writers.

About the Author

I started writing with my sister and a friend of ours back in high school. We enjoyed it and even finished one of our projects. One day in the bookstore I picked up a book and thought, even I could do better than this! So in college, I wrote on my own and ran up against the traditional print publishing process.

Let the grand experiment begin! In the Shadow of Demeter is my experiment (yes, I majored in the S part of STEM, sorry) in self-publishing. If it goes well, my next book, Lorelei and the Airship is ready to go.

Read more at https://vicmalachai.wixsite.com/my-site.